D1316664

THE
CAVEREL
CLAIM

Also by Peter Rawlinson

Non-fiction
Price Too High to Pay: An Autobiography
The Jesuit Factor: A Personal Investigation

Fiction
The Colombia Syndicate
Hatred and Contempt
His Brother's Keeper
Indictment for Murder

THE
CAVEREL
CLAIM

Peter Rawlinson

St. Martin's Press ⋈ New York

THOMAS DUNNE BOOKS.
An imprint of St. Martin's Press

Library of Congress Cataloging-in-Publication Data

Rawlinson, Peter.
  The Caverel claim / Peter Rawlinson.
    p.   cm.
  "Thomas Dunne books."
  ISBN 0-312-19343-2
  I. Title.
  PR6068.A925C38   1998
  823'.914—dc21

                                        98-44121
                                        CIP

First published in Great Britain by Constable & Company Ltd

First U.S. Edition: December 1998

10 9 8 7 6 5 4 3 2

Dedicated

to

the memory of Arthur Orton, alias Tomas Castro,
alias Roger Charles Doughty Tichborne, Baronet,
The Tichborne Claimant
1834–1898

GENEALOGICAL TABLE OF THE CAVEREL FAMILY

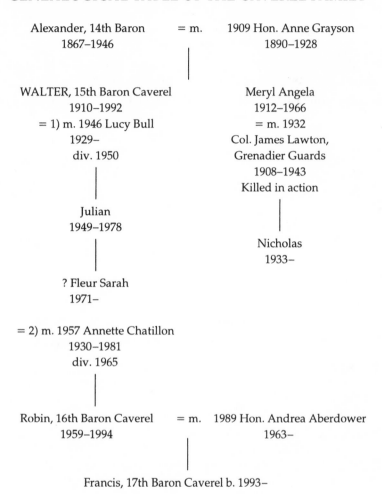

Alexander, 14th Baron   = m.   1909 Hon. Anne Grayson
1867–1946   1890–1928

WALTER, 15th Baron Caverel   Meryl Angela
1910–1992   1912–1966
= 1) m. 1946 Lucy Bull   = m. 1932
1929–   Col. James Lawton,
div. 1950   Grenadier Guards
                                 1908–1943
                              Killed in action

Julian
1949–1978   Nicholas
                              1933–

? Fleur Sarah
1971–

= 2) m. 1957 Annette Chatillon
1930–1981
div. 1965

Robin, 16th Baron Caverel   = m.   1989 Hon. Andrea Aberdower
1959–1994   1963–

Francis, 17th Baron Caverel b. 1993–

Prologue

The man was obviously dying. Grey skin hung on his body like sacking, his face cadaverous, barely recognisable as the restless, reckless companion of eighteen months before. Now only the eyes seemed alive.

None of the doctors knew why he should be as he was. None of the drugs they had pumped into him had any effect. It was a virus, they said, and nothing seemed able to halt it. They could not say how he could have contracted it. In hospital he had told them he wanted to die at home and so his friend had brought him back to the Victorian house which they shared in the Haight. Now he lay in a king-size double bed in the bedroom on the top floor, the shutters closed against the fierce San Francisco sunshine.

'What day is it?' he asked suddenly.

The man by the bed did not answer immediately. He was as young as his companion, with cropped hair and a dark moustache turned down lugubriously at the sides of his mouth. Instead he continued to dab his dying friend's forehead with a cloth soaking in a basin of iced water. Then, as if starting a new conversation, he said, 'Today is Thursday, 25th May.'

'It was May when we went to the lawyer to make our wills. I remember sitting across the table in the lawyer's office and pointing to you and saying, To my beloved, I hereby bequeath all my worldly goods and everything I possess. The lawyer looked so prim and you so smug that it made me laugh.'

'I also left everything to you.'

The man on the bed stretched out his hand and laid it on the other's. 'You've never had anything except what I gave you.'

'I still left everything I had to you.'

For a time neither spoke.

'You know that I want to be scattered in the Bay. And see it gets into the *Bay Times*. I want my friends here to know. And the lawyer. He must tell London.'

'Does he know whom to tell?'

7

'Yes, another lawyer. The address is with the will.' He paused. 'They'll be happy in London when they get the news.' He turned his head towards the shuttered window. 'The money from there will stop, but there'll be enough for you without it. So long as you behave yourself, which I suppose you won't.'

'There'll be no one else, Julio, not now, not ever.'

'Not now perhaps, not for a little while. But not never.'

There was silence. Then the other said, 'Your mother?'

'She won't care. She didn't approve of what I was, of what you and I are. She'll get to know, eventually.'

'There's no one else I should tell?'

'No. Just our friends and the lawyer in London.'

An hour later Julio said, 'I've always known I'd die young. But I thought it would be from the booze. Not from this – whatever this is.'

The man by the bed bent forward and kissed him.

That was five years before the disease was identified and given a name.

Part I

1

She sat in front of the glass in her dressing-room brushing her long dark hair, pinning it up and peering at her face, her head throbbing. She took two tablets from a small jar and swallowed them, drinking water from a tall glass. Then she shut her eyes and dabbed the lids with cologne before she began to use her eye-liner, thinking of the Gypsy's eyes and the medallion twisting and glinting in the lamplight. She painted her lips bright crimson the better to set them off against the chocolate colour of her skin. Then she rubbed rouge on to her nipples, grimacing at herself in the glass. She stood to fix her G-string as she had six times a week, two shows a night, ever since she was fifteen.

She looked at herself in the tall glass at the end of the small room, naked save for the fake-jewelled triangle glittering between the dark skin of her thighs. She stretched up, planting and securing the plume in her hair. Fastening the bra, she slipped into the dress covered in spangles with the long zip easy to unfasten and stepped into the high-heeled shoes. After a last look she went out into the corridor which ran behind the stage and stood in the wings, waiting for her entrance. The brightness of the lights and the blare of the music pierced her head like a knife.

On stage she went through her routine like an automaton. Afterwards in her dressing-room during the interval between shows, she sipped tea and took more tablets and lay on the padded couch, thinking of the afternoon and the Gypsy with the different-coloured eyes who had put her to sleep.

All her life she'd had an obsession to pierce the curtain between the present and the future. It was an addiction as compelling for her as were drugs for some of her friends in the other dressing-rooms. At one time or another in every city from Paris to Istanbul, she would make her way to some back street into some cheap and shoddy room with the windows curtained to keep out the light, where some elderly woman stared into a luminous bowl or at the cards spread on the table before them, and prophesied. Only once had it been different. In Berlin, when it had been a great room like a tent with painted silver stars on the roof and three figures in black and gold robes wearing the white, beaked masks of Venetian revellers. Only one of the three had spoken and from the pitch of the voice she could not tell if it was a man or a woman.

It had begun when she was a child, squatting at the feet of Minerva, vast and much blacker than herself, as Minerva rattled the bones and read the grubby Tarot cards. One night, very late, Minerva had appeared by her bed. 'I need you, little one,' she had said. With an oil-lamp in one hand and a finger to her lips, Minerva had led her in the moonlight through the front garden, closing the gate carefully, making sure it did not creak. In her bare feet, with her small hand in Minerva's great paw, they had gone up the dirt road to the graveyard at the edge of the village. There on the earth of a newly dug grave Minerva had told her to take off her night-shirt and stand on the grave and stay very still and very quiet. Then the old woman had scooped up dirt from the grave which she put into a small paper bag and tucked into the pocket of her apron, while she shuffled round the grave, three times one way, three times the other, all the while mumbling and crooning to herself or to the spirits she was invoking. And all the while in the centre of the circle stood the small naked figure of the child, facing the moon, with her hands rigid by her sides.

When Minerva had finished, she had taken her in her arms and made her promise that tonight would be their secret; that she had needed the little one to help her help someone who needed help very badly. And the child swore that what had passed would stay a secret between them for ever.

When five years later Minerva died, she had slipped out of the house and stood in the moonlight naked on Minerva's grave. Then she circled it as she had seen Minerva do and took dirt from the grave. But she did not know what to do with the dirt and she didn't know what words to say, except to wish good to the spirits into whose company Minerva had now passed.

Two years later she'd run away from home.

*

Lesley and Payne, solicitors, specialists in European law and commercial international contracts.

After graduating from Sydney University and before joining the family business in Sydney where his father, Randolph Rutherford, was the founder and chairman of one of the great corporations of Australia, Greg Rutherford had been sent to Europe to visit what his mother, who had been born in Surrey, called 'the Old Country'. After only a week in London, Greg had gone with a party of friends to Zermatt for Christmas. He had not returned to London but had remained all winter in Switzerland skiing, and in the spring and early summer he had wandered around the south of France, ending up sharing rooms with three university friends in an apartment on the left bank in Paris. Reports of the goings on there filtered back home to Sydney, mainly from the European executives of the Rutherford Corporation. Randolph was not amused.

'That boy of yours,' he began one morning, 'he's making a bloody fool of himself. Twice he's been in trouble with the Paris police.'

'Our boy,' his wife corrected him in her Home Counties English. 'Yours and mine.'

It was she who had insisted their only son should spend a year or so in Europe, acquiring, she said, the graces. It would give him exposure to European culture and society before being thrown into the rough world of business deals and Australian politics. But through her own social grapevine she too had heard the rumours.

'It's time that young man was given something to do,' her husband growled, 'instead of idling about in cafés and nightclubs. I don't know what culture he's meant to be picking up there.'

'Then send him to London. Tell Jason to keep an eye on him. Let him work with Jason.'

So Randolph arranged with his brother-in-law, portly and punctilious, to take on his nephew as an assistant in order to keep the young man occupied and give him some introduction to the world of international business. Jason had been reluctant, but as Randolph gave his firm much important and lucrative work, he had no choice. So a month before, Greg, resentful but mollified a little by the provision of a flat in Fulham and a second-hand BMW, had started as Jason's 'bag-carrier'.

He was meant to accompany Jason to conferences, when he was on time. He was meant to attend Jason's meetings in the office unless they were very confidential, and take notes. He was meant to come to the office every day if Jason was there, which he did, although he often slipped away early; and he was meant to study the forms of negotiation and the contracts in which the firm specialised. He had been given a small room and the services of a part-time secretary, Helen, a spinster in her late forties who lived with her mother. After the first week she told her mother, with pursed lips, that she found Mr West's nephew's habits and manner 'very Antipodean'. But after a month she began to dream about him.

The receptionists liked him, because of his looks and casual manners, and were happy to field his messages, usually dates to play squash or cricket; and, very soon, dates with girls. But the members of the firm were not so taken with Mr West's nephew. On his first visit to the partners' lunch room, Greg had given them the benefit of his views on the English class system, English manners, English habits, and the English weather. He had not disguised his radical and republican politics. Jason had squirmed. 'You are a visitor to this country, Gregory,' he later admonished him. 'You must be more tactful, more sensitive. You are only here because of the connection this firm has with your father.'

Greg made little secret to his Australian friends of his opinion of his Pommy mother's relations and country. 'A bunch of stuffed shirts,' he said over the cans of Fosters. But he knew that after Paris, he could not afford to make too much of a mess of his time in London.

Greg was in his room, reading the sports page in the newspaper, when the telephone rang.

'A Mr Henry Proctor is on the line for you.'

Henry was a fellow Australian, an actor who picked up a little TV work as an extra in commercials.

'We missed you last night, Henry,' Greg said. 'Where were you?'

'Up north.'

'A good part?'

'No, I've been resting, selling water-softeners. But I've a job in Milan and I'm on the way to the airport. I called, because I've given your name to a friend, a girl I met during a shoot in Paris.'

'Is she pretty?'

'Very. We were in an advert together.'

'What kind of an advert?'

'Some kind of drink. She was one of a bunch of girls on a beach. She's come to London and for some reason she needs an English lawyer. I told her you worked with lawyers and you'd find her one. Her name's Wilson, Sarah Wilson. She's going to call you. Now I've got to run.'

And he was gone.

That afternoon the receptionist telephoned again. 'There's a young lady here to see you.'

'But I'm not expecting anyone.'

'She said someone called Henry fixed it. Her name's Wilson.'

Henry's friend! Here! He'd assumed Henry had given her his home address, not the office.

'I think you'd better come down,' the receptionist said, 'and pretty quick.'

Both the receptionists had been on the telephone when Greg's visitor had come through the swing-doors. The blonde had looked up into a pair of hazel eyes below dark, glossy hair drawn back and fastened at the back of the neck. The mouth was bright red with lipstick, vivid against the dark, chocolate skin. The features were regular but surprisingly small. Now this apparition was sitting in the waiting area, long slim legs crossed beneath a white mini-skirt below a pink, almost see-through blouse.

As Greg came from the lift he saw her, and, startled, his eye fell at once on the curve of her breasts in the light, flimsy blouse and her long, slim legs jutting out from the minute mini-skirt. I must get her out of here, he thought.

As he approached she stood up.

'I'm Greg Rutherford.' He held out his hand. She took it and held it. 'Henry called me about you,' he went on, his hand still in hers. 'Shall we go out for a cup of coffee and you can – '

She interrupted. 'This is an attorneys' office, isn't it?' she asked, her accent American but not pronounced.

'It is but – '

'Henry said you could find me an attorney.'

Greg was conscious that the receptionists were watching and listening. He got his hand free. 'If we slipped out,' he said, 'and went to the café at the corner – '

'No. What I have to say is private. Haven't you an office?'

'Yes, but – '

'Show me.'

Outside his room Margaret, Jason's secretary, was talking to Helen. The two women watched as Greg ushered in his visitor. Once the door was shut the visitor began. 'Henry said you're not an attorney yourself.'

'No, I'm just working here for a few months before – '

'Henry said you'd find me one. I don't have much money but I need an attorney. Is there one here who'd do?'

Greg thought of Jason. He certainly wouldn't do. 'It depends what it's about. The man I work with and the others here do commercial work, international business contracts and so on and – '

'I'll tell you about it. Then you can tell me who to see.'

'I haven't much time this afternoon. Wouldn't it be better if we met this evening at my flat, Miss Wilson and – '

'Wilson's not my real name.' She leaned forward so that her elbows were on his desk and she knew he could see the tops of her breasts. 'My real name's Caverel.'

She paused as though she expected some reaction. 'Fleur Caverel,' she repeated. She seemed surprised when he only stared blankly at her. 'They're a very important English family,' she went on. 'Haven't you heard of them?'

'No, I'm a foreigner here and – '

'Well, they are, they're very important.' She leaned back in her chair, crossing her legs, her hazel eyes on his. 'I've come to London to get what's due to me – my inheritance.'

'I see,' he said weakly. She was gazing at him with such intensity that he dropped his eyes and fixed them on her lips bright red with lipstick. He wasn't often thrown by women.

'A month back I learnt that the ma in South Carolina I thought my real ma was my foster ma. She'd just died, and I was given a letter from my real ma. My foster ma couldn't read or write but my real ma could and she gave the letter to my foster ma to give to me when I was grown. But I'd run off.'

From the moment she'd met him in reception, save for the

walk to the lift and then to his room, she hadn't taken her eyes off him.

'My dad, you see, was English. He left my ma before she had me and my ma died soon after I was born so I never knew either of them. In my ma's letter she'd written there's plenty of money.'

'Why should she think that?'

'Because my dad's a lord.'

'A lord?'

'Yes, well, not then he wasn't, not when he married my ma. But when someone died, he would be. Now I want my dad's share.'

The telephone rang. It was Helen. 'Can you come out for a minute? It's urgent.'

He replaced the receiver. His visitor was going on. 'It's an important name, Caverel. Lord Caverel.'

'Will you excuse me a moment?' he said.

Margaret was with Helen. 'Jason called from the car. He's on his way,' Margaret said. 'What does that woman want?'

'She wants a lawyer to ask about an inheritance,' he said. 'Something about a lord.'

'What lord?' Helen asked.

'Caverel.'

Helen handed him a *Who's Who*. 'It'll be in here. Look it up,' she said.

'Who is there in the office who could help?' he asked.

'We don't do that kind of work in this firm, and certainly not for someone like her,' Margaret said primly.

Greg went back to his room. 'I'm sorry for keeping you. This book has all the names of the important English people.'

'My dad's name was Julian, Julian Caverel,' she said.

He leafed through the pages. 'Caverel,' he read out. 'There is a Caverel. Caverel of Ravenscourt in Wiltshire. Francis, 17th Baron Caverel, son of the 16th baron, Robin, who died last year.' He looked up. 'But he's a child, just turned four, and his father was Robin and his mother is called Andrea, maiden name Aberdower. No mention of anyone called Julian.'

She sat very still, gazing at him. 'No Julian?' she said.

'No.'

There was a pause. He closed the book. Then she said, 'You're not a lawyer. Isn't there anyone here who could help?'

'Not that I know of at the moment, but I'll find out and let you know.'

She stood up. 'I don't think you want to help.'

'Of course I do. I'll find out who's the best for you to see. Tell me where you are staying and I'll get back to you.'

'No, I'll find someone myself. Henry shouldn't have sent me. He's a fool.'

He's a bastard, Greg thought, sending her here and not to the flat. She walked to the door and he opened it for her. As they went to the lift, they passed Helen and Margaret. The lift was small and they had to stand close to each other. All the time she looked up at him. He followed her out into reception. By the glass swing-doors she stopped and turned. 'You've been no bloody help,' she said, 'but you're kind of cute.' She stretched up and kissed him on the lips.

At that moment the rotund, red-faced figure of Jason West bustled through the door. When she turned away from Greg, she and Jason stood face to face. Then Jason stood aside as she swept out, swinging her hips and the bag in her hand.

'Who the devil was that?' Jason asked.

'Someone a friend sent to see me.'

'To see you, Gregory? To see you here, in office hours?'

'She wanted a lawyer and he asked me to find her one.'

'She doesn't look the type we deal with. What did she want a lawyer for?'

Greg walked beside Jason to the lift, wiping the lipstick off his mouth with the back of his hand.

'She says her dead mother wrote in a letter that her father Julian was connected with someone called Lord Caverel but I looked him up and Lord Caverel is a child and his father was called Robin. Then she left. I'd never seen her before.'

Jason pressed the button to the second floor. 'You've never seen her before and she embraced you in the hall, in public, in front of the receptionists! What extraordinary behaviour!'

At home that night, before he went to sleep, Greg lay thinking of his visitor. Later he dreamt about her. It was the kind of dream that Helen, his spinster secretary, dreamt about him.

4

After leaving the office in Bruton Street, Greg's visitor paid off the taxi at a shabby hotel near Paddington station.

A large, fat man was sitting in a corner in the small foyer. He rose when she entered.

'A waste of time,' she said to him in French.

He put his finger to his lips. 'We shall go out. Then you can tell me.'

The sour-looking woman at the desk called out, 'Leave your key, please, Mr Valerian.'

He went to the desk and handed over the key with a bow.

'If anyone should ask for me,' he said in heavily accented English, 'I shall be at the Polish Club in Queen's Gate.'

At the club he steered her to a corner table and lumbered back from the bar with a brandy-and-soda and a large glass of red wine. 'Drink, it will make you feel better. I do not like you to get over-excited. You must stay calm.'

'I am not over-excited and I am calm.'

He took her hand. 'When you have had a sip of wine, you can tell me about it.'

'The actor's a fool. He said his friend would find a lawyer but he didn't want to. All he did was to look it up in a book.'

'Look up what in a book?'

'The family. He said there was no Julian.'

'Nothing more?'

'No.'

'What was he like?'

'Young, good-looking . . .'

He smiled and patted her hand. 'Then that at least was agreeable. But it was worth trying. We'll find a lawyer ourselves. And from now on, you and I must speak only in English. And you, remember, you are Fleur. Only Fleur. I, too, must remember.'

He lit a Gauloise and drank some of the brandy. 'But when we do find a lawyer, he may not be young and good-looking.'

'I'm very tired,' she said.

'I know. Tomorrow you must rest. Leave the search to me.'

But she did not rest longer than the morning. She talked to the woman at the desk who made a telephone call and in the afternoon she took a taxi to an address in Chepstow Villas. Half an hour later she was back in the street. It had been a waste of time, like the visit to Henry's friend. Except that she'd liked the young man. She'd liked the dimple in his chin and the way his hair curled and fell on his forehead when he'd been reading from the book. The woman in the house in Chepstow Villas had been younger than most, with dyed black hair bound by a scarf; the room, as was usual, almost in darkness. It was all shoddy and cheap and after five minutes Fleur had pushed back her chair, put a ten-pound note on the table and left. The woman had looked angry.

On Saturday she stayed in bed. He came to her room in the morning and said he'd be with friends all day. 'They have promised to help,' he said.

On the Sunday morning he knocked on her door. 'When you are ready, I shall be waiting for you in the hall. We go to a restaurant to celebrate. I've found what we were looking for.'

He led her down Praed Street to a small restaurant and handed her a newspaper, opened at the centre-spread.

'Read,' he said. 'It is interesting.'

On the left-hand page was a large picture of the singer, Dukie Brown, in his prime, with his guitar and his hair down to his shoulders. Beneath – 'Pop Star Killer Freed'.

'I went to a concert of his once,' she said, 'years ago, in Budapest. He was good.'

On the opposite page was a picture of Dukie looking older, his hair short, walking between two men; one carrying a briefcase, the other smoking a cigar. 'Dukie with his new manager, Willoughby Blake' was the caption.

She looked up. 'Well?'

He took the newspaper from her and read out: '"On Dukie's right, Michael Stevens, lawyer to the rich and famous." He ran Dukie's defence when Dukie beat the murder rap. My friends spoke to me about him, and here he is in the newspaper. Isn't that remarkable? They tell me to go to him, and now I read about him. He is the one for us.'

'If he'll take it on.'

'He will. My friends say tell him we pay as they do in America, on results. He looks very clever.' He smiled. 'But not very handsome.'

'If you say so.' She pushed back her chair. 'I don't want to eat.'

He leaned across the table and put his hand on hers.

'Please, my dear, do not get ...' He struggled for the right word. 'Do not get agitated. Do not slip into one of your moods. You will if you do not eat.'

'I am not agitated and I'm not hungry.'

'Listen, my dear. What we have to do will take patience and courage. You must be sensible and stay calm and strong.'

She looked at him. 'I know. But I get frightened and today I have one of my headaches.' She got to her feet. 'I'll see you later at the hotel. You arrange about the lawyer.'

She picked up her bag and left. When she had gone, he sighed and shook his head. It would not be easy to keep her calm and determined.

Fleur walked in the park. By the Round Pond, she sat on the grass, plucking at the clover, watching the kites flying high above her and the children playing around her.

So now it had really begun. Once it was in the hands of lawyers, there could be no turning back. Although it was warm in the sun, she felt cold.

5

Andrea Caverel threw back the bedclothes and lowered herself from the canopied, four-poster bed. When she'd found her slippers she crossed the room to the tall, high window and pulled back the curtains. The early morning sun was shining brightly on the neat, clipped lawn which ran down to the walled flower garden. Beyond the pleasure garden, on slightly rising ground, was the Folly, a strange mass of shafts of stone formed into a grotto, built at the end of the eighteenth century when the house itself was not a hundred years old. The near part of the flower garden was full of red and yellow roses. Beyond was her own blue and white garden, which she'd planted when she'd first come to Ravenscourt the year before Robin had been killed. She'd been working in her garden when she'd heard the sound of people running and the voices calling her and the shock of what they had to say. By then it was autumn, and with a sudden morning fog swirling in thick banks across Salisbury Plain, Robin had crashed head-on into the back of a lorry and died instantaneously. Francis was three. Not many hours of any day passed when she did not remember, and every time she felt a stab of pain. After nine months, the pain was no duller.

She heard Alice and Francis passing along the corridor outside her door on their way to breakfast. Alice was the girl from County Wexford Andrea's cousin had found to help with Francis. She was twenty-three, stumpy, with round, red cheeks and straggly red hair to match. She laughed a lot and sang, and treated Andrea like an elder sister. Already Andrea loved her. She was chattering away now to Francis in her soft, sing-song voice as they passed Andrea's door on their way to the great staircase where they'd go down to the hall and along the side corridor past the dining-room to the kitchen. It was quite a distance from kitchen to dining-room; in the old days the meals were brought by a file of footmen and kitchen maids. Now it was rarely used. Francis and Alice ate their meals in the kitchen; if Andrea was with them, next door, in what had been the butler's pantry.

Andrea went into the bathroom. While the bath was filling, she looked at herself in the glass above the basin, pulling back her pale, fine blonde hair from her forehead. Soon she would be thirty-two. There were dark rings under her eyes. I look forty, she said to herself.

It was Sunday and lying in the bath she thought of the day ahead. It was to be the first time she'd entertained since she'd been widowed and it was going to be quite an occasion. It had been her idea to revive what had once been an old tradition, the annual family cricket match and summer party which had been abandoned at the start of World War II and not restarted when Robin's father, Walter, had inherited in 1946 and shut the house and gone to live abroad. But today Ravenscourt was to be on show. There was to be a lunch in a marquee for the teams and special guests, followed by tea for everyone and a reception in the Long Gallery at the end of the game. It was to be her way of announcing to the county that she was going to stay on, that the Caverels were going to live at Ravenscourt as they had for over three hundred years. It was also her way of trying to make some amends for the trouble caused recently by the present manager of the estate, Robin's older cousin, Nicholas Lawton, the son of Walter's sister.

She was drying herself when she heard Alice at the bedroom door.

'Telephone, Lady Caverel. It's himself, Major Lawton, fussing and worrying as usual.'

'What does he want? I'm not dressed.'

'He says he's done the seating plan for your table for lunch. If you want to change it, you must let him know as soon as you come to the ground.'

Andrea groaned. They'd settled all that yesterday. He was to do the seating. He knew the neighbours better than she.

'He says please be at the ground before eleven.'

'Tell him I shall.'

When Robin had died, Andrea had turned to Nicholas. He was Robin's nearest relative and he lived in the dower house on the edge of the estate. A retired soldier and a widower with a stiff and self-conscious manner but he was good-hearted and meant well. Above all he cared – about the family, of which he was a part, and about Ravenscourt where the Caverels had lived for centuries and where he himself had been born. When he had taken over the management of the estate, he was determined, as he said, to put it to rights and make it pay. He dismissed the incompetent land agents who had been in charge since Walter's day and kept on by the easy-going Robin. With the lawyers and accountants, he negotiated with the Revenue, until by the sale of some pictures and outlying farms, much progress had been made in settling death duties. He had installed a tea-room and shop in the stable-block and arranged for the house to be opened to the public on two days a week from Easter to the end of September. By careful management he had staunched the haemorrhage of capital which had been going on for years as in his crisp, military fashion he had overhauled every department of the estate. Within a few months he had made such economies and improvements that if there was no further drain on resources, the accountants and lawyers considered the future of Andrea and Francis in the family home was assured.

But it had been at a cost. Men from families who had worked on the estate for generations were laid off; work schedules were tightened; tenants' obligations were enforced. And as Alice – who had heard it from the women from the village who came to clean – passed on to Andrea, he had gone about it in such a way that there were now groups who met regularly in the local pubs, and grumbled and criticised. The Major, they were saying, was a bloody dictator, too much the soldier, too hard-headed. Because of him, Alice told Andrea, the family was not popular.

It was in an attempt to still some of the local feeling that she had planned the revival of the cricket match and the reception which would enable her to invite many of the locals to the house. She had told Nicholas he must include in the home team several from the village eleven and he was to make sure that all the players, their families, the spectators, the neighbours and the tenants were given tea and invited to the Long Gallery after the game was over. Andrea prayed that the weather stayed fine and that all went well.

It was past nine o'clock when she came to the kitchen, a cavern of a room in which she had recently installed an Aga. There still remained the long deal table running almost the length of the room and the hooks in the walls and the tall dressers. As she drank her coffee, she listened to Mrs Mason's morning catalogue of woes. It was the same day in and day out – too much fetching and carrying in such a barrack of a house, too much difficulty trying to cook in such a vast, old-fashioned kitchen.

Andrea resisted the temptation to snap at her. There was only herself and Alice and Francis, while two women came daily from the village to clean. Nor was Mason, her husband, over-worked. He was meant to be a handyman-houseman, but she hadn't entertained since Robin's death and Mason refused to do any outside work, and sometimes even found excuses not to drive her in her car. He had his own, which he was forever tinkering with and polishing. I must find another couple, Andrea said to herself as she listened to Mrs Mason's grumbles, but today wasn't the day to quarrel. The reception in the evening was being done by caterers but necessarily it involved the Masons.

She took Francis out to play in the rose garden and looked up at the clear blue sky. It was going to be a fine June day: Ravenscourt would be looking its best.

Nicholas Lawton, grey hair, grey military moustache, his back straight as a ramrod like the Guardsman he had been, was standing on the steps of the pavilion. He was already in his white flannels and blue blazar with brass buttons, a panama hat perched on his head. From his pocket he took out his check list and a pencil.

Wet weather drill. He could cross that off.

The pitch. It seemed well prepared and properly marked. Peachey the head gardener had seen to that.

The catering. The previous evening a white marquee had been erected close to the small pavilion. He'd check that in a minute.

Finally, the team. He glanced at his watch.

'The cars from London will be arriving soon,' he called out to Peachey who was carrying deck-chairs from the pavilion. 'Eleven o'clock start, sharp.'

Peachey nodded. Nicholas turned and looked back towards the house, a great pile of rose-coloured brick two hundred yards from where he was standing, separated from the park and the cricket ground by an iron rail. He had been born there in his grandfather's time and his first memories were of the nursery on the top floor. When he was a child his mother used to bring him back to her home every holiday. When he was small, he used to stand before his window on summer evenings, watching the house martins skimming and diving under the eaves, looking out across the park and pretending that one day, when his old grandfather died, it would all belong to him. The two were very close, the old man often leading the child around the garden and the estate, telling him stories of Caverels of long ago. But it had not been long before he understood that his name was not Caverel; that he was only the son of the daughter, and that his Uncle Walter, his mother's older brother, would inherit; and after Walter, Walter's family. But when Walter had succeeded, he had preferred his villa near Antibes and wintering in the sunshine of the Cape, and Ravenscourt had been shut. A series of surly caretakers had been installed in a few rooms above the stable-block and agents from Salisbury brought in to manage the land.

Fifteen years later and five years ago, Nicholas, by then a widower, had retired from the army and come to live in the dower house at the edge of the park which had been left him by his mother. Walter had always been jealous of the relationship between grandfather and small grandson and the agents had been instructed that Major Lawton was to be kept away from the closed and shuttered house. He was to have no business with the estate. But eighteen months after Nicholas had left the army and come to live in the park, Walter had died in his villa in France. His son, Robin, had resigned from the Foreign Office and returned from Rome with Andrea and their small son, Francis. The house had been reopened.

Robin was easy; he got on well with everyone but he was no manager so he kept on the Salisbury agents and the neglect of the estate continued. When Robin had been killed Nicholas found he had been named as an executor, and Andrea had turned to him. So for a time, even if only as steward, Nicholas saw the fulfilment of part of his childhood's dream. Until Francis reached his majority, he was effectively the master of the Ravenscourt estate.

He looked again at his watch. Soon people would be arriving to settle into the deck-chairs and, for those not invited to lunch in the marquee, eat their picnics. It was going to cost a packet, he reflected grimly, as he wandered across to the marquee. The lunch, and the tea with strawberries and cream, then the reception. But Andrea had insisted.

The waitresses were laying the round tables with the catering manager in his white shirt-sleeves and black trousers.

'Serve Pimms and beer to the spectators in the deck-chairs at twelve thirty,' Nicholas said. 'We'll break for lunch at one fifteen.'

Up the drive was coming a procession of cars, being directed to the field set aside as the car-park.

It had been only on the previous evening that Greg Rutherford had been asked if he was free to play. The visiting team were one short, and someone he'd played against the week before had given his name. He'd be picked up, he'd been told, and given a lift.

In the car on the way down, Greg asked Sandys, who had collected him, where they were heading.

'Donhead St Philip, on the borders of Wiltshire and Dorset. I was sent a sketch map for the last few miles.'

Just outside Tisbury, Sandys handed it to Greg. 'You'll have to direct me from now on,' he said.

It was then that Greg saw the name – Ravenscourt.

'Isn't that where a family called Caverel live?' he asked.

'Yes. Do you know them?'

'I've heard of them. Lord Caverel and all that?'

'I believe so.'

'Lords and ladies and scones and tea. I suppose it'll be pretty stuffy. Do you think we'll play with a tennis ball?'

Sandys looked at him. 'It's a game of cricket,' he said. 'And we're their guests.'

'I was only joking,' Greg replied. They drove on in silence.

Later, at lunch at the centre table, the Lord Lieutenant's wife leaned across to speak to Andrea who was seated opposite her, next to the Lord Lieutenant.

'How is Francis?' she enquired.

'Very well,' Andrea replied. 'He's becoming quite a handful.'

'Is he four yet?'

'Last month.'

'I hope we'll see him later. I'm so glad you're staying on. It's good to have the family back in Ravenscourt.'

Greg, at his table towards the edge of the tent, was next to Eve, Nicholas' secretary.

'Is the wife here?'

She looked at him coolly. 'The wife? Do you mean Lady Caverel?'

'I guess I do.'

'She's at the centre table, opposite Major Lawton and next to the tall man with the glasses.'

Greg saw the back of the blonde head. A moment later she turned and he saw her full face. A very English face, he thought, with the English complexion beneath the fair hair. But there were dark rings beneath her eyes and her hand fluttered repeatedly to her neck, playing with a plain gold necklace as she talked and listened, mostly listened. She was sitting very straight in her chair. She reminded him of a thoroughbred, fine-boned, nervous, a world apart from the vivid, dark-skinned American from whom he'd first heard about the Caverels.

In the afternoon and towards evening, it looked as if the home team were going to win until Greg came in. Eventually he made the winning hit for the visitors, a boundary high above the bowler's head.

The guests assembled for the reception in the Long Gallery, a tall narrow room running the length of the south face of the house, with two bow windows overlooking the rose garden and opposite a great fireplace surrounded by carvings by Grinling Gibbons. Greg wandered into the hall, glass in hand.

'My name's Oliver Goodbody. You, I'm told, are Greg Rutherford, from Sydney.'

Greg had been joined by a tall, thin elderly man with aquiline features and a full head of white hair, formally dressed in a dark grey flannel suit, walking with a stick.

'You won the game for the visitors.'

'It wasn't too difficult,' Greg replied.

'You certainly looked as if you were enjoying yourself.'

'The bowling wasn't up to much.'

'Not for you at any rate. Well, we all enjoyed watching you, even those of us who wanted the home team to win. Are you over here for long?'

'For a year. I'm working as a sort of assistant in a law firm in London until I go home, although I'm not a lawyer myself.'

'Which law firm is that?'

'The one my dad uses, Lesley and Payne. Jason West, the senior partner, is my uncle.'

'I know him well. I have a meeting with him tomorrow. I'm a lawyer too. I look after the family's affairs.'

Oliver Goodbody gazed up at the portraits lining the walls. 'It's a fine collection, isn't it? Up there above the staircase are two Reynolds, a Gainsborough, and a Ramsay. They're a handsome lot.'

'Very. When they were sitting for their portraits, my ancestors were being shipped out to Van Diemen's Land in chains.'

34

Oliver looked at him. Greg laughed. 'Actually,' he said, 'my family went out in the 1860s, bringing a carriage and a cow.'

Oliver smiled.

'Are there portraits of all the Caverels?' Greg added.

'Every Lord Caverel, except for the last two.'

'So there's no portrait of the one who was killed in the accident?'

'Robin? No, neither he nor his father, Walter. No one bothered to paint Walter Caverel – a very disagreeable fellow – and, sadly, his son, Robin, did not live long enough.'

'Is Caverel a common name in England?' Greg asked.

'Not very, but I expect you'd find some in the telephone book.'

'Do you know if there was one called Julian?'

Oliver Goodbody looked at him. 'Why do you ask?'

'Somebody mentioned a Julian Caverel to me recently.'

'Who was that?'

'I can't remember. I just seem to recollect the name.'

There was silence. Then Goodbody said quietly, 'Yes, there was a Julian Caverel. He died many years ago. He's not much talked of in the family.'

He turned away. 'I must get back to the party,' he said over his shoulder.

Greg remained for a moment in the hall. What relation could Julian Caverel have been to the little boy's father, Robin? And what would he have inherited which had so interested the American girl who called herself Fleur Caverel and who had once been known as Sarah Wilson?

He went back into the salon to find Sandys and tell him he had to get back to London. They pushed their way through the throng to find Andrea who had Francis by the hand.

'Nicholas says he wished you'd been playing for us,' Andrea said to Greg.

'I'd have been very happy to. I'm a mercenary.'

'Have you managed to have a look around the house?'

'Some of it. But I have to get back to London.'

Andrea put out her hand and Greg took it. 'Goodbye, and thank you for your hospitality,' he said.

In the hall Greg waited for Sandys, looking again at the portraits. A fine bunch of villains, he thought.

'You're in a damned hurry,' Sandys grumbled when he had joined him.

'I'm sorry, but I have to get back.'

From the steps outside the front door, Oliver Goodbody watched as the young man who had spoken about Julian Caverel crossed the park on his way to the car.

6

On the Monday Jason West came to the offices of Goodbody's in Lincoln's Inn Fields to discuss with Oliver Goodbody a development project in Covent Garden in which both firms were involved.

When Jason was about to leave, Oliver said casually, 'I met a young relative of yours at the cricket at Ravenscourt yesterday, Greg Rutherford.'

'Gregory? Yes, he's my sister's boy, from Sydney. He's with me for a few months so that he can get some knowledge of international dealing before starting in his father's business in Australia.' He paused. 'He's a rather provocative young man.'

'He's a very good cricketer. I was interested because he told me someone had been speaking to him about the Caverel family. Do you know who that could have been?'

'I've no idea,' West replied. Then he remembered. 'Oh, yes. A young woman came to see him a few days ago. A rather extraordinary young woman, I seem to remember. Gregory told me it was something to do with the Caverels.'

When Jason had gone, Oliver returned to his desk and began to make a note.

Ever since he had become the senior partner at the age of forty-five, more than twenty-five years ago, Oliver Goodbody had looked after the affairs of the Caverels, as his father had before him. There were now few in the direct line but many distant connections, and there was little in the lives of any of them of which Oliver Goodbody was not aware. He drafted their marriage settlements, advised on their divorces, made their wills, and guided some through their bankruptcies. He made it his business to know as much as possible about all of them and anything of any interest, even gossip, was carefully recorded in his files. Some items were quite trivial; a young second cousin who'd got drunk at a Commem ball at Oxford and been banned from driving; an older even more distant cousin in difficulties with Lloyd's. Other matters he noted were of more importance, such as Robin Caverel's affair in Rome four years ago while his wife, Andrea was at her father's home in Shropshire for the birth of their child, Francis. Andrea had not known of it, certainly not at the time. But Oliver had – and it too had been recorded in his neat handwriting and filed away in the safe in his office. Now he added to the file his conversation with the young Australian at Ravenscourt and the suggestion by Jason West that the Australian's enquiry about Julian Caverel had been prompted by a visit from a young woman. When he had locked it away, he collected his hat and stick and went slowly down the old wooden staircase to the taxi which regularly took him from the office at the end of each day. He directed the driver to take him to Eaton Square.

Oliver Goodbody spent weekends at his home in Whitchurch in Hampshire, an early Victorian rectory which he much loved. He had lived there with Jennifer, his wife. There were no children and it was there that Jennifer, by then a chronic invalid, had died five years ago. But for twenty years, on every Monday and Thursday evening, Oliver Goodbody visited an apartment in Eaton Square. In the old days he would spend the night. Now he only dined before going on to his own small flat in Kensington.

A tall, handsome woman, her dark hair shot with grey, opened the door and kissed him on both cheeks.

'You look tired,' she said.

'It's been a long day.'

In the small library off the hall, she poured him a whisky-and-soda. 'A difficult one?'

'So, so. Something I've learnt has worried me a little.'

Anne Tremain waited in silence. Then as he said no more, she continued, 'About your precious Caverels, I suppose.' He looked at her in mock surprise and she smiled. 'Is it ever anything else? You're obsessed by that family, Oliver.'

'They're a part of my professional life, an important part.'

'They're more than that, and you know it.'

She was right, of course. The Caverels had been more than that to him ever since as a schoolboy he'd been taken by his father to Ravenscourt before World War II. They had dined with a footman behind every chair and he'd sat silent, observing. At the head of the table was the old Lord Caverel, the last of the family to have sat in Cabinet. To Oliver, he was awe-inspiring, magnificent in his green velvet smoking-jacket. At the other end of the long table lounged his son, Walter. When the men were alone, the schoolboy with them, and the port was being circulated, Walter had lit a cigarette.

'If my port is so inferior you feel you must smoke while you drink it, you might at least remember to pass it.'

The words and the tone of the old man had imprinted themselves on Oliver's memory. Walter had flushed and pushed the decanter to Oliver's father on his left. But to the schoolboy son of his friend and family solicitor the old man had been kindly, walking him past the family portraits, telling him about each of them and of the part they had played in the country's history. Ever since that evening, Oliver had been under the spell of Ravenscourt.

'It's not so much the people,' he said at last to Anne, 'it's Ravenscourt. I care lest it be turned into an institution for I care who lives in it. I grieved when Walter shut it up and it stood empty and neglected. I used to go down from time to time, just to look around. I made the excuse that I'd come for documents from the muniments room, and the caretaker would open up the library for me. When I was alone I used to talk to the empty place which for three hundred years had been the centre of so much life, and I promised that some day it would come alive again, that some day the family would return.' He looked down into his glass. 'I suppose Ravenscourt does obsess me, as you call it. I would like to think of Caverels in the house their ancestors built and where at one time great matters of state were discussed and decided.'

'Not any more.'

'No, not since the turn of the century. Until then, they had all played a great part.'

'Walter ended that?'

'He did. Robin, unlike his father, was agreeable enough. And he had the sense to open up the house. But he had no great talent. There's no place nowadays for the family except in the county.'

'I never understand why you worry so.'

'I think it's my sense of history, of tradition. I like to think of them there, the descendants living where their ancestors had lived, and now that Nicholas has taken charge, the family should be there until well into the twenty-first century. That'll see me out.'

'The good and faithful servant.'

'Certainly not,' he said. 'The good and faithful adviser.'

'Then what's worrying you?'

'Someone's been enquiring about them.'

'Why shouldn't they?'

'It's just a little odd. I had what I can only call a premonition that after Walter Caverel died there'd be trouble.'

'About what?'

'Can't you guess?'

'Julian?'

'Yes, but when Walter did die, and when Robin succeeded and then was killed in that accident, there was nothing. Everything seemed settled. My premonition was proved false.'

'And now you've heard something?'

'Yes. I've heard that a young woman has been making enquiries.'

'What did she want?'

'I don't know – yet. But it's strange, and it has disturbed me.'

7

Later that same week, a tall, sandy-haired man in a dark blue lightweight suit checked in at the BA Club Class desk at Gatwick airport. At eleven thirty, he boarded the flight.

Several hours later, after changing aircraft at Charlottesville, he disembarked at Charleston and took a taxi to the Four Seasons Hotel. When he entered the foyer, a tall, thin man with a white moustache and over-long white hair rose from a chair to greet him.

'Jed Blaker. You're from Willoughby Blake?'

The newcomer nodded and was led to the desk. 'Mr Jameson's room, please,' the thin man said.

'Certainly, Judge,' the clerk replied.

Ten days after his arrival in Charleston, Richard Jameson was shown to his room in Claridge Hotel, Buenos Aires. He was handed a message. He looked at his watch. It was mid-afternoon. He should be able to catch Michael Stevens at his office in London before he went home. Jameson made the call.

Next morning he took a taxi to a modest house in the suburbs. He rang the bell and a maid showed him to a sitting-room and told him to wait. He wandered round the room inspecting it. He picked up two photographs in silver frames standing together on a small table and examined each in turn. The first was of a dark, handsome young man in breeches and riding-boots astride a polo pony; the second of a young woman, inclined to plumpness, her figure well displayed in a minuscule bikini, standing under a sun umbrella on a beach. He put them back on the table and went to another in the far corner of the room, a photograph of a child with long blonde hair. He could not tell if it were a girl or a boy. After half an hour a short elderly woman, very stout and heavily made-up, came through door.

'Jameson,' he said as he got to his feet. 'From London. I telephoned earlier.'

The woman looked at him and then waddled across the room to a sideboard. 'Want a drink?'

'No, thank you,' he replied. He heard her throwing the ice into the long glass and saw her reach for the vodka bottle. She turned and came slowly back to where he was standing. She looked him up and down and drank before she flopped into an armchair. 'Sit down,' she said and drank again. He noticed her fat arms and the swollen wrist and the fingers covered in bangles and rings. Fakes, like the glass beads round her neck. She had a mean, narrow mouth which she had tried to enlarge with lipstick.

'They say London's bloody awful now,' she said. 'Rapes, muggings, strikes.'

'The streets are not so safe as they were.'

'It's a lifetime since I was in London.' She whirled the ice in her glass with a finger and drank. 'How did you find me?'

'We knew your married name.'

'I didn't think anyone did.'

'What I've come about is important.'

'It may be to you, my lad, but is it to me? That's the sixty-four thousand dollar question, ain't it?'

'I think you'll find it will be.'

'Maybe. How did you get my name?'

'From the divorce papers.'

'Which? The first, from that shit, Walter? That farce? They gave me the divorce, think of that. Me!' She laughed, her chin quivering over the flesh of her neck. 'You couldn't've got my name from that. It must've been from the second.' She stared at him over the rim of the glass. 'That mattered. That was from the horseman.'

He was surprised to see a look of pain on her grotesque features.

'No one ever mattered except him.' She jerked her head towards the table with the photograph of the man in riding-boots.

'It was from the particulars of that divorce that I was led to you here.'

'So you got it from the lawyers? Bloodsuckers. Sell anything for money, after they've stolen all yours.' She held out her glass. 'Fill it up, sonny. Vodka, on the rocks.'

He took the glass and went to the sideboard. He'd been told he'd better come before lunch, that it would be useless to come later.

'They were good times, those days with the horseman.' She took the glass from him. 'And the nights, specially the nights. He had imagination, that one did. I was thin then. Can you believe that?' She jerked her head again to the table with the photographs. 'That's me.'

She lay back in her chair. 'So you've come all the way from little old London town just to see little old me. It's a bloody long way. And a bloody long time ago.' She drank and looked at him over the rim of her glass.

'So you want to know about my boy, Julio?' she said at last.

41

He nodded. 'That little bugger.' She eyed him again. 'What's in it for me?'

8

Nicholas Lawton was in Brinkley's wood, high up at the top of the down, with Headley, the head forester. It was raining, a fine late August rain, the first since the drought of June and July.

'We needed this badly,' Nicholas said to Headley.

'Not enough,' Headley replied.

'The forecasters say it'll keep up.'

Headley spat. 'Can't trust them forecasts.' He looked up at the sky between the tops of the trees. 'It'll clear soon.'

Nicholas wanted to get rid of George Headley. He was a trouble-maker and a drinker, but Headleys had worked for Caverels at Ravenscourt for generations and the fellow's uncle had been head forester before him. George had got the job during the time of the Salisbury agents and had been left by them to do as he liked. Which was as little as he could. Nor had Robin Caverel given him any trouble. Everything had been fine, until Major Lawton had taken over. In the village pub, the Caverel Arms, where he drank with Peachey, the head gardener, and Mason, the male half of the couple in the house, George Headley had made himself the leader of the circle of grumblers. Several nights a week they sat together in the bar, joined by those whom the Lawton reforms had made redundant and by others who feared their jobs were under threat.

As the two men pushed through the wet undergrowth, Nicholas pondered how soon he would be able to replace the surly, lazy Headley with Rowley, a serious young man just back from an apprenticeship on a neighbouring estate. Headley was thinking how he'd get his own back were he to be sacked. Emerging from the belt of trees, they came to a point where the ground fell away steeply to a cart track far below. The rain poured off the brims of their caps and down their waterproof capes as Nicholas pointed to the plantation of spruce on the slope on the opposite hill and said it ought to be thinned, implying neglect. Suddenly, on the track far below them, they saw a small car coming from their left, travelling fast, throwing up mud and water from the ruts and pot-holes, leaping and skidding as it careered down the track.

'Who is that maniac?' Nicholas said. 'Whatever is he doing?'

Headley's eyes were sharper. 'It's her ladyship,' he said.

'That's not her car,' Nicholas protested.

'No. It's Mary's.' Mary was one of the cleaners who came from the village to help in the house. 'She must've taken it. She's in a hurry. Something's up.'

'She'll be looking for me,' Nicholas said.

He turned and, followed by the forester, broke back through the trees and undergrowth towards the point where the track would enter the wood after winding up the hill. Well before they reached it, they heard the noise of the engine in low gear as the car laboured up the hill. When they emerged from the wood, they could see it coming over the brow three hundred yards away, sliding and slipping in the narrow ride between the trees.

'For God's sake,' Nicholas said. 'She'll skid off the track and hit a tree.'

He stood in the centre of the ride, pulling off his drenched cap and waving it; he stepped back into the bushes as the car slithered to a halt a few yards from him. Andrea put her head out of the window. 'Nicholas,' she shouted, 'Nicholas.'

He trotted towards her, the rain pouring from his unprotected head. 'Whatever's the matter?'

'Get in,' she said. When he had lowered his wet frame on to the seat of the small car, she thrust a letter at him. 'This came this morning.'

Headley had remained where he was, watching. Something's up all right, he thought with satisfaction.

In the car Nicholas took the letter and smoothed it, resting it on the dashboard in front of him.

'Dear Mrs Caverel,' it began. 'By thus addressing you we mean no discourtesy but only that this is the correct way by which you should be addressed.'

He looked at the heading. Michael Stevens and Co., Solicitors and Commissioners for Oaths. Above the date he saw not 'The Lady Caverel' but 'The Hon. Mrs Robin Caverel, Ravenscourt, Wiltshire'.

43

He read on. 'According to the instructions we have received from our client, backed we may add by the information we have gained through our own researches, it appears that you have no right and never had any right to the title of "The Lady Caverel". For you are not and never have been the wife of a baron, for your husband was never a peer and had no right to the title which he assumed in his lifetime. Nor has your son, Francis, on the death of his father, the Honourable Robin Caverel, the right now to be called or to call himself Lord Caverel. Above all, neither you, your late husband nor your child has any right to be in possession of the estate and property entitled Ravenscourt.'

'Have you ever heard of them?' Andrea said. 'Why are they writing like this?'

'Let me finish it,' he said.

'Our reason for making the above statement is that we act for Miss Fleur Caverel who was born in South Carolina, USA, on 26th March 1971, the daughter of the Hon. Julian Caverel and his wife, Florence, née Wilson.'

Nicholas raised his eyes from the letter and looked through the rain-spotted windscreen at the ride ahead, remembering a scene almost thirty years ago. He'd been in a taxi making its way through the heavy traffic in the King's Road on his way to Chelsea Barracks, and he was late. He had leaned forward to peer through the window over the driver's shoulder to see how they were getting on and he'd seen Julian, on a pedestrian crossing, hanging on to the arm of a tall man, with a short pointed beard, a black beret on his head, and a cape above narrow black trousers. Julian was looking up into the man's face for all the world like a girl looking up into the face of her boyfriend. His mouth appeared to be painted. As they crossed in front of the taxi, he rested his head against his companion's shoulder. Then the pair disappeared into the crowd on the pavement and the taxi had moved on. That was the last time Nicholas had set eyes on Julian Caverel.

He turned back to the letter, the second page.

'As doubtless you are aware, the Caverel barony is one of those peerages created by Writ descendible to the heirs general of whomsoever first received a Writ of Summons to Parliament and then took his seat in the House of Lords. In other words, the

Caverel barony is one which a female can inherit. As the daughter of the Hon. Julian Caverel, the elder son of Walter the 15th Lord Caverel, it is Miss Fleur who was the rightful heiress to the barony when her grandfather Walter Caverel died, taking precedence over her uncle the younger child of the 15th Lord Caverel, Robin, your late husband. Thus it was Miss Fleur and not the Hon. Robin Caverel who on the death of her grandfather was entitled to all the estates attached to the barony, including the family seat, Ravenscourt.

'Your use of the title of Lady Caverel arises from the no doubt sincere but wrongful usurpation of the title by your late husband which we accept that he did while ignorant of the existence of his niece. However we must now invite you to acknowledge Miss Caverel, as she is presently styled, as the true and rightful heiress to her grandfather and thus to all the settled land and estate of the Caverel barony, and we must require you without too lengthy a delay to vacate the estate and the house of Ravenscourt where you and your son, Master Francis Caverel, are presently residing.

'Our client will require a full and complete account of all monies which have passed since your late husband wrongfully took possession of the settled land, up to the date when you hand over possession and our client enters into her inheritance.

'Failing your formal acceptance of the rights of our client, we are instructed to make an early application to the court for a declaration that Fleur Caverel is entitled to possession of the said Ravenscourt estate and house, and once in possession of such an order from the court our client will petition the Crown for her right to a Writ of Summons to take her rightful place in the House of Lords as the Baroness Caverel.'

'Who are these people?' Andrea repeated.

Nicholas could see the tall figure of Headley at the edge of the wood, dark and sinister against the trees.

Julian, the homosexual son of the fashion model who had run off with an Argentinian polo player, the son whom Walter Caverel had never acknowledged as his. Now a young woman was claiming to be Julian's daughter.

'Lawyers, of course,' he said savagely. 'We must get back to the house and call Oliver Goodbody.'

45

Andrea switched on the engine and the car jerked forward down the track, splattering Headley with mud as he stood aside and watched it go.

'What does it mean?' she asked.

'It means war,' he replied grimly, 'war to the death.'

9

Willoughby Blake and Michael Stevens were in a taxi on their way to dine in a favourite haunt of Willoughby's. They were discussing Dukie Brown. After the publicity of his release, Willoughby said, he had started well enough but interest had now waned. Brown himself was the reason. 'Too moody, too erratic. Sometimes he goes well; at other times, not a spark and the show's a flop. The word's got round you never know how he'll do and it's a risk booking him.'

'He needs time,' Stevens replied. 'Three years is a long time away.'

Willoughby grunted. 'I'm sending him overseas. If he refuses, I'm through.'

Stevens had looked after Dukie for a long time, ever since he'd got him off the murder rap, and had visited him during the years in prison. He was fond of Dukie but he wouldn't argue. If Willoughby Blake was going to chuck Dukie, there was nothing he could do.

In the restaurant, Willoughby ordered a grouse, roasted, very under-done, and a bottle of Château Pichon Longueville 1976. Stevens ordered a grilled sole, declined the wine and drank Perrier. As Willoughby ate, he gossiped happily about some of his more notorious clients. When he had pushed aside the cadaver of his grouse and ordered coffee, he took out a cigar. He put a match to it, carefully examining the end to make sure it was properly lit. A plume of blue smoke floated up above his head.

'Now, about young Sarah Wilson.' Then he corrected himself. 'No, not Sarah Wilson. Fleur Caverel. That's her name and that's what we call her. Miss Fleur Caverel, heiress to the Caverel estates and barony.' Stevens nodded. 'This is big, Michael, very big.' Stevens sipped his coffee, watching Blake over the rim of the cup. 'I've had a call from Jameson. He's located the grandmother in BA, and he's bringing her to London. She'll acknowledge Fleur Caverel as her granddaughter.'

'But they haven't met.'

Willoughby winked. 'A photograph, Michael, she's been shown a photograph, a true likeness of her long lost granddaughter. But Jameson says the old girl will need watching. She has a taste for vodka.' Willoughby knocked the ash from his cigar. 'Like her as a house guest, Michael, to save on costs?' He laughed happily. 'Don't worry, I intend to roll out the red carpet and put the old dear into an hotel. She's Fleur Caverel's little grandma who has crossed the ocean to be beside the long lost heiress, and she's going to be looked after.'

'Will she make a good witness in court? That's all that matters.'

'That's up to you, Michael. You're in charge of the law. My job is to assemble the cast – and prepare the public.'

He signalled to the waiter and ordered brandy. 'But there is someone around who we do not need,' he went on. Stevens knew who he meant. 'Paul Valerian. We must get rid of him.'

'How can we? I know he's not very prepossessing – '

'Prepossessing! There's the lawyer for you. He's fat, he's ugly, he can hardly speak the Queen's English and he looks a villain. If he's around when we produce her, he'll do immense damage.'

'He's the client. Or rather, they are the clients. It's their case. He found me. He came to me.'

'And you did very well, old son, by coming to me. But I want the Pole out. He must go. He has some hold over that girl. It's not good, it's not healthy. He's a Svengali. We've got to get her away from him – and quickly.'

'She's with him now in Paddington. She won't leave him. She trusts him. She's his friend.'

'But not, I judge, his mistress,' Willoughby mused. 'At least no longer, though she may have been at one time in the past.' He struck the table with the flat of his hand, making the coffee cups rattle. 'But we can do without Mr Valerian both in the run-up to court and at court. He's greasy, he stinks of liquor and he looks a crook whether he is one or isn't. The family lawyers would have a field-day with him – not to mention the press.'

'How do we get rid of him?'

'Pay him off, tell him he's harming her chances by staying around. From now on this is our show, Michael, and that's the way it's got to stay.'

Your show, you mean, Stevens thought. You and your people have taken it over.

'He'll want a lot of money,' he said. 'He believes the family will negotiate a settlement.'

'Will they?'

'How can they? They might pay a little to get her to go away if she will irrevocably renounce her claim, to rid themselves of a nuisance. But it wouldn't be enough for him. It'll end in a court case, and he'll be beside her when it does.'

'If we're to succeed, he has to be eliminated. Get him to your office, promise him a share. Tell him we're all more likely to get something if he clears off.'

'And if he refuses?'

'We'll cross that bridge when we come to it. Talk to him. See how he takes it. I suppose that in the life she was leading, she had to have someone to look after her, but it's odd she chose someone so repulsive.' Willoughby looked amusedly at Stevens. 'Now if it had been you, Michael, I could understand.'

Stevens, embarrassed, drank from his coffee cup.

'Thinking of trying your luck with her yourself, Michael?'

'Of course not.'

Michael Stevens lived an impeccable existence in an expensive villa in north London with his plump, serious wife and two earnest children.

'Just pulling your leg, old son. Have you had any reaction from the family?'

'No, and I didn't expect to, not yet. I'll hear in a few days. I have to give them time.'

'No, old cock, you do not have to give them time. Call their lawyers tomorrow and tell them to reply pronto or we go public.'

'What do you mean, go public?'

'I mean that I intend very shortly to introduce the lost heiress to the Great British Public. The time has come for us to launch her and to help us along, we need public opinion on her side.'

'It will be for a court to decide, a judge will decide, not the public.'

'Don't underestimate the GBP, Michael, and the effect of public opinion, even upon such unimpeachable characters as Her Majesty's judges. They won't say so. They can't show it, but they'll feel it, provided public opinion is properly targeted. They'll understand. They watch the telly, you know.'

He leaned back in his chair, looking benevolently at Stevens. 'Have you begun court proceedings?'

'No, of course not. As I told you, I must wait until I get a reply from the family.'

'Exactly. So there's no worry about contempt of court and no objection to telling the little lady's story to the world. The hacks'll love it – and love her.'

He again rocked back on the back legs of his chair, his eyes turned up on the smoke from his cigar above his head. 'And when we tell her story, the toffs'll be rubbished, you'll see, rubbished.' He brought down his chair with a bang and leaned forward. 'This is big, Michael, bigger than anything you and I have handled before. Think of that estate, the rolling acres, the pictures, the silver, the porcelain, it's worth a king's ransom. That young lady's going to be very, very rich – and so, Michael, are we.'

'Nothing is hers yet,' Stevens said. 'Maybe nothing ever will be.'

'It will, one day, and that day is not too distant. Then it'll all be hers – and ours. I know it'll come to a court case, but before it does I'm going to make sure the world knows all about her – and likes what it hears.' He wagged his cigar at Stevens. 'The sympathy factor, old cock, the perception of what's fair, whether it is or whether it's not. Beautiful young black barred from barony and fortune by a bunch of toffee-nosed snobs. Can't you see the headlines? Beautiful, just beautiful. What we have to do at this moment in time, as the pundits say, is to create an image, a politically correct image, of the deprived, snubbed, humble but beautiful young female black, an image so powerful, so sympathetic, so politically correct it might even induce the family to throw in the towel.'

'They won't do that.'

'Perhaps not, but they'll feel the pressure and it'll scare them. They won't be used to it and they won't like it. Have you ever experienced a rent-a-crowd of hacks outside your home, Michael, with the telephoto lens on the bathroom curtains?'

Stevens played with the spoon of his coffee cup. Willoughby laughed again. 'No, of course not. But when the Great British Public and the Great British Media learn all about the heiress denied her rights because of her sex and her race, the family may just think again.'

He stubbed out his cigar. 'I've set up a press conference for next week, so whether you've heard from the family or not, next week I go public. And when I do, I'll go public in style.'

10

Dukie Brown lit a cigarette. Then he ruffled the blonde head that lay on his shoulder. 'All right?' he said.

The head turned; a snub nose, freckles and the eyes, when they opened, very light blue.

'I've a date with the Almighty this morning,' he said, inhaling.

'Sod him,' said the girl. They were lying naked under an embroidered duvet on a large double mattress on the floor. Every now and then the whole building shook as the trains entered and left King's Cross station. It was a large, wide room, a great polished table in the centre with an elaborate silver centre-piece. At the far end was a Victorian bath tub on legs with clawed feet; a door near to it led into an enclosed loo. Against one wall was an electric cooker and a sink; opposite, on the other side was a large iron stove. The whole served for bed, bath, cooking and eating.

Dukie stubbed out the cigarette into the ashtray on the floor beside him. 'Time to move, Clem,' he said.

His hands behind his head, he watched her walk naked across the room and disappear into the loo. When she emerged, she turned on the bath and sat on the edge yawning and stretching. He threw aside the duvet and went to the sink. He looked at himself in the glass. Christ, he thought. His hair was longer now, not as long as in his prime but curling respectably at the back of his neck. He hadn't shaved for five days; today he thought he would. Not in honour of the Almighty, but because he felt like it.

Dukie left Clem at a café and went alone to the offices in the Shepherd's Market. He sat in reception on a black leather sofa, watched by the receptionist behind her desk. She was in her late twenties, a brunette, with a good figure which she worked on but a bad complexion. She liked Dukie Brown. She always had. As a kid she'd loved his music and she still did. She had agonised for him during his trial and had enthused when the boss had taken him on after his release. Now she was suffering as his come-back faltered and the engagements only came in fits and starts. She knew what he was going to be told.

'Coffee, Dukie?' she asked.

'No thanks, love. What time is it?'

'Eleven fifteen.'

'What time did he say?'

'Eleven, but there's been a crisis,' she lied. 'He's been badly caught up all morning.'

Dukie stood up. 'I'll come back later.'

'Oh no,' she said quickly, 'don't leave, I'm sure he won't be long. Do stay, Dukie, do.'

Her concern touched him. 'Why?' he said. 'Why should you care?'

She blushed. 'I just do,' she said. He smiled and leaned across her desk, gripping the edges with his hands, his head towards hers.

'Hullo, hullo,' a voice boomed. 'What's going on? Dukie Brown making love to my lovely Pru?'

Dukie straightened up and half turned. Willoughby put an arm round him. 'Sorry to have kept you, old son, but I see you haven't been wasting your time.' He laughed genially, slapping Dukie on the back. 'Come into the inner sanctum, old cock. I've plans for you, the chance of a lifetime.'

And with his arm still around Dukie, he led the pop star into his room.

Clem was still at the café. Dukie slipped on to the bench beside her. 'Want anything?' she asked.

51

'Wine,' he replied. He only drank red wine, and that in the evening.

'This early?'

'I need it.' Clem beckoned the waiter.

'What is it then?' she asked after she'd ordered.

'A tour, several months.'

'Here you go,' said the waiter, putting the two glasses on the table.

'The States?'

'No such luck. Ozzie-land.'

'Do you have to?'

'The last chance saloon. Otherwise, he says, he's through. He's fixed Perth, Adelaide, Melbourne, Sydney, Brisbane, up to the north then back south to Auckland. Home via the Cape and Jo'burg. Months.'

She was silent. Then she asked. 'And me?'

He took her hand. 'You're part of the baggage. You're on if you want to.'

'What's Oz like?'

'Sun, sand, ocean, chips everywhere, especially on shoulders. Good blokes, better sheilas.'

'I'll come,' she said.

After Dukie had left, Willoughby put through a call to Stevens. 'Have you seen Valerian?'

'He came round this morning. He says he's the client, or rather he and she are the clients. They've hired us, he said, or rather me. He doesn't know what you're doing in it.'

'Doesn't he just?'

'He says it's a simple negotiation with the family, see what they'll pay to settle. If that fails, it's a legal claim. A job for a lawyer, he said.'

'Did you explain to him what we want?'

'As best I could.'

'Did you talk money?'

'No, he wasn't interested. But he understood what I was getting at. He said if I was worried about his ugly mug I wasn't to worry as he wouldn't be a witness. He said he was here to help her as he always had.'

For a time there was silence. Then Willoughby said, 'He'll have his price. Keep trying.'

11

With one hand gripping the banister, the other his two sticks, Mordecai Ledbury worked his way down the narrow circular stair of the dining club to the basement floor where there was an open fire in the sitting area and beyond, in another room, the circular table where the members dined. If the descent was slow, the ascent later in the evening would be slower, and if anyone offered to help, they would be answered with a growl and an angry jerk of the great head. As a result those members not fleet enough to get ahead of him when he struggled to his feet from his chair as he prepared to leave had to fall in behind him and follow patiently as the crab-like figure made its way slowly up the narrow staircase. From the back, the hump and the head growing neckless out of the broad shoulders made him appear even more misshapen than did his front where the twisted face was at least illuminated by dark, restless eyes. Some, generally women, were sometimes privileged to see a strangely beautiful smile, but usually it was only his voice, low and melodious, that compensated for the distortion of face and figure. Like the womanising, squint-eyed John Wilkes in the eighteenth century, he said what he needed was time, and at first it was usually politeness that made the listener stay; then fascination; and finally, for one or two women, passion.

However, the members of Penns, the dining club whose stair he was now descending and where he dined every Wednesday, never saw that side of Mordecai Ledbury QC, only brusqueness and a caustic wit, usually at their expense. As a result, most avoided him; the newer members because of his appearance; the older because they feared his ill-temper and the savagery of his talk.

The conventions of the place demanded that when dining all sat at a single central table set in the candle-lit dining area where James, the steward, put their places – which he did in the order in which they had given their order. On a Wednesday the wiser members either dined early or waited until the steward tipped them off that Mr Ledbury had finished. It was the new or the unwary who found themselves sitting beside him, and the wise then ate in silence. Among them were many brave if now elderly warriors who had won every decoration for valour, but they blanched when they found they had been placed next to Mordecai Ledbury at the dining-table at Penns.

On this particular evening when he emerged from the stairs into the sitting-room there were only one or two members reading newspapers; from the hum of conversation from the dining-room, most were already at table. But in the furthest corner, reading from a narrow black notebook, a tall whisky-and-soda in front of him, was Oliver Goodbody. Mordecai limped across the room and lowered himself into an armchair in front of him.

The pair made a striking contrast; Oliver upright and slender with aquiline features and a full head of silver hair; Mordecai hunched and saturnine, with what hair he had plastered in streaks across his large head.

James, unbidden, brought a pint of champagne in a silver tankard and Mordecai began to drink, not sipping but gulping as if it were ale.

'I had a retainer delivered to your chambers this afternoon,' Oliver began.

'So I've heard.'

'It's a case of particular importance to me personally.'

Mordecai looked at him over the rim of his tankard. 'My clerk said it was a retainer for the Caverel family.'

'It is. I've been their solicitor and adviser for very many years, as was my father before me. I've known them all, even as far back as the great-grandfather of the present Lord Caverel, who is a child. I'm very close to the whole family.'

Mordecai raised his thick, black eyebrows. 'It's never wise for the lawyer engaged in litigation to be too involved personally,' he growled.

'That's my business,' Oliver said.

Mordecai bowed, smiling slightly at the sharpness of the reply.

'The defendant to any proceedings which may be commenced – ' Oliver continued.

Mordecai interrupted. 'There are none as yet?'

'No, but there will be. The formal defendant will be the child and it will be a claim for possession of Ravenscourt and all its lands and treasures brought in the name of a young woman who says she's the rightful heiress to all the settled land – and to the barony.'

Mordecai drank from his tankard. 'Then I'm not your man.'

'Yes, you are. It is the kind of case in which you excel.'

Mordecai Ledbury was the most formidable cross-examiner of the day. He was helped by his appearance – the hunched back, the twisted face under the dirty, grey wig usually perched askew on his enormous head, the two walking-sticks laid on the bench in front of him which were noisily snatched when he moved along the barristers' bench. The sight of him rising to cross-examine made most witnesses uneasy. But as an advocate he was flawed, for his bad temper led him at times to cross-examine too fiercely, which could alienate juries and judges. He only ever appeared in the Common Law courts, occasionally at the Old Bailey, and was never briefed in cases which required abstruse legal argument before an appellate court. Recently his practice had declined. Whereas it was once axiomatic that Mordecai Ledbury would be one of the counsel briefed in every prominent libel suit, now it was not. He had angered too many newspaper managements by the savagery of his cross-examination of editors and journalists or by the insults he showered on proprietors; and he had frightened off plaintiffs' solicitors by his quarrelling with the court. He had few personal friends either in the profession or outside it. He never attended functions at the Inns of Court or mixed with fellow members of the bar. He was part of no social circle. Penns was his only club. Oliver Goodbody was unique in that, perhaps once every two months, he dined with Mordecai on a Wednesday.

Mordecai put down his tankard on the table with a bang, beckoning the steward to bring more drink. He turned back to Oliver. 'If you've got yourself too involved with the troubles of this family, you're a damned fool. And you're an even greater fool to brief me in a case about inheritance law and a peerage claim.'

'I know which counsel I need to brief,' Oliver replied. 'I've retained you because I think you're the best man to do what will have to be done.'

'What you need is a quiet, reliable, Chancery lawyer guaranteed to be polite to the judge. I've never appeared in the Chancery Division in my life. I ought to reject your retainer in order to save your skin.'

'I can look after my own skin, Mordecai.'

'Can you? You're retaining me because we are what passes for friends and we're both getting old and once upon a time won battles together and you probably think I'm not doing so much work as once I did and that I need the money. Well, I don't, and if I did, I wouldn't take your charity.'

'Now it's you who are being the fool. There's no question of charity. I want you because I think you're the best man for the job.'

'It will mean arguing law and keeping one's temper with some boy or girl of a judge who's hardly out of short pants or petticoats. No, the man you need is Percy Braythwaite. If you're sensible you'll brief Percy, not me.'

Oliver leaned forward, a flush now on his pale face. 'You're wrong, and anyhow Braythwaite's been retained by the other side. He's not the man to represent the family. But he's certainly the best man to represent the claimant. He'll provide the villains with some cloak of respectability. No, I want you, Mordecai – you, at your best.'

Mordecai looked down at the tankard. For a time he said nothing. 'Me, at my best,' he said at last. 'The old me, what I once was.'

'Nonsense, what you are today.' Oliver stretched out his hand and laid it on the other's arm. 'You're the only man at the bar who can do what will be needed – which is to expose a conspiracy by a pack of unscrupulous rogues.'

Mordecai looked up at him, an eyebrow cocked. Oliver went on, 'A conspiracy by a gang who are using a young girl to get their clutches on a vast estate and a great deal of money. You're the right man to expose them.'

Mordecai's dark eyes were searching Oliver's face. For quite a time he said nothing. Then he said, 'You're very deep into this, Oliver. I hope for your sake that is wise.' He sat back in his chair. 'I'm hungry. James,' he shouted. 'We want to order.'

Mordecai bent forward so that his chin rested on his two hands holding one of his sticks, his eyes on the floor. 'A battle royal,' he said with one of his rare smiles. 'So that's what you're after.' He looked up at Oliver. 'You will have to provide me with ammunition if we are to destroy what you say is a conspiracy.'

'I shall.'

'Then we'd better celebrate now, before it begins – in case we're weeping when it's over.'

He banged the floor loudly with the ferrule of his stick.

12

Stevens talked to Paul Valerian a second time. All that Valerian would agree was that when Fleur got possession of the estate, generous fees, greater than the lawyer could reasonably expect, would be paid. Not a penny more. When he was informed, Willoughby was angry. Stevens was being too amenable. He would send Jameson. He was determined to get rid of Paul Valerian and when they had, he'd take Fleur Caverel under his wing – and keep her there.

Richard Jameson and Paul Valerian met in a bar near Paddington station. Valerian was slouched over a glass of brandy; Jameson sitting very stiff before an untouched glass of soda water.

'Ten thousand pounds, immediately,' Jameson said. 'It will be paid whenever you wish and it will be yours whatever the result. You take it – and go.'

Valerian put down his glass, leaned across the table and poked a stubby finger in Jameson's chest. Jameson drew back, icy.

'Fleur has been my friend for a long, long time. We began this together and we'll finish it together. We are partners. You cannot separate us.'

'It is ten thousand pounds certain, even if at the trial her claim is dismissed and she gets nothing.'

'My answer remains no.'

'Be reasonable, Mr Valerian. My principal believes that she has less chance of success if you remain.'

Valerian shook his head. 'I know what he's after. He's after her. He wants to get his hands on her, and then he'll cheat her out of everything. I'll not allow it. My answer is no, no, no.'

Jameson got slowly to his feet. 'My principal won't like your attitude. And my principal is very important – and very powerful.'

Valerian looked up at him 'Is that a threat?'

'No, it is advice.'

'I don't need advice from you. I know what that man is after. Go back and tell him no. And leave me alone.'

Jameson reported to Willoughby. 'Give him a few days,' Willoughby said. 'Then one more attempt, one last offer.'

'And if he still refuses?'

Willoughby looked at Jameson long and hard and shrugged.

13

Greg was having a swim in his lunch break when he had a message to call the office. It was urgent. Cursing, he clambered out of the pool and with a towel round him went to the telephone. Margaret told him he had to be back by two to take an urgent call.

'From home?' Greg asked.

'How should I know?' Margaret snapped. 'All I know is you're to be here. Jason will be at a meeting.'

But the call wasn't from Sydney. It was from Lincoln's Inn Fields.

'Mr Oliver Goodbody for you.' For a moment Greg was puzzled. Then he remembered the tall, elderly man who had chatted to him in the hall at Ravenscourt.

'We met at the cricket when you were looking at the Caverel portraits,' the silken voice began.

'I remember,' Greg replied. 'The Poms in wigs on the staircase.'

Oliver laughed. 'Exactly. You may remember you asked me about Julian Caverel, and Jason West tells me your interest in him was aroused by a visit from a young woman.'

Not a day had passed since that visit when Greg's thoughts about her had not been aroused. 'Oh, yes,' he said guardedly.

'I think I told you then that I act for the Caverel family.'

'You did.'

'Well, we have had a letter from a firm of lawyers making a quite extraordinary claim on behalf of a young woman. I believe she might be the same young woman who visited you.'

'Oh, yes.' So she had found lawyers.

'I wondered', the smooth tones continued, 'if you and I could have a talk about what was said when she saw you.' There was a long pause.

'Hullo, are you still there?' Goodbody asked.

'Yep,' Greg replied at last. 'I am.'

'We could meet wherever's convenient for you, either here at my office or – '

'What do you want to talk about?'

'What she said to you. You may be the first person she spoke to about Julian Caverel after she arrived in London, and as we now have this claim by her lawyers – '

'Who did you say her lawyers were?' Greg asked. If he had their name, he'd be able to trace her.

'Michael Stevens and Co. of Clarges Street. In view of their letter, it is important to learn exactly what she was saying when she first arrived in this country. I would very much like to talk and hear your report of – '

'No way,' said Greg. 'No way.'

This time it was Oliver Goodbody who paused. 'Do I understand that you are declining to talk to me about what was said when she spoke to you about Julian Caverel?'

'You understand right,' Greg said. 'What was said was private.'

This time the pause was even longer. The voice went on coldly, 'You appreciate that if this ever comes to litigation, you could be forced to tell a court what was said? You would be brought to court under a subpoena.'

'Sure, I understand. But I told you that what was said was private. Between her and me. So you just subpoena me. I'll look forward to it.'

Greg replaced the receiver. He sat back in his chair. So she'd gone ahead. Already she had the stuffed shirts twittering. He'd be damned if he'd lift a finger to help any of them against her. But if she wanted help, that would be different.

He asked in the office about Michael Stevens and Co. and then looked up their number. When he'd got through, he asked for Miss Fleur Caverel's address. He was refused it. He asked to leave a message for her and gave his name and telephone number. From the tone at the other end of the line, he knew Fleur would never get it. Then he thought of Henry Proctor. Henry was back from Milan.

'Lunch, tomorrow,' Greg said.

'Why?' said Henry.

'You'll see.'

'There's no such thing as a free – '

'I know, and this one isn't either. Morton's, one o'clock, Berkeley Square. I've got an acting job for you.'

Later that afternoon Jason sent for him. 'I've just spoken to Oliver Goodbody, Gregory. I gather you have refused to meet him and tell him what that young woman said about the Caverels when she came to see you – the young woman who embraced you in the hall.'

'That's correct.'

'But why won't you?'

'Privilege,' said Greg. 'She came to consult me.'

'Don't be ridiculous, you're not a lawyer.'

'Perhaps not. Still, it was private. What she said was confidential.' And that was all he would say.

In the afternoon of the following day, Henry presented himself at the offices of Michael Stevens and Co. He asked if he could see Mr Stevens' secretary. It was about Miss Caverel, he said, and it was important.

To the secretary Henry was at his most winning. 'I'd be so grateful for your help. Miss Caverel and I are old friends. We worked together last year, acting, you know, in Paris,' he added grandly, so grandly that the secretary thought she ought to have recognised him. 'I've been abroad in Italy, doing a part in a film which is being shot there, and I've lost contact with Fleur. I was told I might be able to get hold of her through you. Could you ask her to get in touch with me?'

'I'm not sure . . .' the secretary began.

Henry turned on his grandest manner. 'She and I talked only a week or so ago when she first arrived in London, just before I had to go to Milan. She wanted me to fix something for her. I took down her number but I've mislaid it. Now I need to see her. I believe I may be able to help her.'

'In what way?'

'Just help her. She'll understand. Tell her Henry, Henry Proctor, was asking for her. Ask her to call me.'

Henry had done well, for that evening Fleur rang.

'Darling,' Henry began, 'I'm just back from Milan, a far better job than the one in Paris last year. Much more money. Do let's meet and have a talk. Where are you staying?'

'At a hotel in Paddington, with a friend. By the way,' she added quickly, 'your friend was no bloody use.'

'Oh, I'm sorry.' For a moment Henry hesitated. Then he ploughed on. 'But I gather you're fixed up all right now. I'd just love to see you again. I'm across the park in Fulham. Come and have a drink tomorrow evening. I have some news for you.'

'What kind of news?'

'Come round and find out. It'll amuse you.' He gave her the address. 'Flat No. 8, the third bell. I'm on the first floor.'

Later he rang Greg. 'She doesn't think much of you, and she said she was here with a friend. But she has the address. Now you owe me.'

The next evening Greg stood at the window looking down at the street. She came by taxi, and he saw the top of her glossy head as she paid off the cab. He retreated back into the room in case she looked up. The bell rang; he pressed the buzzer and stood by the door waiting. There was a knock. He opened the door.

'You!' she exclaimed. 'I came to see Henry. What are you doing here? Where's Henry?'

'He's not here just at present,' he said cheerfully. 'But come on in.' She stood where she was, looking at him. 'Henry asked me to let you in. He's been called away.'

'Henry said he had some news for me,' she said. 'When will he be back?'

'Not long now.'

Slowly she entered the room and he closed the door behind her. She looked around, at the photographs on the chimney-piece, at the sporting magazines on the table. 'This isn't Henry's place,' she said, her back to him.

'No, it's mine,' he said breezily. 'I got Henry to ask you.'

She swung round. 'Are you working for the Caverels?' she said quickly.

'No, of course not. It's nothing to do with any of that.'

'Then what is it to do with?' She began to walk to the door. He stood with his back to it.

'All I know about your claim is what you told me. I hope you win, and if I could help, I'd like to.'

She stopped. 'Then why – ' she began.

'I just wanted to see you, and I didn't know where you were. Then I heard that Stevens' were your lawyers so I rang up but I knew they'd never pass on my message so I got Henry to ask you here.'

She was staring at him. 'You talk like Henry,' she said.

'He's Australian, like me.'

She started to walk again towards the door, forcing him to step aside. 'Don't be mad,' he said grinning. 'I don't mean any harm, at least not what I'd call harm. I just wanted to see you again.'

She turned. 'Why?'

'Guess why.'

She was staring at him. 'Why?' she repeated.

'Because I think you're – I think you're quite wonderful.'

Her eyes were still on him, her face still serious. He was still smiling. 'I think you're great, terrific, marvellous. I fell in love with you the moment we met and I had to see you again. That's why.'

She half smiled. 'Well, now that you are seeing me again, are you still in love?'

'More than ever. I'd do anything for you.'

'You didn't last time we met.'

'I know. I just couldn't think. I'm new in London, like you.'

'Did you believe what I told you?'

'Of course I did.'

For several seconds she stood staring at him; then she walked from the door and began to prowl round, examining the pictures and the photographs, fiddling with objects on the tables. After

62

she had circled the room, she sat on the sofa, drawing up her long legs beneath her.

He went to the side table. 'A drink?'

She shook her head. He opened a can of beer, his back towards her. 'I hear you found a very good lawyer.'

'No thanks to you.'

'In the office where I work, the office you came to, they say he's bloody sharp.'

'I hope he is. And he has a PR man who works with him, called Willoughby Blake. Have you heard of him? He's famous.' He shook his head. 'But my friend doesn't trust Blake. He says Blake wants to get rid of him and take me over.'

'Will you let him?'

'My friend won't.'

He looked down at the can in his hand. 'Is all this so very important to you?'

'I told you. I want my rights.'

'But what does that mean? Suppose it goes through the courts, appeals and everything, and in the end you get your father's estate? Then what? Do you want to stay here, live all your life in England, in the damp and the cold and the rain, with all these toffee-nosed Poms with their plummy voices? Do you really want to live in that great barrack of a house?'

'If it's mine, I do.'

'Have you seen the place?' She shook her head. 'I have,' he went on, 'just after I'd seen you, I was asked to play cricket there. It's vast. I couldn't live in it. I wouldn't want to.'

She stretched her arms high above her head. 'Can't you see me in a castle, sitting on a throne, wearing a crown?' She began to laugh. 'Wouldn't I look great?'

'You'd look great in anything anywhere. But is that what you really want?'

'I want what's mine.'

He shrugged. 'Well, if that's what you really want, that's good. Then fight for it, go and get it and don't let a bunch of stuffed shirts keep you from getting it.'

'I'm not going to. And when I win, my friend says I'll be very rich.'

'Who is your friend?'

'That's my business. Are Australians always so nosy?'

'Usually.'

She stared at him, looking him up and down. He grinned back at her. 'Do you really like the way I look?' she asked.

'I certainly do.'

'You think I'm beautiful?'

'I think you're more than beautiful. As I said, I think you're wonderful. That's why I got you here.'

'You said you wanted to get to know me.'

'Of course.'

Suddenly she was serious. 'Do you? Or is it that you just like what you see?'

'No,' he said, 'I want to get to know you, all about you. But I do very much like what I see.'

She stretched both hands high above her head again. 'Who knows what anyone else is like. No one ever knows.'

'They find out, if they care enough.'

Suddenly she said, 'I get headaches, bad headaches.'

'I'm sorry. Have you one now?'

'No, not now. I get them, though.'

She got up and went to the window looking down at the street. 'Do you know what I was doing before all this began?'

'Henry said you were a dancer. That's why you were in the advert with him.'

'I was in that advert 'cos I'm black, and they needed some black girls in grass skirts to go with the palm-trees and they hired us from the cabarets.'

She came back to where she'd been on the sofa and leaned against the cushions. 'I was a stripper. I've been a stripper since I was a kid. That's how I lived, taking my clothes off in clubs all over Europe – Paris, Berlin, Cannes, Budapest. Most of Europe must have seen me. All of me.'

'What of it?' he said.

'After the show we'd have to sit with the punters, chatting them up, making them buy champagne.' She paused. 'You know what that means?' He nodded. 'Some were all right.' She got to her feet. 'I think I will have that drink now,' she said.

She went to the drinks table, her back to him. 'You know, I quite fancied you when I saw you, even though you weren't any bloody use. The dimple in your chin. I like that.'

He heard the ice going into a glass. When she turned she had a glass half-filled with ice in one hand, the vodka bottle in the other. She poured some vodka over the ice, a lot of vodka. 'You're pretty sure of yourself, aren't you?'

'On the surface,' he said grinning again at her. 'Only on the surface.'

She put down the vodka bottle and drank from her glass. 'Seeing you again', he went on cheerfully, 'makes me feel good, very, very good.'

'I like your voice.'

'Poms don't.'

'Poms?'

'English.'

'You're not English, are you?'

'No, I told you. I'm an Ozzie. But my mother's English.'

'If my ma's right, so was my dad. I'm half English too.' She drank again. 'I don't feel it.'

'Nor do I,' he replied. He wondered why she said 'If my ma's right.' Wasn't she certain?

She came towards where he was on the sofa and bent and rested her hand on the side of his face. Then she kissed him on the forehead. He tried to pull her to him but she drew away and strolled again round the room, drinking as she went. She paused at the far end.

'Three doors,' she said. 'What's in there?'

'The kitchen.' She walked to the next door. 'Bathroom,' he said, 'and loo.'

The third door she opened and stood in the doorway, looking at the bed. She raised her glass, drank and walked inside. When he came to the door, she was sitting on the bed.

'You didn't know about me, about what I used to do, when you asked me here, did you?' she said. 'Or had you guessed?' He shook his head.

She drank again from her glass and then put it on the table beside the bed. 'Don't be scared,' she said, beckoning him.

She came at him like a hurricane, forcing him on to his back, riding him, then switching him over so that she lay beneath him, then back again, her nails scratching his sides, his shoulders. But she kept her mouth away from him. When she was on top of him and rose and fell, she had her eyes shut and was murmuring.

Only when it was over did she let him kiss her on the lips. They lay side by side, his hand on her thigh.

'I needed that,' she said.

He took his hand away abruptly. 'Was that all it meant?'

She turned her head to him. 'No, I was teasing. It was different.'

'Different! From what?'

'From other times.' She bent and kissed him gently on the lips. 'Do you believe in fortune-tellers?'

'No, do you?'

'In a way.'

'In what way?'

'I like to be told what's going to happen.'

'Did they tell you about me, that I was going to happen?'

'Of course, a dark man with a dimple would come into my life. No, I mean the real future, what's really going to happen.'

'It's nonsense,' he said.

'Is it? Are you so sure?' When she heard herself saying that, she remembered the Gypsy in Paris asking the same question and asking was it the past or the future she'd seen. And she'd replied it was only a dream, just a dream.

She turned on her side and saw the clock by the bed. 'I have to go,' she said. 'I have to get back to the hotel, to my friend.' He was going to speak but she put her finger on his lips. 'Don't worry. He's just a friend.'

He watched as she went naked from the room to the bathroom. She had made love as no one had ever made love with him before. Then he thought of what she'd told him about herself and the clubs and the punters. He swung his legs off the bed, put on his robe and in the sitting-room poured himself some vodka and drank it neat.

She reappeared, dressed. He pulled her to him but she broke away. 'Why do you have to go?'

'The lawyer's coming tonight. Nowadays it's nothing but meetings, people asking questions, other people taking notes. I have to do what they say now. But I shan't when I'm rich.'

'Where can I find you?' he asked.

'No,' she said. 'It's too difficult. They mustn't find out about us. The lawyer says I must be careful. He says I may be followed.'

'Who by?'

'By the family lawyers.'

'Why?'

'To see what I get up to. They'd like to catch me out. I'll get in touch with you here.'

She had indeed been followed, by a stout, neat little man in a dark suit, carrying an umbrella. He had sat in the café opposite watching the door of the house she'd entered, waiting for her to emerge. When she did, he followed her back to the hotel in Paddington, but while he had been waiting he had examined the names in the plates beside the bells on the front door and made a note on a pad with a small gold pencil. He'd come back later and check out the people who lived in the flats. It would, of course, be a man she'd been with. He had no doubt of that.

14

At about the same time on the same evening, when Fleur was with Greg at his flat in Fulham, Richard Jameson eventually caught up with Paul Valerian in a Polish restaurant in Knightsbridge. Jameson had been looking for him all day. He had come to deliver Willoughby Blake's final offer.

Valerian had been in the restaurant since noon, lunching, drinking, playing chess with cronies, but by six o'clock he was alone, a brandy glass and a newspaper before him, the chess board pushed aside. He looked up when Jameson approached. His eyes were rheumy and bloodshot.

'You again,' he said thickly.

Jameson drew up a chair. He was carrying a black briefcase which he laid on the table. 'I have here', he said, 'fifteen thousand pounds.' He opened the case, and showed Valerian the bundles of banknotes.

'That's a lot of money to be carrying around,' Valerian replied.

'It is. You can take it from me now, this instant, and you can be in Paris by tomorrow morning. This way, whatever happens, you have for certain fifteen thousand pounds. It is in fifty-pound notes. All you have to do is take it.' He closed the lid of the case and pushed it across the table towards Valerian.

Valerian stared at him through his bloodshot eyes. He must have been drinking all day, Jameson thought.

'I told you. I'm not interested.'

'So you said, but this is an even larger sum than what we talked about when last we met. To prove they are in earnest I have brought the money to you. It's their final offer.'

Valerian pushed the case back across the table towards Jameson. 'What do they think they are doing, offering me money? Whose money is it?'

'It is my principal's money. He's so serious about wanting you to go home to Paris that he is willing to pay you this very large sum to persuade you to leave. If you stay, he believes that the young woman may not succeed. He is prepared to pay this money to you because he thinks that it is in her best interests you should go.'

'Why should I? Why doesn't he go? Who says it's in her best interests that I go? I am her friend. He is not. She needs me. It's me who is in charge of this, not him, not you. It's me who began it and it's me who'll end it. I'm doing the paying, not them, and when it's over, I'll pay them for what they do for her, as I arranged with the lawyer. Now go back to your boss and tell him that, once and for all.'

He tried to rise. Jameson put his hand on his sleeve.

'Be sensible. Do what they ask, do it if it's only for the young woman's sake.' He paused and then said slowly, 'She's your friend. Do it for her sake, and for yours. They mean it. They want you to go.'

Valerian shook off Jameson's hand, staring blearily at him. 'Take your hands off me. I've had enough of the lot of you.'

He stumbled to his feet. 'Tomorrow I find other lawyers. There's plenty of other lawyers who'll take us on. We don't need you.' He bent and shook a finger under Jameson's nose. 'Go home and you tell them that tomorrow I take Fleur to other lawyers. Tell Stevens and Blake I don't want to see them again. Tell them they're finished.'

He turned and wove his way unsteadily past the empty tables and out into the street. Jameson followed. On the escalator of the Knightsbridge underground, Jameson stood a few steps above. He was quite close when they joined the crowd on the platform.

Valerian shouldered his way aggressively to the front until he was standing on the edge of the platform.

A little later the Piccadilly line stopped running. There had been an accident at Knightsbridge. A man had fallen in front of a train. At the time the station had been packed with commuters and shoppers on their way home, a mass of people several rows deep who were crushed together on the platform. From behind more had poured down the escalator, struggling and pushing to get on to the platform. Afterwards all that anyone could remember was that the man, a large man, very stout, had been seen suddenly to lurch forward and fall. Some said he was drunk. He certainly smelt of drink. He must have lost his balance, they said, pushed forward by the pressure of the crowd behind him. Others said he could have deliberately thrown himself in front of the train.

No one took any notice of the tall sandy-haired man with the black briefcase who had been among the crowd near the front of the platform and who after the accident had pushed his way back to the exit, as had so many when they realised that for some time no more west-bound trains would be running from Knightsbridge. Later the dead man was identified from papers on him as Paul Valerian, born in Warsaw, with a French passport and an address in Paris. No one knew where he was staying in London.

15

From time to time Paul Valerian had taken Fleur in the evening to a small restaurant near Paddington station, but usually she preferred to be on her own. If there were no meetings, she sometimes lay in bed all day, nursing her migraine in her darkened room while Paul was out with fellow Poles at their clubs or restaurants. After she'd got back from being with Greg, she found a message for her that the evening meeting with Stevens and his clerk had been cancelled and she went to bed.

At seven o'clock next morning she was woken by the telephone. Mr Willoughby Blake, the woman at the desk said, was on his way up to her room. She had only time to fling on a dressing-gown before he was at her door. When she opened it, he took her by both hands.

'Come and sit, my dear. I'm sorry to come so early but I've something to tell you.' He led her to the bed. 'I'm afraid I have bad news.'

She sat on the edge of her bed, and he drew up a chair. Speaking very gently he told her of the accident at Knightsbridge underground station and that Paul was dead. She stared at him, silent and wide-eyed. He took her hand. 'I am sorry, so very sorry. I know what a shock this must be and I wanted you to hear the news from me and from no one else. I came as soon as I heard. You must let me do what I can to help.'

On his way to her he had rehearsed what to say. He expected hysterics. Over the past weeks he had seen how agitated she could become, suddenly, unexpectedly, sometimes over trivialities, and he was prepared for total collapse when she heard what he had to tell her. But instead she just stared at him, wide-eyed, sitting bolt upright, rigid and frozen.

Her stillness and silence surprised him. Had she taken in what he had been saying? He repeated, very gently, that her friend, Paul, was dead. Still she said nothing, her eyes fixed on his. He was puzzled by the absence of any reaction, so for a time he too sat in silence, holding both her small hands in his. Was her silence due to shock? Or was it fear of a future without the friend who had guided and protected her? Then he began again.

'I know how close Paul was to you and how dear you were to him. You will miss him grievously and so shall we, but sadly we have to accept that he has gone, and you and Michael and I must carry on as best we can. We shall no longer have the advantage of his inspiration and leadership but I promise that Michael and I will do everything in our power to help and support you. We must not allow this terrible tragedy to stop us from winning for you what is rightfully yours.'

He was pleased with this little speech. He studied her face, her beautiful, dark face, and looked into her hazel eyes, still quite free of tears. He dropped his eyes to the flimsy dressing-gown above her nightdress barely covering her shoulders and breasts.

She turned her head away from him towards the small window in the narrow, shabby room. She'll be thinking of Valerian, he thought. Perhaps now the hysterics will begin?

She was indeed thinking of Paul Valerian, remembering the scent of brandy and Gauloise cigarettes that had so nauseated her and which now she would never again have to endure. But she was also remembering times past, happy times in many cities, Istanbul, Berlin, Paris, when he had looked after her, helped her and, in his own way, worshipped her. He had been a good friend.

'His passing', she heard Willoughby say, 'means that Michael and I will now work all the harder for you and I promise that we shall. We shall miss him, but he would have wanted you to go on even if he will not be beside you when you get what is yours, as I am certain that you will.'

It was true, she thought, Paul would have wanted her to go on. He had urged her on when she'd hesitated. He had told her what she must do. He had provided the money. Having got so far he would not want her to abandon it.

She turned her head back to Willoughby, who now spoke even more sadly and gently as he approached the real reason he had been so anxious to be the first to bring her the news.

'What makes it so tragic is that only yesterday we were discussing an agreement between us. Paul understood that the costs of the claim would be great and would increase as litigation approached, and we were talking about how best we could share those costs; and when we had won, how we would share the winnings. He had insisted, although we were of course friends, that we must put our relationship on to a proper business footing so as to avoid any risk of any misunderstanding in the future. He was so sensible, so wise, and this is what we were engaged in doing just before he died.'

'Where will he be buried?' she asked abruptly, the first words she had spoken.

Willoughby thought for a moment. 'There will have to be an inquest. There always has to be when a death has been – ' He was going to say 'violent', but he checked himself. 'When death

71

is due to an accident. Michael Stevens will look after it. He will deal with the Coroner's office. As to burial, where do you think he would have liked to rest? Here or in Paris?'

She shook her head. 'Whichever is quickest, that's all I want.'

'Stevens will arrange it. There is also the question of his belongings – '

'He has none.'

'He must have some, clothes, personal effects. Do you know of any relatives in France? He owned the club in Paris. There will be a will. Perhaps you – '

'I want nothing,' she burst out, pulling her hands away. 'I want nothing of his.'

'Of course. But where did he live in Paris?'

'At the club, above the club.'

'We'll see to it that everything is done properly. There will be no need for you to worry.' Then he went on more briskly. 'But to return to what I was saying, when you feel you are ready for business, you and I and Michael Stevens must meet. Just the three of us, alas, no longer four, to settle the agreement Paul had in mind.'

She remembered Paul's warnings. That Blake wanted to take her over and would cheat her. But what could she do? Who could help her? Greg? From the moment she'd cast eyes on Greg she'd been attracted to him, and their sudden love-making had given her a sense of fulfilment, a release from the tensions and anxieties of the past months. But could he take the place of Paul, the place which Willoughby Blake was now offering to fill?

'Whatever happens,' she heard him say, 'we must do what Paul would have wished, and that is to press on.' He stood up. 'My dear,' he said, looking at her very kindly, and she saw how handsome he looked with his bronzed face and silver hair, how prosperous in his silk, cream shirt and blue tie and well-cut suit. 'Will you let me take you from here? I think it would be best for you to leave this place where you were with him. Come with me to the hotel in Kensington where I have taken rooms. You can be there with your grandmother who is flying from the Argentine. She is old. I have engaged a companion for her, a Mrs Campion. She is at the hotel already and I know she'd be happy to look after you as well.' He looked around the room. 'It will be much nicer at Kensington than here, more comfortable. And you

72

will not be alone but with friends. I can send later for your things.'

She looked down at her hands folded in her lap. She couldn't involve Greg. There would be too much explaining. And would he have the money? For a moment she thought of abandoning it, of running away. But where to go? There was only the old life in the clubs. Could she face a return to that after she had broken from it? No, she knew she had to go on, and if she was to go on, there was no alternative to Blake and Stevens.

'I'll come,' she said. 'I'd like to leave here.'

When she had dressed, she joined Willoughby in the foyer, not even bringing her small suitcase. He said he'd send for everything. The pinched receptionist was not at her desk. Willoughby had seen to that. He had laid out more money and told the woman about the accident and that Mr Valerian was dead. His lawyer would come later to look after everything, settle the bill, collect the belongings.

Willoughby led Fleur to his car. At the large, opulent Kensington Park Hotel, Mrs Campion settled her in bed in a bright, airy room, so very different from the drab little room she had just left. She brought her some pills. 'You'll be glad of these. They will help you get over the shock.'

She drew the curtains and left.

Fleur curled up in the bed. Poor Paul, poor drunken old Paul. I hope he didn't suffer.

All that day and all the following night she dozed in the comfort of the great bed and the attentions of Mrs Campion. At some time, in the middle of the night, she thought her door opened and light flooded into the room. She thought she heard a voice say, 'Is the black bitch in here?' But it was probably a dream.

She slept long into the next morning. It was early afternoon when Willoughby came into her room and sat beside her bed.

'How did you sleep?'

'Very well. But I thought someone came into my room in the middle of the night.'

He shook his head. 'I'm sure not, unless it was Mrs Campion to see if you were all right. I expect you were dreaming. The pills Mrs Campion gave you were very strong. Now you must rest some more. Do not hesitate to ask if you need anything.'

He spoke gently and he made her feel safe. Before, she'd been wary of him. Now she knew she would have to rely on him – until it was over. When it was over, she'd go to Greg.

In the evening, Willoughby returned. 'If you're well enough, I'm afraid I must trouble you with a little business. First, your grandmother has arrived. She's anxious to see you but she is exhausted after her long journey from South America and has gone to bed. Tomorrow you will meet. Next, Stevens has agreed to look after the inquest. When that is over, he thinks it better that the body should be taken to Paris. He's in touch with the assistant manager at the club. But he keeps insisting that as soon as you are well enough, we must put our relationship on a business basis. He keeps talking about cost. Expenses, he says, are mounting, especially the legal fees and the maintenance of you and your grandmother here in the hotel. He is right, but tiresome, like all lawyers. I told him you won't be fit for business for a day or so and we can discuss it when you're stronger.'

He rose and walked to the window. 'There is, I'm afraid, something I should tell you about your grandmother.' He turned and looked back to the bed. 'She will be a very important witness, because she's the one member of the family who is supporting you. Michael Stevens says her evidence will be vital. But she has a little problem. Probably because she's lived so much alone, she does – well, she does like to drink, sometimes too much. So we must look after her.'

He walked from the window to the bed. Fleur, in her night-dress, was sitting up, the bedclothes thrown back, her arms around her knees. Willoughby could see her breasts. She knew he could, but she didn't cover them. 'I'm sure you'll do what you can to help her.'

'Of course,' she said.

'Well, that's enough business for one day and I'm sorry, my dear, I have had to trouble you with it. Now you must rest. If there's anything you want, anything at all, just tell Mrs Campion.'

He leaned over the bed and she looked up at him. He would like to kiss me, she thought.

'I have one of my headaches,' she said.

He took her hand. 'Then be sure you rest and stay quiet.'

In the sitting-room of the suite, Willoughby said to Margaret

Campion, 'See how she is tomorrow. She must meet the Senora as soon as the old woman is in a fit state, and then in a few days, we must get her to Stevens.'

Next day Mrs Campion helped Fleur to get up. When she was dressed she went into the sitting-room where she was grabbed by a short, fat, painted old woman and buried in a great embrace. It was still morning, but over the scent Fleur got the whiff of alcohol. Mrs Campion stood discreetly at the far end of the room.

'My darlink,' the old woman began, 'my little darlink, my Julio's little baby whom I have never seen. Come, my darlink, come and sit with your old grandmamma and tell her all about yourself.' She pulled Fleur down beside her on the sofa, still holding Fleur's hands, and thrust her face into Fleur's. 'You are beautiful, my darlink, you are quite beautiful, such pretty eyes and hair – and not nearly as black as I expected.' She kissed Fleur's cheek. 'I know we're going to be friends, very, very good friends. And you are going to look after your poor old grandmamma for the rest of her poor old life.'

Only routine interest was shown in the inquest on the accidental death of Paul Valerian, a visitor from Paris. The autopsy had shown that he was full of alcohol. After the inquest the body was shipped home, where Jean, the assistant manager at Valerian's club, made the arrangements for the burial. The club was mortgaged and heavily in debt and after the funeral expenses, there would be little left. But there was a will – and a wife, long separated from him, an elderly Polish woman who'd been a cleaner in the Cathedral of Notre Dame. Jean's lawyer had got in touch with her and she came to the funeral but stood apart from Jean and three others who had come from the club. They did not know the widow and ignored her.

There was, however, one other person at the burial, a stranger to all of them, a stout, neat little man, wearing a dark raincoat and black hat and carrying a rolled umbrella. He kept to the path some way from the grave, watching. When the coffin had been lowered and the earth poured on it and the mourners from the club had drifted away, he crossed the grass and approached the widow, raising his hat, telling her he was from London. When he expressed his condolences, she shrugged. He said he had known Mr Valerian in England, and after they had talked a little by the grave, he told her he had a taxi waiting and offered her a lift home. She accepted gratefully. On the way he suggested they have some coffee or tea, so the taxi dropped them at a café. Later, after a meal and some wine, he took her home.

A few days after the burial, Fleur, now settled into the suite of rooms in the Kensington hotel, was taken by Willoughby to Stevens' office. There the formal, confidential agreement between the three was executed. In consideration of unlimited legal and representational support by Stevens and Co., including the cost of briefing counsel to appear at all stages in the hearing of her claim up to and including the trial and any appeal and any application to the Committee of Privileges of the House of Lords; and for the advice and special arrangements made on her behalf to promote her claim and for her maintenance and an allowance for her personal needs provided by Willoughby Blake Associates, Fleur Caverel, the claimant to the Caverel estates and barony, agreed that all or any of the assets which she might receive arising from the prosecution of her claim were to be divided equally between herself, her lawyer Michael Stevens, and Mr Willoughby Blake. Willoughby, however, made a point of insisting that the house itself, Ravenscourt, apart from its contents, must be excluded. The house, he said, should be for the claimant alone. It was the home of her ancestors. He did not explain how it could be maintained on only a third of the revenue of the estate.

Back in the sitting-room at the hotel, he ordered champagne. The Senora declined the champagne and drank from a tumbler of what she said was water but which Mrs Campion knew was vodka. Fleur sat curled up on the sofa, sipping the wine, conscious that Willoughby was looking at her legs.

Willoughby raised his glass. 'A toast,' he said, 'let us drink a toast to the claimant, the future Baroness Caverel of Ravens-court.' They all drank. 'Very soon,' he went on, 'I shall have the honour of introducing the Caverel Claimant to the public.' He bent and kissed Fleur's hand. 'Then, my dear, you will be famous. Later you will be rich.'

16

There were empty seats and Richard Jameson could have sat but he preferred to stand at the back where he could keep an eye on everybody and everything. He leaned against the wall, his arms folded, as still and motionless as ever, his eyes on the audience and, beyond them, on the figures on the stage.

His special charge was the Senora. It was he who had located her and it was he who had suggested his cousin as her companion, a Mrs Campion, whom the Senora had at first resented. But as Mrs Campion had discreetly helped over the supply of vodka, the Senora had accepted her. Now she stood in the wings unseen by the audience while the Senora sat behind a table on the dais under the lights, a tangle of dyed orange hair above beads and bangles and an electric blue dress cut low showing the wrinkled skin of her chest and arms. She kept swinging the beads round her neck, smiling and bowing, now and then patting the hand of Fleur who was seated beside her. The professional make-up artist Willoughby had brought to the hotel to prepare Fleur and the Senora had done as well as she could with the old woman but her work to the mouth had not remained unsmudged for long, for when she had been finished, the Senora had waddled off to her bedroom. At the studio, she had gone to the Ladies and returned bearing a glass of colourless liquid which she carried on to the stage with her. She had then called for a carafe, which certainly contained only water for it was brought to her by one of the attendants.

Although many of the chairs set out for the audience were unoccupied, Willoughby was content. 'It's quality that counts,' he said. Representatives from each of the two best-selling daily tabloids and Sundays, stringers for *Der Spiegel* and *Paris Match*, and a pair from the *Black Banner*, a local weekly circulating in Hackney – Jameson had been sent to recruit the last. 'You should come,' he'd told them. 'It's a race thing.' Willoughby himself had got the two-man crew from Channel 4 with a camera and a boom mike, which accounted for the lights under which the three on the platform were sitting. As they faced the audience, Willoughby, his silver hair neatly coifed, bronzed under his make-up, wearing his light grey suit and bright blue tie with a red carnation in his buttonhole, was on the right. In the centre was Fleur, in a pale blouse which set off her chocolate skin, and a short black skirt. She wore no lipstick and no jewellery, not even ear-rings.

'Vulnerable, a little bewildered,' Willoughby had said, 'that's what we want.'

With her hands clasped on the table in front of her, Fleur made a striking contrast to the flamboyant and outrageous old woman on her left.

Two days earlier Willoughby had taken her to a photographer and ordered head and shoulder pictures, sepia, rather misty, old-fashioned pictures, and these he had distributed with the hand-out before the platform party had appeared.

Willoughby now began, not standing, talking easily, professionally, into the microphone, welcoming everyone, telling them they'd been asked here to meet Fleur Caverel and hear the extraordinary story of how a simple young woman had come to learn that she was the rightful heiress to one of the oldest titles in the British peerage.

'Until a few weeks ago,' Willoughby said, 'this young woman ...' Here he took Fleur's hand and looked at her but she kept her eyes lowered. '... this beautiful young lady believed she was the child of humble, elderly parents who had raised her in the countryside in South Carolina in the United States. But three months ago, in the office of an attorney in Charleston, she was handed a letter written by her real mother on her death-bed over twenty-five years before. The attorney told her that the old woman who she believed was her real mother was in fact her foster mother. From the letter she learnt that her name was not Sarah Wilson, but Fleur Caverel, the daughter of Julian Caverel, the elder son of the 15th Baron Caverel of Ravenscourt in the county of Wiltshire, in England.'

Willoughby paused and looked round his audience. Most, he noted with satisfaction, had their heads buried in their notebooks.

'Julian Caverel, whose parents were divorced,' he went on, 'had been brought up during his early years by his mother who

78

was living in Buenos Aires in the Argentine. When he was a young man, he'd spent a few years in England but soon left for the USA where he wandered across the continent from state to state, supplementing an allowance paid to him from England by playing the piano in clubs and bars. In 1970 in South Carolina he met and fell in love with a girl from Beaufort County. He married her and conceived a child. But he was a feckless and irresponsible young man, and before his wife had even borne his child, he had disappeared, abandoning his pregnant wife who never heard from him again. In 1978 he himself died in San Francisco.

'His daughter, who was born in 1971, had been christened Fleur by her mother who herself died soon after, and the baby was taken in and raised under the name of Sarah by Mr and Mrs Wilson, a devout chapel-going couple with no children of their own. But the little girl being brought up in St John's Parish, Beaufort County, South Carolina, was in reality a half-English orphan, her existence unknown to any other member of her family. Save for one, and the knowledge of that person was only vague and uncertain.'

Willoughby paused. 'After he had left South America, Julian, with his usual fecklessness, rarely communicated with his mother, but in or about 1971 he sent her a postcard, with no address, in which he wrote quite casually that he'd been informed that he was to be the father of a child. She never heard from him again and knew no more of the grandchild of which her son had written, whether it was a boy or a girl or indeed whether it was ever born. Ten days ago she arrived in London from South America, and met the granddaughter she had never seen. She is with us today – the Senora Lucia Martinez.'

At the mention of her name, the Senora made as if to get to her feet but found difficulty in shifting her bulk out of her chair. Willoughby hurried on, so the Senora had to be content with a wave and a series of majestic bows.

'Three years ago, Walter, Julian's old father, the 15th Baron Caverel, at last died, many years after his elder son, and his younger son, Robin, born of a later marriage, and unaware of the existence of any child by his deceased elder half-brother, assumed the title, took up residence in Ravenscourt, the ancestral seat of the Caverel family, and took his place in the House of

Lords. But Robin had little enjoyment of his estate. Two years later he was tragically killed in a car accident and was in turn succeeded by his infant son, Francis. However, unknown to either of them, there existed an heir with a superior title, this young lady, Miss Fleur Caverel.'

Jameson was only half listening; his eye was fixed on the Senora who, when she was not smiling at the audience or at her granddaughter, was, he saw, sipping more and more frequently from the glass in front of her.

A man's voice suddenly interrupted Willoughby, a journalist in the front row who asked if the family had been told of Fleur's existence and of her claim.

'They have,' Willoughby replied, 'and, we acknowledge, it must have come as quite a shock. But let me make clear, Miss Caverel, as we must call her for the present, accepts that the family was quite unaware of her existence when Robin and later his son assumed the title and took possession of Ravenscourt.'

'What has been their reaction?' another asked.

'We're waiting to hear from them.'

'Hasn't there been any contact? Hasn't Fleur been to see them?' a woman reporter asked.

'No, not as yet.'

'Why not?'

'She has not yet been to see them because, as a stranger to this country and unaccustomed to our ways and forms, she knew nothing of titles and estates and when she arrived in this country she chose to seek advice. As an American, or as someone raised in America, she did what all good Americans do.' He grinned knowingly. 'She went to see a lawyer, and that lawyer, the distinguished solicitor, Mr Michael Stevens, decided to lodge her claim officially and formally by letter.'

'What happens if the family rejects her claim?' the woman reporter went on.

'I hope they won't. There can be no doubt that Fleur is the child of the elder son and accordingly she takes precedence over a younger son and his family, and this is a barony which a woman can inherit.'

'But what if they don't accept her?' the journalist persisted.

'Then it will become a matter for the courts to decide, to the advantage of none save the lawyers. But as I said, we trust it won't, for there can be no doubt who Fleur is, and to support her and vouch for her is none other than her own grandmother.'

Willoughby paused to look down at his notes and the Senora seized her opportunity. This time she didn't attempt to rise.

'I am so happee,' she announced loudly in a stagey Latin accent, 'so happee to have found my darlink little granddaughter, my Julio's little Fleur. Julio's daughter.' She pronounced it 'Shoolio'. She grabbed Fleur's hand. 'I am so proud after all these years to be with this little one. Since the death of my darling Shoolio, I have been so much alone, so lonely, so unhappee. Now I have my Fleur, my Shoolio's little daughter, my own grand-daughter and – '

'Where's the postcard?'

The question came from a man sitting to one side of the audience, at the end of a row about five from the front, a stout, neat little man in a dark suit, with a notebook on his knee and a bowler hat and a rolled umbrella on the floor beside his chair.

Startled, the Senora put her hand to the beads swinging in front of her ample breast and peered in the direction of where the question had come. 'What was that? What did he say?'

'I said where's the postcard you say your son wrote to you about him expecting a child?'

Willoughby intervened. 'Unhappily the Senora no longer has it. It was after all written quarter of a century ago and – '

'She's not South American at all, is she? She's English, isn't she?'

The Senora had her hand to her ear. 'What's he saying? I can't hear what he's saying.'

'I said you're English, aren't you?' the man repeated more loudly.

'What do you mean? I'm Argentinian from Buenos Aires. My name is Martinez. I arrived in London, when was it, a week ago. I live in the Argentine. I've lived there for years and years and – '

'But you're English.'

The Senora took a swig from the glass. 'Well,' she said, her South American accent not now so pronounced, 'if you're askin' was I born in England, I was. And that was more years ago than I care to remember.' She laughed but it sounded forced. She went on, 'I don't think of myself as English. I 'aven't been back

81

'ere for years. I've lived in the Argentine for what seems to me like a century.' She giggled again, not very convincingly. 'My name, as you have heard, is not English. My name is Martinez.'

'Your name used to be Bull, didn't it, Lucy Bull, from Berners Road, Clapham?'

Willoughby felt he'd better intervene again. 'However long the Senora may have been away from this country,' he began gallantly, 'we're all delighted to welcome her back to the land of her birth and delighted she has come all this way to join us this afternoon – '

'How is the girl sitting beside you your granddaughter?' the stout little man called out.

Willoughby answered for her. 'Miss Caverel is the Senora's granddaughter because Miss Caverel is the daughter of the Senora's son.'

'Is she? How do you know? Julian Caverel was a well-known homosexual, wasn't he? Didn't he die of what's now known as Aids?'

'Look here,' Willoughby began, by now quite rattled. 'I don't know which newspaper you represent or who you are but – '

'Even if she is the homosexual's daughter, which is unlikely, on which side of the blanket was she born? Can she tell us that?'

'That's quite enough – ' began Willoughby.

'And if it comes to that, even if the former Lucy Bull is Julian's mother, who was Julian's father? Tell us that, madam.'

''Ow dare you!' the Senora shouted back, struggling to rise from her chair.

'It wasn't Walter Caverel, was it? He wasn't Julian's dad, was he? Just tell us who was Julian's dad?'

The Senora had managed to extricate her bulk out of her chair, knocking it over behind her. She had the glass of liquid in one hand; with the other she swung the glass beads fiercely round her neck. She bent forward, her face red with rage. 'You fuckin' little bastard,' she shouted, the accent now not South American but South London. ''Ow dare you, 'ow dare you come 'ere and insult me! I know who you are. You're a fuckin' messenger boy from those fuckin' Caverels. They sent you 'ere to bad-mouth me. I know them, those fuckin' snobs,' she shouted, redder in the face than ever.

'Who was Julian's dad?' the stout little man repeated.

'Shut your face, you arse-creeping little bastard. You've been sent here to insult me because those toffee-nosed shits'll stop at nothing to keep their hands on what they've stolen from my little girl. They won't 'ave her because she's black, that's why the buggers want to stop 'er getting what's 'ers. They don't think she's good enough for them, isn't that it? Just as I wasn't good enough when I was with that swine Walter. She's just a nigger, that's what those fuckin' snobs are saying, like they said I was just a tart. Well, you just tell them that she's my Julian's kid even if she is a nigra, and to hell with them, them fuckin' lords and ladies.'

She swung her arm back. Some of the liquid from the glass fell on Fleur and on to the table before the Senora flung the glass towards the questioner. It barely reached the front row of the audience who, seeing it come, ducked and put their hands over their faces as the glass crashed and broke on the floor in front of them. They got to their feet but ducked again when they saw that the Senora had now grabbed the carafe. It didn't get as far as the glass, but exploded on the floor with an impressive crack.

Willoughby was now on his feet. Jameson started to run up the side aisle to get to the platform. As he did so, he brushed past the questioner who had slipped from his place and, umbrella in hand, was walking quietly to the door at the back of the room.

'It's all right, it's all right,' Willoughby was shouting through the microphone. 'Everyone keep calm, please keep calm.'

The Senora was still yelling when Jameson leaped on to the platform. She tried to slap his face but he grabbed her, pinning her arms to her side and hustled her, still struggling, through the door at the back of the platform. Once out of sight, Mrs Campion held the Senora's arms while Jameson struck the old woman in the face three times, first with his open hand; then twice with the side. Mrs Campion let the old woman slide to the floor and they both stood over her as she lay at their feet.

On the platform, Willoughby had put his arm around Fleur. 'It's all right, my dear, it's all right.'

She looked up into his face. She was laughing. She was still laughing when he escorted her off the stage.

*

83

At the hotel in Kensington, a doctor was summoned to examine the Senora, who was unable to speak. He pronounced that her jaw was dislocated, perhaps broken. She'd had a bad fall, Jameson told him, stumbling off the platform and falling on her face. She was taken by ambulance to a private clinic in St John's Wood.

Later in the evening, Willoughby joined Michael Stevens in his office.

'In her inimitable and colourful way, the old darling said what none of us could possibly have said.' He smiled and lit a cigar. 'She was spot on, bless her old soul. Let's take a look at the TV.'

There was a short clip on the Channel 4 seven o'clock news bulletin, but only about the claim for the title and estates by the lost daughter of the lost heir. There were pictures of the platform party before the conference had begun and no reference to the fracas or the Senora's words, except to report that in the course of the conference the claimant's grandmother referred with considerable hostility to the aristocratic Caverel family into which she had once been married. Close-ups of the girl made clear that the claimant for the ancient Caverel title and estates was black.

'I've had a word or two so it'll be better in tomorrow's tabloids,' Willoughby said. 'You'll see.'

And next morning Stevens did see. The Senora's words, with a few suitable asterisks, were fully reported. The story of the Caverel Claim, as it came to be called, was carried by every newspaper, including the broadsheets. There were many reproductions of the wistful photograph of Fleur and one of the tabloids had an imaginative picture of what was meant to be a share-cropper's cabin with a large, black 'mammy' seated in front of the door, with the caption, 'Birthplace of Caverel claimant'. There were photographs of Ravenscourt, with some of the hall and staircase with the portraits of the Caverel ancestors. There was a picture of Andrea with Francis on her knee, which had been taken by a photographer from a local newspaper when Robin had inherited; and an old one of Major Nicholas Lawton, in his scarlet tunic and bearskin cap. He was described as the member of the family now managing the Caverel estates and beside his picture was that of a dismissed estate worker standing by the cottage from which he was shortly to be evicted. There was a formal statement from the family's solicitors, Messrs

Goodbody, that the claim would be strenuously defended. 'Classic Court Case Looms. Challenge to Ancient Title. A Fortune at Stake' was one of the more reserved headlines. 'Black girl seeks title and fortune from toffs. Snobs and cheats charge. Court battle ahead' was the headline in the *Daily News*.

'Splendid,' Willoughby said cheerfully to Michael Stevens. 'And all thanks to the old darling.'

'But what will she be like when she comes to court?' Stevens asked. 'What kind of a witness would she make? It's a judge who'll decide,' he muttered.

'I know, old son, I know. But that little introduction to the Great British Public won't have done any harm. The Albert Hall to a china orange, our little conference has rattled the family. And over the weeks to come, old cock, there'll be a few more rattles. You'll see. I've only just begun.'

17

In the afternoon of the following day, another conference of a different and more staid kind assembled at four thirty in the room of Mordecai Ledbury QC in King's Bench Walk in the Temple. Oliver Goodbody entered, followed by Nicholas Lawton and one other – a short, stout, middle-aged man with an agreeable rather cherubic face, dressed in a tight-fitting dark suit. He was the man who had witnessed Fleur's visit to Greg in Fulham, who had attended Paul Valerian's funeral in Paris and who had asked the questions at Willoughby Blake's press conference.

Mordecai was seated behind a vast eighteenth-century desk. He did not rise but waved to them to take a seat. Oliver Goodbody lowered himself into a red-leather armchair on his left, crossed his long legs and placed both hands on the gold knob of his cane.

'Mr Rogers,' he said, indicating the stout little man.

Mordecai nodded, and Mr Rogers bowed as he took a chair beside Oliver. The barrister, with his dark, swarthy skin, his outsize head bald except for the few strands of hair brushed across it and his prominent hooked nose above his thin twisted lips and high white stiff collar, reminded Mr Rogers of a vulture. And at the thought, Mr Rogers smiled happily to himself.

Nicholas was on Mordecai's right, perched bolt upright on a straight-backed Regency chair. He was wearing the blue and red tie of the Guards Division.

When they were all seated, Mordecai's clerk, Robins, drew the curtains across the windows behind Mordecai's chair and turned on a television set at the far end of the room. 'Begin,' said Mordecai, and in silence they watched the short tape of the broadcast of Willoughby Blake's press conference.

'Again,' said Mordecai when it ended. He had it played three more times before he signalled Robins to switch off the set and leave. As the door closed behind the clerk, Mordecai bent his head to read the copies of the newspapers spread on his desk in front of him. 'Repeat, if you please, Mr Rogers,' he said, 'the report you made to Mr Goodbody.'

Mr Rogers gave his account of what had happened at the press conference. When he had finished, Mordecai said, 'The tabloids at least seem to have got most of it, with a suitable display of asterisks.' He looked up. 'Did anyone at the conference know you?'

'Not that I am aware.'

'You had disrupted their proceedings. Did no one attempt to stop you as you left?'

'No.'

Mordecai grunted and leaned back in his chair. 'Blake will be well satisfied,' he said grimly.

'Satisfied?' interjected Nicholas, looking at Mordecai with surprise. 'I'd have thought the whole show was a disaster.'

Mordecai turned his head towards him. This, he presumed, was the military cousin who, Oliver said, was managing the estate; and making enemies. 'I said that Blake will be satisfied,' Mordecai repeated slowly. 'He got all he wanted.' He paused, still looking at Nicholas. 'Are you contradicting me?'

'No, of course not,' Nicholas said hastily. 'Only it seemed to me that it was a fiasco.'

'Then you haven't grasped the significance. The grandmother said things Blake could never have said himself. As a result he achieved more than he could have hoped for. She focused this case where Blake intends it shall remain – on race and class. Race because the claimant is black and the Caverels white; class because she comes from a humble background and is poor and the Caverels are aristocrats and rich.'

'I sent Mr Rogers and I told him the questions I wished asked,' Oliver said. 'I decided to show Blake that we were aware of what they were up to – and that we knew the kind of people we are dealing with. I wanted to test how serious they are.'

Mordecai shook his head. 'Blake's purpose was to secure public attention and whip up public opinion. He hopes that if the media is sufficiently manipulated and takes up the cause, this might influence some weak judge – and if the pressure is strong enough, frighten off the family.'

'If he thinks that, then he's off his head,' said Nicholas.

Mordecai swivelled round in his chair to face him.

'Is he? Have you any idea what you and the family will undergo when the campaign gets under way? Public hostility, hounding by reporters and photographers, your private lives put under a microscope? Are you ready for that?'

'You know perfectly well, Mordecai,' Oliver intervened, 'there is no question of the family surrendering to this fraudulent claim.'

Mordecai pushed the newspapers on his desk to one side. 'Very well. But have any of you considered the possibility that this young woman is genuine? That she is Julian Caverel's daughter?'

'She's not,' Nicholas replied. 'She's a fraud.'

Mordecai looked up at the ceiling, then down at his hands folded on the desk. 'So you say.'

'Yes,' said Oliver, 'that is what Nicholas has said and it is what you will say in court, Mordecai, and you will say it loud and clear.'

For a time no one spoke. Mr Rogers was watching Mordecai from the corner of his sharp little eye. Eventually Mordecai broke the silence. 'Has there been any DNA testing?'

'There's no purpose. Julian died twenty years ago in San Francisco,' Oliver said. 'He was cremated and his ashes scattered in the Bay. The alleged mother died more than twenty years ago and was buried in a cemetery which was flooded in the hurricane of 1989. Her corpse cannot be identified.'

'The grandmother? The child? What about them?'

'Any DNA testing on them would be inconclusive.'

'It would, I venture to suggest, be more than inconclusive,' Mr Rogers said, his fingers pressed together across his chest. 'In the absence of any remains of the father and mother, DNA could not establish whether the young woman is their daughter, even were the remains of the half-brother, Robin Caverel, in existence, which I gather they also are not, and despite the existence of young Francis.'

Mordecai stared at him balefully. 'You know what you are talking about?'

Mr Rogers bowed gravely. 'I do. I have some knowledge, some experience of this.'

There was a long pause. Then Mordecai went on, 'The claimant certainly appears to be of mixed blood.'

'She does,' said Oliver. 'But she could be anybody. We say first, she is not Julian's daughter. Second, if they prove she is, she was a bastard. Third we say that Julian was not the son of Walter, the 15th Baron Caverel who never acknowledged him during his lifetime.'

There was another long silence. Mordecai again examined the ceiling. He said at last, 'The alternative is what you think is the unthinkable. That she is the rightful heiress.'

Nicholas uncrossed and crossed his legs, staring straight ahead of him as though he were on parade. Mr Rogers settled himself more comfortably in his chair, the tips of his fingers now together under his chin. He closed his eyes and looked like an observer to whom the discussion afforded merely some wry amusement. Mordecai was watching him. 'Well, Mr Rogers,' he said, irritated, 'can we provoke you into saying something, apart from giving us a lesson on DNA? It was you who provoked the old woman at the press conference.'

Mr Rogers smiled and shrugged. He folded his small white hands over his tight-fitting waistcoat. 'I don't think that at this stage there is anything more I can usefully contribute. At the press conference I acted on instructions.'

Mordecai shrugged. 'Very well,' he said at last. 'So if she is not Julian's daughter, who is she and where has she come from?'

'She could be anyone and she could have come from any-where,' Nicholas broke in. 'Someone has put her up to it.'

Mordecai turned to him. 'You may be right, Major Lawton. It is true that Julian was the improbable father of any child, but if he did not conceive this child, who did?'

'It could have been anyone. If any of the story is true.'

'I am examining the possibilities, Major Lawton,' Mordecai growled. 'We are here to review the case we shall have to meet in court.'

Nicholas shifted in his chair. 'Of course,' he said.

'So who was the white man who seduced this girl's mother twenty-five years ago and induced her to believe he was Lord Caverel's heir?' Mordecai looked at Nicholas. 'If, of course, he did.' He turned back to Oliver. 'But if he did, why should he do that if he were not Julian Caverel?'

'That assumes', Oliver replied, 'that there's any truth in any of the story.'

'Isn't it fanciful to imagine that it is all invention? Lies by the foster mother, lies from the real mother?'

Oliver leaned forward in his chair. 'No, it is not. We don't know what the mother or the foster mother actually said or wrote. All we know is what the girl says they said and wrote. There may or may not have been a white man who fathered the child. But whoever it was, it was not Julian Caverel. The story is invention, with the girl telling lies she's been taught to tell by the conspirators who see a chance to get their hands on a great estate and a great fortune.'

Mordecai looked down at his hands folded on the desk. 'Assume the girl is telling the truth at least as far as this part of the story is concerned. Assume the mother had an affair with some man, some Englishman who was not Julian but who held himself out to be Julian Caverel and convinced the mother that he was. If that is so, then there has to be an Englishman in Beaufort County twenty-five years ago who seduced the black woman and conceived a child after telling her a story about a wealthy family and a lord in England.'

He paused, looking at the other three in turn. 'But why in heaven's name should he want to tell such a story?'

Oliver answered. 'I knew Julian. I tell you he never fathered any child.'

Mordecai grunted. 'That the man was homosexual doesn't mean he couldn't conceive a child.'

'Of course it doesn't, but throughout his life Julian was never known to have shown any interest in any woman. Why then should there suddenly appear a woman from South Carolina – or rather the ghost of a woman because she is conveniently dead – on whose behalf it is claimed that the homosexual Julian fathered on her a child? And what is the corroboration of this story? The foster mother who took in the child? Where is she? Also dead.'

'There is a letter.'

'No one has seen that letter. It was not produced at the press conference. I doubt if it exists. Who is to say who wrote that letter, if there ever was a letter?'

'The lawyer in Charleston?'

'Perhaps, but at the moment we have only the young woman's word for any of it, and when it comes to court, it will be for her to prove she is who she claims she is, namely the legitimate daughter of the legitimate elder son of the then Lord Caverel. And when she seeks to do that, your task, Mordecai, will be to challenge that story, probe her background, her previous life, her backers and financiers and expose where they came from and why. I've briefed you, Mordecai, because the story is a pack of lies and because you are the best qualified counsel practising at the bar to expose what is nothing less than a conspiracy.'

When Oliver had finished, Mordecai lowered his head. 'Then you'll have to supply me with documents and facts and witnesses,' he said quietly. 'I cannot cross-examine on your unsubstantiated suspicions.'

'That is why I have retained Mr Rogers.'

Mr Rogers bowed. Mordecai looked at him and grunted; then turned back to Oliver. 'They will produce records of Julian's marriage and the birth of the daughter.'

'No doubt,' Oliver replied. 'But how genuine they'll be is another matter. I don't imagine it's very difficult to manufacture such documents in Beaufort County.'

Mordecai turned back to Mr Rogers. 'Then it's up to you, Mr Rogers,' he growled. 'Without facts, without witnesses, we shall fail. The fate of this family is in your hands.'

'So it appears.'

'Have you sufficient ...' Mordecai was going to say 'experience' but paused. 'Have you sufficient resources to undertake these enquiries?'

'If he hasn't, we shall see that he has,' Oliver replied.

'The estate', Nicholas began, 'is not – '

Oliver interrupted. 'I know. The estate, despite its intrinsic value and wealth, has not much ready cash. Sales will have to be made, land, pictures. A very large sum will have to be raised.'

'What will the court make of trustees', Mordecai said almost to himself, 'who sell the family silver to finance resistance to the claim of a lady whom the court eventually declares to be the genuine heir?'

'You keep suggesting she's the genuine heir,' Nicholas broke in. 'She's an adventuress, an impostor.' He bent forward, his face suddenly red and angry. 'I don't understand why you can't see that she is. I thought you were hired on behalf of the family to be on the side of the family.'

'That is offensive, Major Lawton,' Mordecai snarled.

'Nicholas! Mordecai!' Oliver interjected, but Mordecai was not to be stopped.

'I hoped that Major Lawton had the wits to appreciate that the purpose of this consultation is to examine the case that will be brought against us and that if we aren't prepared and ready to meet it, then Lady Caverel and her child will be thrown on to the street and the black girl, with Blake and the drunken grandmother, will be in possession.'

There came a loud scrape of a chair being pushed back. Mr Rogers was on his feet. Mordecai swung round and bent forward to look at him. 'What the devil do you want?'

'I must be on my way.' To Oliver he said, 'I shall be in touch, Mr Goodbody.'

'You know where to find me,' said Oliver.

'I do.'

'If you are leaving us, let me give you some advice,' said Mordecai.

Mr Rogers looked at him steadily. 'I'm always very ready to listen to advice,' he said coolly.

'If this is a conspiracy,' Mordecai growled, 'as Mr Goodbody believes it is, and if these conspirators catch up with you, you'd better take care.'

'I shall,' Rogers replied gravely.

'Do you know anything about any of them?'

'I know of Blake and I have come across some of his associates.

One of his henchmen especially is not . . .' He paused and sought for the appropriate word. '. . . is not the most respectable of citizens. So I shall be careful.' He bowed to Oliver and across the room to Nicholas. 'Good afternoon, gentlemen,' he said.

'Anything you need, get in touch with me either at the office or at home, in London or the country. You know where to find me,' repeated Oliver.

'And if there's trouble,' added Nicholas, 'you know where to find me.'

Mr Rogers liked the military so he did not smile at Nicholas' offer. He bowed gravely. 'Thank you, Major Lawton. I have had experience of what you call trouble and I have some expertise in avoiding it.'

'If these gentlemen are right,' growled Mordecai, 'you'll need all the expertise you've got.'

Mr Rogers stared at him as coolly as before and it was Mordecai who dropped his eyes. Mr Rogers swung round on his heel and began to walk to the door. Then he stopped and turned again. 'If you will forgive me, perhaps you gentlemen ought to be considering not so much whose daughter she may be but whether she is who she says she is.'

He left the room, moving deftly, almost like a cat, balanced perfectly on his small, well-shod feet. When the door had closed behind him, Mordecai turned to Oliver. 'Who the devil is he?'

'He's the best,' Oliver replied, using the same words Stevens had used some weeks ago to Dukie Brown about Willoughby Blake.

On leaving the Temple, Oliver and Nicholas shared a taxi.

'I didn't like that fellow,' Nicholas said.

'Many don't.'

'Why did you brief him?'

'Because he's the best for what needs to be done. If you think he's offensive to us whose side he's paid to be on, wait until you see him with the enemy.'

'Was he right when he implied you should never have sent that little man to the press conference?'

'That's his opinion, given after the event. I wanted those criminals to understand what they're up against.'

'He was bloody rude to me.'

'He is to many. That's the risk we take in briefing him.'

'And the little man? You said he was the best. Best at what?'

'At finding out.'

'Where was he going when he left?'

'I leave that to him. Europe, the Americas, wherever he has to.'

'I suppose he charges a fortune.'

'He does, and so does Mordecai. To defend this claim will cost the estate a great deal of money. So you'd better start selecting the treasures you'll have to sell.'

Nicholas looked out of the window of the cab. They sat in silence. Then Oliver asked, 'How is Andrea?'

'Calmer now.'

'She'll need to be strong,' said Oliver. 'It'll get much rougher, for her and for all of us. Especially when Blake really gets going and really whips up the media.' He stared out of the window of the cab. 'Ravenscourt is part of my life. It has been ever since I first went there when I was a boy. For you, it probably means even more, since you are attached to it by ties of blood. But I tell you, I shall do everything, everything that is needed, everything in my power, to make sure it remains in the family.'

18

Unlike Richard Jameson some weeks earlier, Mr Rogers on his arrival at Charleston in South Carolina did not check into the Four Seasons Hotel; nor was he met by anyone resembling a Southern senator who was addressed as Judge. He had exchanged his black suit for a crumpled light fawn one which fitted so tightly across his frame that the middle button was seriously strained. On arrival he was met by no one, and from the airport he took a taxi to a modest hotel in a side street. Before retiring for the night, he sat at the bar drinking tall glasses of Jack Daniels on the rocks while engaging in friendly chat with the barman.

The next morning he spent much time on the telephone and at

noon received his first visitor, a grey-haired black man who drove up to the hotel in a battered 1985 Chevrolet. The visitor, Clover Harrison, was soon sitting with Mr Rogers in the bar eating a sandwich and drinking beer served by the same friendly and chatty barman. After an hour, Mr Rogers and Clover Harrison left in the ancient car. In the afternoon they paid a visit to a shack with a corrugated tin roof outside which they sat at a wooden table sipping a mixture of lemonade and sarsparilla with two elderly women and a very ancient man who spoke little. They then drove on to visit the local Baptist chapel and drank tea at the home of its pastor. Back in the city, they passed the evening going from piano bar to jazz club, Mr Rogers consuming a prodigious quantity of bourbon without it apparently affecting him in the slightest. Clover Harrison did the talking; Mr Rogers the paying.

It was at the last of the jazz clubs that they received some information which took them the following morning to a small, neat house in the city's western suburbs where they spent several hours drinking coffee on the front porch with a middle-aged black woman. She was a widow and lived alone. They then retraced their steps to the hospital in Charleston and a doctor's office, and after more visits in the afternoon and early evening to other houses Mr Rogers was delivered back to his hotel where once more he began telephoning. For the next seventy-two hours this was the pattern of his days and nights, and he never once ventured outside the hotel except in the company of Clover Harrison. Twice again they visited the middle-aged woman with whom they had drunk coffee, and with whom at their last meeting Mr Rogers left several pages of manuscript written in his neat handwriting. But one place they did not visit was the office of a Mr Jerome Walker, attorney-at-law, the frail and elderly black lawyer who had placed the advertisement for Sarah Wilson in the Paris edition of the *Herald Tribune*. Mr Walker was ill, and according to Clover Harrison failing fast. But that did not prevent Mr Walker from hearing of the presence in town of an inquisitive gentleman from London; and Judge Jed Blaker, as he was called although he had retired from the bench, was duly informed.

On the fourth day after Mr Rogers' arrival, Clover Harrison

picked him up at the hotel and drove him to the airport and bade him farewell. From Charleston Mr Rogers flew west to San Francisco, missing by only a few hours the arrival of another visitor from London, Richard Jameson, who checked into the Four Seasons Hotel and who spent the rest of that evening and several days thereafter in the company of Judge Jed Blaker.

At San Francisco airport Mr Rogers was met by a lean, craggy-faced woman with cropped black hair speckled with grey, dressed in a check shirt and ill-fitting pants. 'Jules,' she said, thrusting out a hand and snatching his bag from him. She marched him to a cab which delivered them to an open air car-park some way from the airport. In her bottle-green XJS soft-top convertible Jaguar, Jules lit a cheroot and they sat talking for the best part of an hour.

As she started the engine before moving off, she handed him a card. 'Eleven o'clock,' she said, looking him over. He was still in his fawn suit which stretched so tightly over his stomach. 'Shirt and pants,' she added.

At the Sheraton Palace, a far more up-market hotel than Mr Rogers had frequented in Charleston, she sat in the car and watched as his stout figure stepped lightly up the steps and disappeared into the hotel, accompanied by a porter carrying his bag.

Shortly after eleven o'clock that evening, Mr Rogers, now more comfortably but somewhat incongruously dressed in a flowered shirt and white trousers, took a taxi to the address on the card. At the door of the club he presented it to the doorman and was admitted. The place was dark and very crowded, lit almost solely by the coloured lights flickering on and off on the dance-floor. He pushed his way to the bar, ordered bourbon, and observed the dancers.

A middle-aged, moustachioed couple glided past. They were wearing light grey suits with ties and white shirts, so that Mr Rogers thought that perhaps it had been unnecessary to spend his clients' money purchasing his new outfit. But he soon saw that most of the other dancers of either or indeterminate gender were in shirts and pants, except for some very tall, beefily built, heavily made-up dancers in elaborate ball-gowns. For ten minutes he watched; then he saw Jules coming towards him leading by the hand a slender Oriental figure, a head shorter than she. When they were a few yards from Mr Rogers, Jules pecked the cheek of her small partner who immediately turned away.

Jules beckoned, and Mr Rogers followed her to an empty table, slightly raised, guarded from the dance-floor by a brass rail. From time to time dancers leaned over the rail and spoke to Jules and embraced her. Each time she introduced Mr Rogers. 'Harry,' she said, 'from London, England.'

After half an hour they were joined by the person whom Mr Rogers had come to meet, a grey-haired man who walked with a stick. He was skeletally thin, had a grey moustache turned down at the corners of his mouth and wore, Mr Rogers noted ruefully, a shirt of a far more conservative design than that which he had purchased in the hotel shop. As soon as the newcomer had seated himself at their table, Jules imperiously waved away any who approached. After an hour of conversation, Mr Rogers left and took a cab back to his hotel.

Next morning, he abandoned his extravagantly flowered shirt for one of a plain dark blue, but slung from his shoulder a leather bag. When Jules collected him, he had already taken a long call from Charleston during which Clover Harrison told him of the arrival of Jameson. Mr Rogers advised him to leave town until he was certain that Jameson had departed.

Like his activities in Charleston, Mr Rogers' visit to San Francisco settled into a pattern; by day, a series of visits to the Castro and the Haight and elsewhere, usually to apartments up winding, outside stairs and small, white or pink box-like houses, wreathed in climbing roses and orange blossom; by night visits to clubs. The registry office and the hospital and several law offices were also visited but it was in the apartment of the thin man and his younger companion that Mr Rogers spent most time. On the third morning after his arrival, he put a call through to the friendly barman at the hotel where he'd stayed in Charleston and asked the barman to check Clover Harrison's address to make sure he had left town. Later the barman reported that he had been round to Mr Harrison's rooms and been told by the owner of the drug-store that Mr Harrison was away but the apartment had recently been broken into.

It was a thoughtful Mr Rogers who left with Jules for the airport, once again attired in his tight-fitting fawn suit. He flew east to Atlanta, ignoring other reservations in his name on flights to LA and to Boston. In Atlanta he boarded a flight to Miami where, on arrival, he hired a car and drove to West Palm Beach. After more calls from a call-box, he drove to the WPB airport, handed in the car and reported to the offices of Caribbean Ferry Services. He was left to wait, drinking coffee and watching television. After two hours, he was conducted from the offices to a Beachmaster turbo-prop executive jet warming up on the apron. During the flight, Mr Rogers sat alone in the cabin behind the two pilots, writing. On arrival at Belize he joined a Vargas flight to Rio. He stayed the night at the airport hotel and next day flew on to Buenos Aires.

After two days in BA, and with no sign that he had been followed south by Richard Jameson, he flew back across the Atlantic, and reported to Oliver Goodbody in Oliver's flat in Kensington. A day later he was on his travels again, this time to Europe.

19

Brought to a sudden halt by the traffic as she breasted the hill just east of Stonehenge, Valerie Spencer snapped down the sunvisor and examined herself in the looking-glass. She pushed her short dark hair into place on her temples and smoothed the skin at the corners of her mouth. Too many lines, she thought; too deep now to disguise.

The car in front began to move and she pushed up the visor. She would stop to fix her face before she got to the house.

Yesterday the appointment had been confirmed. She'd made her pitch two days before, unexpectedly catching the woman on the telephone, telling her that all they wanted was background, just an interview about the kind of family they were. Everyone's talking about the Caverel claim, Valerie had said. An interview would give her a chance, Valerie added, to present herself to the public. Her paper had three million readers and an interview would give her the opportunity to show them what kind of woman it was who was facing a claim which might turn her and her child out of doors. To Valerie's surprise, for there could be little doubt in most people's minds on which side her paper, the *Daily News*, would stand, her call had been returned. Would it really be general background, just about her and the family? Of course, nothing more, just a profile of you and the family home. Very well, the voice said. She'd be pleased to receive Miss Spencer at eleven o'clock at Ravenscourt.

'Receive!' Valerie snorted when she'd put down the receiver. 'Does she think she's the Queen Mother!'

Press interest in the Caverel claim, as Valerie had said on the telephone, had grown. The incongruity of a claimant with a background of black America and European night-clubs and the aristocratic family living in the vast Palladian mansion in Wiltshire was intriguing editors and readers. Although no proceedings had as yet been begun, they were obviously imminent and lawyers warned that the stories had to be handled discreetly. So the press concentrated mainly on the personalities. On one side, the half-black, exotic girl with a mysterious past who was supported by an eccentric and, rumour had it, alcoholic grandmother who had not been seen since she'd made a scene at the press conference; and on the other, the ancient but obscure and apparently dim aristocratic family consisting of an infant with an insignificant mother, supported by an unpopular military cousin who was running the estate. It was because Willoughby Blake had seen to it that so many of the stories presented such a sympathetic picture of the claimant that Andrea had, apparently, consented to be interviewed.

Valerie Spencer had done her homework: sending for the cuttings; looking up the family history and background in the reference books; checking the dates and places of the husband's diplomatic career and reading the reports of his death in the car crash. She spoke to the paper's man in Rome and he filled her in on the political and financial crises and scandals in Italy when Robin Caverel had been at the Embassy. He also told her the gossip concerning Robin's brief Roman love affair. Everyone knew about it, he said, except the English wife who at the time was in England having her baby. He sounded so knowing that for a moment Valerie almost felt sorry for the wife. But not for long. It was a useful tip. She'd have no scruple in using it. Other people's pain gave neither her nor her editor sleepless nights.

Basically, the editor said, the piece had to be about the woman as widow and mother facing a claim which might push her on to the street and not about whom her dead husband had been bonking. But 'Give it bite, darling,' he had added. 'You know how to handle these sort of stories about these sort of people.' The story of the affair might provide just what was needed, for Robin Caverel's lover was well known to the pages of *Hello!* and other glossy magazines.

As Valerie Spencer drove past Stonehenge she wondered idly what it must be like to have the threat of eviction hanging over one's head. But if she was threatened with eviction, all she'd do would be to find another flat in Battersea. She smiled when she compared her flat to what she'd heard about Ravenscourt, but she stopped smiling when she thought of the woman's child. She never smiled when she thought about children. She would have liked to have had a child. But in her twenties and thirties there had never been time. The battle in the jungle of what was Fleet Street and was now Dockland had absorbed her whole life. Forty-nine next birthday, she was probably too old now to bear a child. And anyway, there was no one to give her one. There had been no one since January when Sam had moved out.

After Stonehenge, the traffic thinned and she drove fast across the plain. She pulled into a lay-by and studied the map. It wasn't far now; it would be eleven when she got there. Would she be offered lunch? There'd been no mention of it on the telephone. The editor had also warned her about the retired soldier who ran the estate – perhaps the woman might insist he be present during the interview. Valerie wouldn't mind. Last year she'd done a feature, three articles, on London men's clubs, one of which had been ingenuous enough to allow her the run of the premises and produced specimen members for her to interview. They hadn't recognised themselves when they read what she'd written. Upper-class toffs with bristly moustaches, plummy voices, oyster eyes. She had a tape-recorder; they hadn't, so they couldn't deny what she said they had said. And each had a drink in his hand when he'd been photographed. Hadn't she asked them to? But for Valerie the series had been a triumph. So if the military cousin forced himself into the interview, she wouldn't discourage it. She could deal with him. But she wouldn't like a lawyer. Then she'd have to be more careful.

She checked the small tape-recorder in her bag, making sure it was loaded and working. Next she confirmed on the car telephone that Graham, the photographer, was at the Caverel Arms. She hadn't wanted to arrive with a photographer. She wanted time with the woman first. Then she'd send for Graham. He could be at the house in a couple of minutes. She had told him to be at the pub by ten forty-five and wait. And he was. She said she'd call him when she'd fixed it up.

Lastly, she fixed her face, grimacing into the mirror and groaning to herself. She hoped the woman she was to interview was not too attractive.

As soon as she rang the bell, the door was opened by a tall, thin woman in her mid-thirties with fine, blonde hair. 'Lady Caverel?' Valerie enquired.

'Yes. Please come in.'

Andrea led the way and Valerie followed her into the hall with its black and white tiled floor, looking up at the ceiling high above her head and at the sweeping stair which led up to the dome with the portraits on the walls.

'Family pictures?'

'Yes.'

One day, Valerie thought with amusement, there might be a portrait of the black girl.

Andrea had dark rings under her eyes. She was pretty in a pallid, county sort of way, Valerie thought, but she looked worn. She obviously didn't take much trouble with herself. Valerie followed her into a small square library, the walls lined with fitted bookshelves. Sporting prints were on any wall free of books.

Andrea closed the door behind them. She looked tense and Valerie was tempted to say something to put her at her ease. I'm not going to bite you, she wanted to say, but then Valerie, the professional, thought she'd get more out of her if the woman did stay tense. And perhaps she was going to bite!

'May I sit?' was all she said.

'Please do.' Andrea went to a side table by the window. 'Would you like some coffee?'

100

'Thank you.' When Valerie tasted it, she put it aside. It was lukewarm. There had been no mention of anyone joining them and Valerie took out her notebook and tape. 'Before we start, can I ask you out of curiosity why you agreed to see me?'

Andrea looked down at her hands. 'You were the only one who asked.'

Valerie laughed. 'But even so, why did you agree?'

'Because I'd like to show the public I'm not an ogre, and that there's another side to the story which the public haven't been told.'

Valerie smiled and nodded her head. There were several photographs in silver frames in different parts of the room, one on the chimney-piece. 'Your husband and your son?' she asked.

'Yes.'

'They're very handsome.' Then Valerie went on briskly, 'Well, I expect you're busy and I mustn't keep you, so shall we start?' She switched on the small tape which she put on one of the arms of the chair. Her notebook, in which she'd written a series of headings, was on the other. 'Can we begin with you and your family, and come to the Caverels later?'

'Of course.' Andrea was sitting on the edge of the sofa, her hands clasped around her knees.

'Your maiden name was Aberdower, wasn't it?' Andrea nodded. 'The men in your family seem to have lived a lot abroad, India or Africa in the days of the Empire and the Raj?'

'Yes, quite a few were in the Indian Civil or Colonial Service – or were soldiers. I had one great-uncle in the Indian army and another in the Sudan political service.'

'Lording it over the natives?' Valerie smiled sweetly.

Andrea did not reply. 'But your father was a sailor, a captain, RN?'

'Yes.'

'Tell me about your grandparents, Lord and Lady Aberdower. When you were a small child, you often stayed with them?'

'Often.' Andrea smiled, remembering. 'On their farm in Africa. It was very beautiful.'

'That was in the White Highlands in Kenya?'

'Yes, just below Mount Kenya.'

'You liked it there?'

'I loved it. My father was so often away at sea and my mother had died when I was very young. So for a few years from about the age of three my grandparents almost brought me up.'

'You loved them very much?'

'Very much.'

Valerie consulted her notes. 'You were eight at the time of the massacre?'

Andrea nodded.

'When the gang attacked the house, killed two of the servants and then got to your grandparents. They . . .' She was going to say what she'd read in the cuttings that the gang had done. Two old people tortured to get the key of the safe, mutilated, finally their throats cut. Instead she asked, 'Where were you at the time?'

'With friends, at another farm. I'd spent the night with them, about twenty miles away.'

'And the next day, not knowing what had happened, they brought you back home and you ran into the house and found them – the bodies of your grandfather and grandmother?'

There had been many cuttings on the grandfather, a former Governor of Bermuda, and plenty on what had happened in the bedroom in the farmhouse in the White Highlands below Mount Kenya.

'Did that turn you against Africans, against blacks?'

'No. Only against murderers and gangsters.'

'Your grandfather and grandmother had many black servants, I suppose?'

'Several. I had a black ayah, a nanny who looked after me.'

'Were you fond of her?'

'Very.'

'What happened to her?'

Andrea looked surprised. 'How do you mean?'

'Well, when you were older, did you see her?'

'No, she went back to her people. I was very fond of her.'

'After she left, did you ever look her up when she'd returned to the townships?'

'No.'

'You just dropped her? She just passed out of your life?' The sniff was not lost on Andrea. Valerie studied her notes and then

102

went on, 'Would you say that all the blacks you've ever come across have been servants? Have you ever had any black friends?'

Andrea's hand was at her neck, playing with the necklace. 'Not a close friend. Have you?'

'Yes, I have.' Valerie thought of standing by the bedroom door while Sam was bent over the bed packing his case and then watching him walk down the front path with that easy, athletic lope carrying his guitar. And her relief that at last he'd gone. But it was true. He had been a close friend, once.

'Has it come as an extra shock to you', Valerie went on, 'that the claim to the Caverel barony and to your house, to Ravenscourt, is being brought by a black woman?'

'Certainly not, not because she's black. The claim itself is a great shock, because it's a lie, it's a plot and she – ' She stopped, remembering what she'd told herself she must not say. Valerie waited but Andrea, a little colour now in her pale cheeks, said no more.

'Would you mind if a black woman became the Baroness Caverel and lived in this house?'

'I would mind anyone living in this house other than my son and me. Of course I would.'

'I'm told we shouldn't really discuss what they call the merits of the case but – '

'There aren't any merits, not in their case,' Andrea interrupted. 'It's all lies.'

'Of course,' said Valerie. 'But just suppose the young woman *does* succeed in establishing her right to this house and the estate, what will you do?'

'I haven't thought. I don't know. But she won't.'

'But if she did,' Valerie persisted, 'and you had to leave Ravenscourt, where would you take your son?'

Andrea thought for a moment. Then she said simply, 'To friends.' She added, 'But that won't happen. This is Francis' and my home. Francis' ancestors have lived here for hundreds of years and when he's grown up, he'll live here. It's his inheritance and she'll never be able to take this from us.'

'But if she convinces the court that she's the rightful heir, that would make her your niece by marriage and your little boy's first cousin. Would you not talk with her and see if you could not persuade her to let you and your child stay on and all live here together?'

'Never.'

'You're not a Caverel by blood. Why does this place mean so much to you?'

'Because it was my husband's and now it's my son's. It's his inheritance and I'll do everything I can to stop these people getting their hands on it and driving us out.'

'Will you be called to give evidence if it comes to a trial?'

'I don't know. I will gladly, if they need me.'

Valerie ticked off another of the headings in her notebook. 'Perhaps we're talking too much about the claim, so let me ask you more about yourself. Where did you meet your husband?'

'In Sussex, one weekend. He was playing polo at Cowdray Park and we'd gone over to watch and he came back to the house where I was staying for dinner.'

'Where were you working at the time?'

'I wasn't working.'

'You didn't have a job!' The last word was emphasised.

'No, I did not.'

'But if you were not working, what were you doing?'

'I was visiting.'

'A fashionable young lady of leisure!' The sneer was pronounced. 'Well, as you had no work and had never had any work, let's talk about your husband's work.'

Andrea's normally pale face was now slightly flushed.

'How soon after your marriage', Valerie went on, 'did you go to Rome?'

'Two years. During the first two years of our marriage Robin was in the office in London, the Foreign Office.'

'And your son, Francis, was he born in Italy?'

'No, in Shropshire, where my father and stepmother then lived.'

'But he was conceived when you were in Rome?' Andrea nodded. 'Did you enjoy living in Rome?'

'Very much.'

'Were you very social, entertaining and being entertained?'

'Quite a lot. It was part of his job.'

'Did you enjoy that?'

104

'Some of it. Some was tiresome. It always is.'

'Dancing, wining, dining, that seems to have been the pattern of your whole life?'

'That was part of our life in Rome. As I said, it was part of the job.'

'But as far as I can gather, that has always been your life.'

'Not at all. At the Embassy we were expected to entertain and to visit. I could speak Italian. When I was growing up I had learnt three languages, French, German and Italian. What languages do you speak?'

'Only English.' The question had annoyed Valerie. She's a toffee-nosed, stuck-up little prig, she thought. She decided to play the Rome card.

'May I ask you a personal question?'

'If you want to.'

'It is rather personal,' Valerie went on. Andrea said nothing; merely stared at her. 'Was your marriage to Robin Caverel a happy marriage?'

The slight flush had fled from Andrea's cheek. 'Of course it was. Why do you ask?'

'I just wondered. So many marriages aren't these days, and living in Rome, they say, can play havoc with Anglo-Saxon marriages.' Andrea was sitting bolt upright, her hands beside her. Valerie went on silkily, 'In Rome you must have had many good friends.'

Andrea remained silent. 'Wasn't one of your very best friends the socially famous – I was going to say notorious but that wouldn't be quite fair.' Valerie laughed and went on, 'No, that fashionable lady, Isabella, the Marquesa di Bonavincini, so often featured in *Hello!*' She paused, then added, smiling, 'No, of course I've got that wrong. Isabella, I understand, was more a friend, indeed she was, they say, a very close friend of your husband. Do tell me about him and her.'

Valerie had looked down at her notebook when she spoke that last sentence so she did not see that Andrea had risen to her feet. Valerie was still smiling when she looked up and saw Andrea, white with fury, striding towards her. She stopped smiling when Andrea snatched the notebook from her hand and the tape-recorder from the arm of the chair. Ripping open the small machine and pulling out the tape, Andrea threw it into the fireplace and, tearing the pages from the notebook, flung the book at Valerie, hitting her in the face. 'Get out,' she said. Valerie put a hand to her cheek. Andrea tore in two the pages she'd ripped from the notebook and flung them over Valerie's head. There was a spot of blood at the corner of Valerie's mouth. 'Get out of my house,' Andrea said.

Valerie leaned down beside her chair and picked up her bag. Taking out a tissue, she dabbed the corner of her mouth. 'That was very silly,' she said. 'I can remember all that was said and what I can't remember, I shall invent.'

'Get out,' Andrea repeated, opening the library door.

Valerie rose. 'Don't bother to show me out,' she said as she walked past.

In the hall she purposely spent time, looking up at the portraits on the staircase, watched by Andrea standing by the library door. Finally with her hand on the front door, she said, 'You're a very foolish woman. Now I shall do all I can to see that you get what is coming to you.' Then she was gone.

When Andrea returned to the library, Nicholas Lawton was bent over the fireplace. He'd come through a door disguised with the false backs of books by the right of the fireplace. He retrieved Valerie's pocket recorder and put it into his pocket. He put his finger to his lips and went over to the side table and took from behind one of the photographs in a thick silver frame a larger tape-recorder. He stopped the tape; rewound it in part and played a sentence or two of Valerie's and Andrea's conversation. Andrea was still by the door.

'We should never have let her come,' he said.

He took Andrea by the arm and led her to a chair. 'They like to hurt, especially people like us. At least they will not be able to print any lies. I'll telephone Oliver.'

Valerie drove fast to the village. In the pub Graham gave her a drink. 'I'll crucify her,' she kept saying. All the way back to London she thought up the arrogant, racist phrases that she would put into Andrea's mouth about blacks and natives and servants. But when she'd got back to the office, the editor said Goodbody's, the solicitors, had been on.

'They have a tape,' he said. 'I'm spiking the story, darling, for the time being. Sorry for the waste of a day but at least you haven't done any writing.'

Valerie had not written. It was all in her mind, where it remained. She'd bide her time. And the time, she knew, would come.

20

Since she had been settled in the luxurious suite in the hotel in Kensington, in what Willoughby called 'the bosom of the family', Fleur was inevitably more and more in his company. He saw to her appearance and wardrobe and took her to restaurants and first nights at the theatre and cinema where they were seen and photographed together, telling her it was all part of the presentation of her. Willoughby alone was allowed to be seen with her in public and in every report he made sure she was described as 'the Caverel Claimant'. Every day he enquired what she was doing, where she was going. If she went out on her own, Mrs Campion was meant to chaperone her. All telephone calls to the suite were routed through Mrs Campion's room. Willoughby kept impressing on her that over the next months all their efforts must be concentrated on preparing for the case, and that included public appearances in his company. Not that he didn't enjoy their outings, he said, but it was business. There'd be time enough to enjoy themselves when the case was won. So Fleur did not dare to get in touch with Greg. When it was over, she kept telling herself, she'd be with him.

One evening after they had returned from supper at the Groucho, they were in the sitting-room while Willoughby smoked a final cigar. He asked her what she planned to do when the estate and Ravenscourt were hers. Sell, she said, if I can. And then go away. And the barony, he asked, what about the barony? She had made a gesture with her fingers. He took her hand and smiled sympathetically.

She still spent days in bed nursing her migraine, but not so many as before, and now and then she'd elude Mrs Campion and slip away to some fortune-teller she'd been told about. One, a medium, she paid to make contact with Paul. But Paul, inconsiderately, was not there. Or if he was, he was keeping himself to himself.

Fleur had not visited the Senora, who was still in the clinic where she was said to be improving from her broken jaw. Willoughby said he hoped her stay might help dry her out. Mrs Campion kept silent. All the pocket money Willoughby gave the Senora was passed on to Mrs Campion so that even in the clinic the flask got filled – and emptied.

Jameson was away in the States, tying up loose ends, Willoughby said, getting Fleur's birth and her father's marriage certificates and arranging for the witnesses who would bring them to court. Fleur was glad Jameson was not with them. She didn't like Jameson. His stillness and silence unsettled her.

Over lunch at Boulestin his friend Harry Price, the editor of the *Daily News*, told Willoughby about the interview of Andrea Caverel by Valerie Spencer and that the *News* was now 'looking after' a couple of the Ravenscourt staff, Headley, a forester, and his friend and drinking companion, Mason. They were now on the pay-roll. He also reported that Major Lawton had been christened the Gauleiter. 'We'll use that when we get another Caverel story to hang it on,' he said.

Willoughby said he'd not have long to wait and two days later he announced to Fleur that he was taking her on an outing. 'It's time for you to become acquainted with the home of your ancestors,' he said. 'You and I are going to pay a visit.'

So on a fine morning in the last week in September, Willoughby and Fleur climbed into the back of a large black limousine which was followed out of London by a Ford Granada from the fleet of the *Daily News*, bearing Graham, the photographer, and Harold, a reporter.

The drive which led to Ravenscourt began beneath a tall, eighteenth-century arch and ran between stone walls banked by tall rhododendron bushes which at that time of year were long past their vivid summer flowering. At the end of the walls, the drive wound through open park land bordered by an iron fence with herds of deer scampering under great oaks, while further up the slopes of the down cattle and sheep were grazing. As they drove through the park, Fleur saw swans sailing majestically on a long sheet of water.

'The work of Capability Brown, my dear,' Willoughby said. 'This is said to be one of his best.'

The drive bent sharply in a curve to the right, and Fleur had her first sight of the huge Palladian house.

'Ravenscourt,' Willoughby said, taking her hand. 'Your father's home.'

Fleur stared, astonished. Greg Rutherford had called it a barracks. To her it looked like a palace.

As they got nearer the drive forked. To the left was a notice on a triangular stand: 'No entry. Car-park to the right at the rear of the house. Entry to the house by the side door only.' The driver began to follow the directions and take the right fork but Willoughby called out, 'Pay no attention to the notice. Take the left fork and drive to the front of the house.'

The driver stopped and reversed. There was just room for the limousine to slip between the notice and the grass verge. The Ford Granada followed.

'Pull up at the bottom of the steps.'

Taking Fleur by the arm, Willoughby led her up the broad stone steps to the great front door. Graham and the reporter ran before them, Graham snapping away with his camera. On the wide stone platform outside the door, Willoughby bowed. 'Your ancestral home, Lady Caverel,' he said.

She giggled. 'No,' he said, 'be serious, he's taking pictures,' and he motioned to Graham to take one of Fleur with her back to the door.

A man came running from the side of the house. 'Hey,' he shouted. 'You can't go in there. You can't park those cars there. The car-park's at the back.'

Willoughby ignored him and pointed to the bell on its long chain hanging beside the front door. 'Pull it,' he said.

Graham took another photograph, with Fleur's hand on the bell. Mason opened the door. Willoughby had Fleur by the elbow. He winked.

'The official tour of the house', Mason began loudly, 'starts at the side door by the car-park.'

Willoughby winked again. 'I know, old son, I know,' he said, 'but this lady's special. She's family.'

He propelled Fleur forward. For a moment Mason stood his

ground and Willoughby wondered if the *News* was paying him enough. Then Mason stepped aside. Once inside, Willoughby saw why Mason had spoken as he had, for around the sides of the circular hall, bordered by a blue rope erected on public opening days, was the tourist line-of-route which led from the public's entrance at the side door near the car-park, along a corridor, into the hall and finally to the foot of the great staircase. Because of the publicity about the Caverel Claim, visitors had flocked to Ravenscourt all summer and today, the last open day of the season, the line-of-route was packed. More tourists were crowded on the stairs beneath the family portraits as they made their way to the state rooms on the first floor. When Willoughby's party entered the hall, many recognised Fleur from her pictures in the papers and nudged each other and pointed.

'Your ancestors, my dear,' said Willoughby loudly, pointing to the portraits.

An elderly woman with a guide's badge pinned to her chest was at the foot of the stairs. She called out, 'Mr Mason, who are these people? What are they doing?'

Willoughby answered her, loud enough for everyone to hear. 'It is Miss Fleur Caverel and her party, come to visit her father's home.'

Graham was busy with his camera, the reporter with his notebook. Fleur looked up at the portraits with the tourists looking at her. The elderly woman called shrilly to another guide at the top of the staircase, 'Fetch Lady Caverel and the Major.'

'Come along, my dear,' said Willoughby stepping over the rope and leading Fleur to the foot of the stairs. 'Excuse me,' he said genially to the elderly guide, pushing past her. 'Excuse us,' he said to the tourists as he pushed past them. 'Sorry to inconvenience you but we're family and we're going up to the family rooms.'

The crush on the stairs was such that it took time for the party to get past, and they paused every now and then while Willoughby chatted up some of the tourists or pointed to a particular portrait and Graham photographed Fleur studying it. By the time they had reached a few steps below the head of the staircase, Andrea was on the landing.

Fleur had been enjoying herself, smiling back at the tourists, joking with Willoughby, but now her smile faded and she halted abruptly, a few stairs below Andrea. The two women stared at each other.

Willoughby, on the stair below Fleur, called out over Fleur's shoulder, 'Good afternoon, ma'am, may I present Miss Fleur Caverel? We thought we should call as I believe this is the last open day of the season and as Ravenscourt is open to the general public, all the more must it be open to the family.' He laughed his stock, genial laugh.

Andrea could see Graham busy with his camera photographing her and Fleur, the reporter behind him taking notes. The tourists, squeezed against the wall, listened, fascinated. Andrea, her face very pale, stared fixedly at Fleur. Fleur dropped her eyes.

'Leave,' Andrea said at last. 'Leave my house at once.'

'Come, come, ma'am,' Willoughby said. 'I don't know why you should say that, unless it's because we haven't paid to come in.' He laughed. 'But we didn't think there was any need for tickets, seeing that Miss Fleur is family.'

Andrea called down to the guide, 'Make sure that Major Lawton is on his way.' The guide disappeared down the corridor.

'Mason,' Andrea called to Mason who was standing in the hall, 'have these people removed immediately.'

She raised her hand and pointed her finger so that it was only inches from Fleur's face. 'Leave my house,' she repeated.

Fleur half turned to Willoughby at her elbow. 'Please,' she said, 'please, let's go. Please, let's leave.'

'If that's your wish, my dear,' Willoughby replied, 'of course we'll leave.' He looked up at Andrea. 'I'm sorry you're so inhospitable and that you find it necessary to be so rude.'

'Get out,' said Andrea. 'Get out of here at once.'

'We shall do as you ask, ma'am, but perhaps sooner than you care to think, it will be you and not Miss Caverel who will have to get out.' He took Fleur's elbow. 'Come along, my dear. You don't seem to be very welcome.' And then he said louder for the benefit of the tourists. 'One day, however, you will. One day, all this will be yours. Then no one will turn you out as you have been turned out today.'

The people on the stairs behind them stood aside as Willoughby, with his hand on Fleur's arm, began to descend. Andrea stood like a statue on the landing. In the hall Willoughby turned and waved good-humouredly to the crowd. Many waved back and called, 'Good luck.' Mason opened the door, Willoughby winked at him once again and they were outside.

'Did you get everything?' Willoughby asked when the door had closed behind them.

'Perfect,' the photographer replied, 'quite perfect.'

Fleur began to run down the steps ahead of them. On the last step she tripped and fell, landing heavily on her hands and knees, sprawling full length on the gravel. The chauffeur came from the car; the other three down the steps.

'Are you all right?' Willoughby cried.

'Just a graze,' she said, 'nothing.'

But there was blood on the palms of her hands and on her knees. They helped her into the car; she began to wipe the gravel from her with a handkerchief and dab at the blood. The chauffeur produced a first-aid kit.

As the cars moved off, Fleur turned and looked back at the house through the rear window. A man had come out of the front door, a tall man with a moustache. He stood there, his hands on his hips, looking at the cars. In the dream with the Gypsy, Fleur remembered, there had been no man. Only a woman.

'I hope that didn't distress you, my dear.' Willoughby patted her on her thigh. 'But it was important that we paid a visit.'

'She was . . .' Fleur began.

'She is Robin Caverel's widow, the woman who calls herself Lady Caverel, your aunt by marriage. Her child is your first cousin.'

Switching on the air-conditioning, he lit a cigar and took her hand in his. Fleur lowered the window beside her. She thought of Paul's Gauloises and the sweet scent of the Gypsy's cigarette when she had woken from her dream.

Next day, under a banner headline 'Thrown Out!', the *Daily News* carried pictures of the heiress being confronted on her visit to her 'ancestral home'. The piece, accompanied by many photographs, was written by Valerie Spencer from the notes taken by the reporter and from her own notes of her interview with Andrea Caverel.

'Rejected and insulted, haughtily ordered from the house like a dishonest servant, the Caverel Claimant was driven sadly away. When she left the home of her ancestors,' Valerie's account concluded, 'Fleur Caverel was weeping. I shall return, she said through her tears. One day I shall return.'

21

'Wherever I go nowadays,' said Jason West, 'I hear or read about that young woman who talked to you about the Caverel family. I've never really understood, Gregory, why you didn't bring the young lady to see me.'

You old fart, Greg thought. You didn't think that when you saw her. 'You weren't at the office,' he said, 'and I thought I'd speak to you when you got back. Then she said she didn't want any help and left.'

'A Chancery action over such an important inheritance would have been most intriguing – and a good advertisement for the firm. It would not have been altogether in our line, of course, but I expect we could have managed. From what I hear, she has an excellent case.' He paused. 'And from her picture, she looks most personable.'

Greg kept his cool, but only just. A very demonstrative young lady! Embracing in the hall! Not at all our type of client! 'She had no money,' was all he said.

'In a negligence case you can act for an impecunious plaintiff with an agreement to be paid out of the damages. It may have been stretching a point, but I don't see why we couldn't have done the same for a young woman who has a very respectable claim to an inheritance.' He examined his nephew over his glasses. 'Your reluctance, Gregory, wasn't, I hope, because of any prejudice on account – on account of her colour? I know that in Australia – '

Greg thought of her in his flat lying naked on his bed. 'Of course not,' he said angrily. He strode to the door.

'Where are you going?' Jason asked querulously. It was early afternoon.

'Out. I'm going out.'

Jason thought yet again that the sooner the young man went home, the better. He would call Sydney to tell them. But he put it off. His brother-in-law would not be pleased if he packed off the son and heir after so short a time under his tutelage. He'd have to put up with the boy for a little longer.

Greg wandered across the park. He'd heard nothing from Fleur. Like Jason, all he could do was read about her. He'd been told by a journalist friend that all enquiries had to go through Willoughby Blake Associates and that she was living at the Kensington Park Hotel. But, the friend said, even at the hotel calls were monitored and put through one of Blake's staff. 'They own her,' he added.

Greg was so irritated by the conversation with Jason he decided that nevertheless he'd try the hotel himself. Mrs Campion answered and when he asked for Fleur, she asked him his business.

'I'm a personal friend. Tell her to call me.' He left his telephone number, not his name. Mrs Campion passed on the message to Willoughby.

That evening Willoughby said to Fleur, 'An Australian has been asking for you. He didn't leave his name.'

'An Australian?'

'That's how he sounded to Mrs Campion.'

'Oh, then that'll be the actor, Henry Proctor.' She was glad to have her back to him. 'We had bit parts in an advert last year in Paris. I suppose he's been reading about me. What did he want?'

'He wants you to telephone him.'

She shook her head. 'He's a bore.'

Willoughby decided that when Jameson got home in three days' time, he'd have him check out 'Henry Proctor' and the number of the caller.

Later that same evening Stevens was put through to Fleur. She took the call in her bedroom.

'I have to take you soon to see your counsel, Sir Percy Braythwaite QC,' he began, 'so I must get from you what is called your proof. I have the notes of what you've told me but I need more about yourself and your early life. I'm having my notes typed up and put in statement form and then I'll send them round. You must check the statement and please add the

'Are we?' she said. She turned away. 'I've a headache. I must get to bed.'

As she was walking to the bedroom door, he said, 'How did you get the money?'

'From a friend.'

'The Australian?'

'Yes.'

'His name's not Proctor, is it?'

'No, it isn't. I've promised to pay him back.'

Next morning at his flat in Fulham, Greg opened an envelope. It contained a bundle of banknotes. There was no message.

23

From her bed Eleanor Braythwaite could see across the garden to the hedge and beyond it the trees which bordered the churchyard. They were now entirely bare of leaves and through the boughs she could see the Norman tower of the parish church. There had been a heavy frost but she was warm in bed and it was Sunday morning. In another hour or so, she'd hear the bells and see Percy cross the lawn and go through the gate into the churchyard. Their house had once been the rectory, which was why, Percy used to say, he had to be so regular an attender at the eleven o'clock service each Sunday morning.

Eleanor settled herself more comfortably against the pillows and took up her book. Downstairs Percy would be having his usual boiled egg. Now that their two sons were grown up and gone, Eleanor was excused Sunday breakfast, coming down only when Percy was at church. When he got back, he always went to his study and worked on his briefs while she prepared the lunch. Afterwards they would go for a walk, accompanied in the old days by the boys and a series of labradors. After a cup of tea, Eleanor would pack the car with the remains of the food she'd brought down on Friday evening from London. By supper-time they'd be in their flat above Percy's chambers in Gray's Inn.

That was their routine while the courts were in session. During the vacations, Christmas was spent at the rectory, to which the boys and their families would come for Christmas day; at Easter, Percy and Eleanor would go to Venice; in the summer to Switzerland to walk. Year in and year out this was the pattern of their lives and Eleanor did not complain. She had lived happily with Percy for thirty years. He was a handsome man in his early sixties, slim with a full head of white hair. Friends who knew them both said that he and Oliver Goodbody could be taken for brothers, although Oliver was in fact some years older.

This weekend Eleanor knew which brief Percy was working on, and it was a brief which fascinated her. At breakfast on the Friday morning in London he had told her that in the afternoon he was to have his first meeting with the Caverel Claimant to go through her statement with her. She was being brought to his chambers by Michael Stevens of Stevens and Co., a firm whose practice did not usually include the kind of work in which Sir Percy Braythwaite QC was so prominent. For Percy was a Chancery lawyer of distinction, one of the old school who could have been a judge had it not been his choice to remain at the bar. He had received his knighthood for presiding over several departmental enquiries, including one into patents and trade-marks which had taken many years. The practice of Stevens and Co., on the other hand, was in the field of divorce, criminal law and libel, very lucrative work, well publicised in the popular Sunday papers but considered by some in the profession as only marginally respectable. Percy's clerk had accordingly been sur-prised when some weeks ago Mr Michael Stevens had delivered a retainer for Sir Percy to represent Miss Fleur Caverel. When the clerk showed in the client and her solicitor in the afternoon of that Friday, Percy had never met either before. Later that evening he and Eleanor had driven to the rectory. Percy had been preoccupied and unusually silent. She always drove and she resisted asking the question she was dying to ask until they had been going for three quarters of an hour when she could resist no longer.

'What did you think of her?'

'Shy, very tense, delightful to look at.'

'Could she be who she claims she is?'

'She could, I suppose.'

'Tell me more about her.'

'Dark, of course, but not very, with small, regular features. Obviously one of her parents was white.'

'You liked her?'

'I did. She's very highly strung. I only hope the strain of the case won't be too much for her.'

'Might it?'

'Not if she's looked after, but the solicitor told me she has no family to support her, except for a weird old grandmother. I wasn't much taken by the solicitor.'

'Are you glad to be representing her?'

'I am. It's an intriguing case, and as I said, I liked her. I think her claim is genuine.' He paused. 'But it's distressing that if she succeeds a young widow and her child will be thrown out of their home.'

'But if she's the rightful heiress, she's entitled to everything. After seeing her, do you think she is?'

'If the evidence they talk about stands up in court, she is the heiress. She impressed me, and I liked her. From the way she carries herself and her manner she could well be a Caverel. I met the grandfather once, old Walter Caverel, many years ago when I was a young man staying with friends at Cap d'Antibes.'

'Was there any family resemblance?'

'I couldn't say, but what I can say is that she has the grace of someone who could have come from a long line of such ancestors. But I'm sorry she's got into the hands of that solicitor.'

'Why do you think they have briefed you?'

Percy laughed. 'If you want me to be frank, it's because I am what I am.'

'Who you are, you mean.'

'Yes. I suppose they think I'm respectable and it's sensible to have someone like me as their counsel.'

'Who is representing the family?'

'That old rascal, Mordecai Ledbury. I don't think he's ever appeared in the Chancery Court. I've never been against him, only heard about him. He's renowned for picking quarrels with opposing counsel and the judge, so it should be quite a contest.'

A battle of opposites, she thought. For the Caverel family, the controversial Mordecai Ledbury; for the girl and her questionable advisers, the respectable Percy Braythwaite. Eleanor made up her mind that come what may Percy must get her a seat in court when the case came to trial.

24

Andrea took Francis into the walled garden. It had been snowing and the snow was lying nearly three inches deep. The sun was shining but it was bitterly cold. The child scampered ahead of her along the path which ran up the centre of the garden, followed by Max, the liver-and-white spaniel. On either side of the path, now buried beneath a blanket of white, were the flower beds which Andrea had planted when she had first come to Ravenscourt. Before Robin had inherited, she had never set foot in Ravenscourt. She had seen it once from a distance from the edge of the park before they were married and they had looked at the empty and shuttered house. When they arrived from Rome and she had seen it close to, the size and scale of it had taken her breath away. She had not recovered when she walked through the vast rooms with the furniture covered in dust-sheets and looked out of the window at the pleasure garden which was a tangle of weeds and the park which was unmown and even uncropped by sheep. At first she felt daunted by all that would have to be done to make it their home, but she was happy to be there.

For she had been glad to get away from Italy. It was in Rome that, for the first time since the murder of her grandparents when she was a child, she had been deeply unhappy. It was when she had brought the newly born Francis back from her father's home in Shropshire that she learnt of Robin's brief love affair. He swore it was over. It was madness, he said. He had been overwhelmed by remorse and the marriage had survived. By the time of the move to Ravenscourt it had become, Andrea thought, as happy as before. So when she first arrived and set foot in the hall and saw on the walls above the great staircase the frames of the portraits hung with dark green sheets, her heart had leaped with excitement. The family had come home, to their rightful place, to the house built by the ancestors of her husband and her son.

She spent the first weeks exploring, planning which rooms to begin to restore and designing her garden. With the help of three women from the village they had battled during that first year to get straight the West Wing where they established the family rooms; next they turned to the library and sitting-room off the rotunda in the centre of the house; finally the state rooms, the great salon and dining saloon. With the gardener, Peachey, and a boy, she had transformed the pleasure garden so that it would eventually become a mass of blue and white foxgloves, delphiniums, veronica, and lobelia; with banks of red roses at one end, white at the other.

As she now followed Francis and the spaniel along the snow-covered path, she thought of that last summer with Robin. It had been a happy time, although a damp, wet summer unlike the summer after his death, the first summer of her widowhood when one scorching day had followed another until the rains had come in late September – and with the rain, the thunderbolt of the claim.

The shock, following so soon after Robin's death, had for a time almost unbalanced her. It had even turned her against the house. As the autumn weeks passed, with the visit of the woman journalist and then the confrontation on the staircase and the mounting campaign in the press, she'd imagined in her misery that it was somehow the work of the house, as though the house resented their presence and the sounds of a child running up and down the great staircase and along the vast corridors; as though it preferred its years of silence and emptiness, and was punishing them. She began to think that it hated them and when recently gales had toppled some of the trees in the park and the wind howled and sang around the chimneys and crashed against the immense windows, she thought she felt a sense of hostility, of malevolence. She had moved her sitting-room from the ground floor to the first floor so that she could be near Francis' nursery, and when he had gone to bed she would sit there with Alice, drinking chocolate in front of the fire. The Masons had their own quarters, a bedroom, bathroom and sitting-room in the East Wing, some way from the family's rooms and the kitchen and pantry on the ground floor. Andrea had never trusted the whining Mrs Mason and her husband, but when she'd said this to Nicholas, he had demurred.

'He's a former policeman. He's a good person to have in the house.'

But the past months had toughened her. Her anger at the effrontery of the claim, the wickedness of the impostor and the people behind her manipulating the media had strengthened her and helped her overcome her imagining about the house. She saw how foolish she'd been to attribute to the house her pain, and she began to make it her friend again. Now it was home, home for her and for Francis, the home of the Caverels; and she would fight with every ounce of strength to keep it, even if it meant bankrupting the estate and themselves. Nicholas had warned that Oliver kept demanding more and more sales in order to pay for the mounting costs of the defence. Sell everything if you have to, she had told him. Do whatever is necessary.

She brushed the snow off a stone bench and sat watching Francis as he tried to make a snowman. She got up to help him but it was growing too cold.

'Come on,' she said and taking him by the hand she led him out of the walled garden.

In the warmth of the vast kitchen, Alice was by the Aga making tea.

'Where's Mrs Mason?' Andrea asked.

'Lying down, wore out by all the work, the poor old soul. We're too demanding, my lady, so I'm getting the tea.' She laughed and catching up Francis swung him around, sitting him on the giant kitchen table.

'I know,' said Andrea. 'The three of us give the two of them far too much to do.'

'The two of you,' Alice said. 'I looks after meself.'

Andrea poured herself some tea as Alice gave Francis a piece of cake. 'How's the fire in the sitting-room?' she asked.

'Fair enough. I put on some more logs on my way down.'

'Supper?'

'She'll be back to do it. He'll be off to the pub later.'

'In this weather?'

'That won't keep him away.'

The telephone on the dresser rang. The telephone in the kitchen was the Masons' outside line, with an extension to their flat.

Alice went on feeding Francis cake. Andrea sat, her hands around her mug of tea. The ringing kept up.

'They've forgotten to switch it through to the flat,' said Alice.

'Can you do it?'

'No, I don't know how.'

It went on ringing. 'You'd better answer it,' Andrea said.

Alice picked up the receiver. 'Who is it?' She made a face at Andrea. 'George Headley, yes?'

Both of them knew what Nicholas thought of Headley.

'No, it's Alice. I'm in the kitchen. Yes, I'm alone.' She winked at Andrea. 'They're in the flat and they've forgotten to switch it through. No, of course I can't. I'm getting tea for Francis. Mason should be here later. All right, I'll give him the message.' She repeated what Headley was saying. 'The friends from London will be at the Plough at Ansleigh at eight. All right. If I don't see him, I'll leave him a note.'

Ansleigh was eight miles from Ravenscourt. At a quarter to eight Andrea sat in her car in the darkness in the car-park of the Plough. She'd been curious about Headley's message. Who were the friends from London that Headley and Mason were to meet? And why at Ansleigh and not at the Caverel Arms in the village? She thought she'd find out for herself.

She parked in the car-park between a van and the wall. There were no other cars. She switched off the lights and the engine. After twenty minutes she saw the headlights of a car coming down the lane, and she ducked below the windshield when the car turned from the lane into the car-park. It drew up on the other side of the van. The lights were switched off and when she heard the slam of the car door, she raised her head and peered through her side window. The front door of the pub opened and she saw the silhouettes of two men. To make sure that these were the friends from London, she waited another ten minutes. No other car came so she went to the side door of the public house. Inside a passage led to a door to the dining-room and beyond that to another door into the bar. The top part of the partition between the two doors was glass, a series of internal windows from which the inside of the bar could be seen. Behind the bar she saw the publican, talking to an elderly man sitting on a stool. At the far end, a couple were playing darts. There was no one else, except for a group of four men seated in front of the fire. One, with his back to her, was Headley. Next to him, also with his back to the bar, was Mason. Facing them were two other men, the friends from London. And she knew them both. One was the photographer, the other the reporter who had been with the young woman when she had been brought to Ravenscourt by the man with grey hair. It had been Mason, Andrea now remembered, who had let the party in through the front door. As she peered through the glass partition, she saw the reporter look around and, seeing they were unobserved, hand an envelope to Mason and another to Headley.

When she opened the bar door and came in, the group by the fire was engrossed in conversation. She walked slowly across the room and stood a few feet from them. The photographer was the first to notice her. He half rose. As he did so, Mason turned. So did the others. Mason got to his feet. She remained quite still, a few feet from them, looking from one to the other. No one spoke. She turned on her heel and left.

She was shaking as she got into the car. She drove straight to the dower house, praying that Nicholas would be there.

The Masons were packed up and gone by noon the following morning, after an angry, ugly scene. Headley was given notice and forbidden the premises or the woods. Until they could find another couple, Nicholas moved into the house.

25

It was ten days before Easter and Mr Rogers was in Venice. During the past winter he had only once returned to London, a fleeting visit during which he did not go to his home in Sanderstead in the suburbs of London but was given a bed in the spare room in Oliver Goodbody's flat in Kensington. The two men talked late into the night and by eight o'clock on the following morning Mr Rogers was on his way to Gatwick airport. From there he flew to Charlottesville and then on to Charleston. He was met by Clover Harrison. In the car Harrison told Mr

Rogers that Judge Blaker had been busy and the sandy-haired Englishman, Jameson, had been back several times. Lawyer Walker had died.

They drove not to the city but to a motel about twenty miles west where they conferred again with the middle-aged black woman Mr Rogers had spoken to at such length during his previous visit.

Mr Rogers did not spend long in South Carolina but soon left for Florida. From Miami he flew to Jamaica, visited Haiti and ended with a swing through the islands, spending a few days in the Leewards and the Windwards and the arc of the Lesser Antilles before returning to Miami. Then he flew north to New York and crossed the Atlantic to Paris. Forty-eight hours later he was in Istanbul where he remained for a week before he began to work his way westward, reaching Venice in early April.

From the airport he took a taxi to the Piazzale Roma where he boarded the vaporetto. It was cold but the sun was shining as he sat in one of the forward seats, observing the familiar sights with satisfaction while the vaporetto zigzagged from station to station along the Grand Canal. As he disembarked at the Accademia and made his way to the Albergo Rosa, a small, rather shabby establishment, he promised himself a few days' holiday over Easter.

There was no restaurant in the Albergo but he found one in the Calle Tollette to eat pasta and drink red wine. While he ate, he propped his newspaper, the *Herald Tribune*, against the flask of wine, studying the personal advertisements one of which many months ago had led to his present argosy. After a cup of strong and very sweet coffee, he paid and left. As he had promised, he took precautions; before emerging into the street he stood in the doorway looking up and down. There was no one about and he set off. As always he had with him the photograph which he carried wherever he went.

The season, he knew, would not begin until after Easter; only the bar would be open but he was seeking the proprietor who resided in an apartment above the club itself.

A week later he was in Rome where his quarters were a pension in the Via Giulia in the old city. The place he sought in this city was an establishment in the Campo dei Fiore, a more up-market club than that he had visited in Venice. But by now it was Holy Week and the club would not open until Easter Monday. Mr Rogers, though not of the Roman faith, had an historical and eschatological bent and he decided to spend the following five days visiting shrines.

On the evening of Easter Monday, his holiday over, he resumed his work and stood on a rusty carpet on raised steps leaning over a rail above a small dance-floor facing a platform on which the band was playing. There were only a few tables occupied along the side of the room and only three or four couples on the dance-floor. He chose a table near the entrance and far from the stage on which the cabaret performers appeared, first a comedian-conjuror, then a single stripper who paraded down the room, boredly casting off her clothes before she disappeared through a curtain beside the band. When the dancing began again, Mr Rogers dispensed several 100,000-lira notes, and as a result was escorted through the curtain behind which the stripper had disappeared and conducted to the director's office. He returned the next day at noon and was taken to several rooming-houses in the city.

On the Wednesday he flew to Berlin where he stayed this time in an expensive hotel, the Maritim Grand Hotel, in the Friedrichstrasse. A registered package from London was waiting for him and after a stay of only twenty-four hours he flew on to Bucharest where on several consecutive days he visited a doctor's office near the Herăstrău Park. From Bucharest he returned once more to Istanbul. Here he spent three days and by early May he had resumed his zigzag tour around the cities of Europe, reaching Amsterdam via Milan at the end of the month. From Amsterdam he set off on what he reckoned would be his last lap. It was a journey which was to take him to the other end of the world.

Part II

26

By ten o'clock in the morning it was already warm and the forecast was for the hot weather to continue. A crowd, many recruited from north London by the staff of the *Black Banner*, had gathered outside the forecourt of the great mock-Gothic building of the Law Courts in the Strand. They were carrying placards – 'Justice for Fleur' and 'Give Fleur her rights'. An army of reporters and camera-men attended them, and all who had any business that day in the courts had to run the gauntlet between the ranks of the noisy demonstrators and the flashing cameras. When Fleur and Willoughby stepped out of the black limousine which had brought them from the hotel in Kensington, they were immediately recognised. Willoughby had made sure they would, and the crowd broke into a great cheer. He put his arm around Fleur and waved happily. Fleur tried to break away but Willoughby held her back and made her turn as the camera-men shouted their instructions. With a last jovial wave, he led her inside.

When Andrea and Nicholas arrived a little later in a taxi, the crowd did not recognise them. But the photographers and camera-men did and, taking their cue from the attentions of the reporters, the crowd realised that these must be the enemy, the family which was denying Fleur her rights, and began to hiss. Nicholas marched a pale-faced Andrea through them without a sideways glance.

Within five minutes of the public being admitted, not a seat was to be had in the public gallery of the court of the Vice Chancellor, the head and senior judge of the Chancery Division, while the court-room below the gallery was packed. Briefless barristers in pristine white wigs crowded into the rows beside and behind the counsel engaged in the case; law clerks and solicitors stood alongside the benches from the entrance doors to the well of the court, while the seats behind counsel were filled with prospective witnesses and the privileged few, such as Eleanor Braythwaite and Oliver's friend Anne Tremain whom the barristers' clerks had managed to smuggle into a seat. By chance the two were put beside each other, neither knowing who the other was nor the connection that had brought each to the court.

Percy Braythwaite had already arrived and was seated in the QCs' row, the front row of counsel's benches. He looked handsome and immaculate in his crisp white linen and well-cut black court coat under his silk gown. On his stand were his notes, while documents from his brief were spread across the desk. Michael Stevens led Fleur to the seats immediately in front of him. Willoughby had handed her over to Stevens in the corridor, and everyone in the court strained to see her, some in the public gallery standing until an usher ordered them to sit.

Willoughby had taken great care and given much thought to her outfit and hair, and she was modestly but smartly dressed in a neat, expensive-looking light linen suit and white silk blouse with a bow at her neck. She wore no hat, little make-up except for a touch of colour on her lips, and no jewellery. She smiled shyly at Percy and, as Willoughby had instructed her, sat and remained very still, looking down at her hands folded in her lap. She appeared calm and composed, but inwardly she was in turmoil. She'd been warned that after Sir Percy had 'opened' the case – that is after he had told the judge the facts and outlined the law – a few witnesses would deal briefly with documentation and she would then be called to give her evidence. She must expect to be in the witness box a long time, Stevens had added. Her evidence could begin today, and on her evidence the result of the claim would depend.

Willoughby had gone to the place which had been kept for him next to the Senora and Mrs Campion. The Senora, neither overdressed nor over made-up, sat looking about her holding Mrs Campion's hand. He smiled at her reassuringly. She looked, he thought with relief, quite respectable. Her stay in the nursing home following her fall appeared to have done her good.

After he had taken his seat, Willoughby every now and then stood, pretending to be looking for someone but really making sure that he'd be noticed by anyone important and by the press who were squeezed into their bench immediately below the witness box. He cut a striking figure in his light grey suit, bright blue tie, a red carnation in his buttonhole and his silver hair brushed high above his sun-tanned – or rather carefully stained – forehead. One or two of the journalists winked at him and he nodded and smiled in reply.

Percy too looked about him but from his seat. He enjoyed the moments before an important case, when the battle was about to begin and the adrenalin was flowing. Especially when, as today, he thought he was on to a winner. 'Rum lot of spectators,' he said over his shoulder to his junior, Harold Welby, sitting directly behind him.

Welby did not bother to look. To him everything about court was distasteful, and he was wondering why on earth he had let his clerk talk him into getting involved in this unsavoury melodrama. For a junior counsel Harold Welby was an elderly man who could have taken silk many years ago if he had wished. But he had not. He was no advocate, and disliked appearing in a court even when he was, as today, sitting behind a Leader. He made an excellent living out of advising and drafting, rarely leaving his chambers in Lincoln's Inn. 'The frippery' of court appearances, as he called it, he left to others. The law was his business; he was the lawyer, they mere advocates, into whom, when he was briefed with them, he pumped the law for them to present.

However, he had a soft spot for Percy Braythwaite; he liked the style with which Percy presented the law that Harold prepared for him. When his clerk, impressed by the size of the fee Michael Stevens had offered, was trying to persuade him to accept the brief as junior counsel to Sir Percy in the Caverel claim, Harold Welby had protested, 'Braythwaite's a gentlemanly enough fellow, but he doesn't know any law.'

'I assume that's why they want you with him, sir, so that you can supply what he doesn't know,' his clerk had said diplomatically. So, to the clerk's relief, Welby had agreed.

Michael Stevens had not briefed Harold Welby only for Welby's knowledge of the law but also because his presence as junior to Percy Braythwaite would add to the standing of the Claimant's legal team. The usual clients of Stevens and Co. were pop stars, fashion models or television personalities engaged in libel actions or criminal defences. The firm was unknown to the sedate and respectable world of Chancery, and it was to make up for this that Michael Stevens had been at such pains and gone to such expense to brief a team of 'blue-chip' counsel. Above all, he knew that they would be well known to the judge who was to try the case, Sir Robert Murray, the Vice Chancellor and Head of the Chancery Division of the High Court.

As his name implied, Sir Robert was a Scot, a well-built, craggy-faced man, the product of Edinburgh Academical and Oriel College, Oxford, where he had acquired a First and won sporting fame as the foremost Rugby Union international of his generation – the centre three-quarter who in his final year had, almost single-handed, won the Calcutta Cup for Scotland against England by scoring a trio of sensational tries. Robert Murray might have been expected to make his career at the Scottish bar in Edinburgh but instead he chose the south and London, influenced not a little by his surprising passion for the daughter of an English earl, Lady Freda Baronby, a young woman frequently in the gossip columns, her name linked to a series of playboys, gamblers and minor Hollywood film actors. Her background was very different from that of the Murrays of Crief in Perthshire. Her childhood had been passed on the family estate in the Welsh Marches; she had learnt her hunting at the family hunting-box in Leicestershire; she spent her summers at the family villa in St-Jean-Cap-Ferrat, and her coming-out ball had been held in the last of the great houses still in private occupation in Belgrave Square.

Robert had met her at a Commem ball at Oxford when he was at the height of his fame as a footballer. She was three years older than he, and she had been amused by the dog-like devotion of the serious young Scotsman. But it was his magnificent physique that impressed her most, and so she smiled on him and overlooked his social pawkiness. She began to bring him into her world of London and county society but, however splendid he looked, he remained awkward and gauche, and her friends secretly, and sometimes not so secretly, smiled at him behind his back, of which he soon became acutely conscious. But Robert Murray was in love. He was also a true son of the manse and his aim was matrimony. So, abandoning his homeland, he got himself called to the bar by Lincoln's Inn, worked furiously at learning his profession and continued his high-minded but clumsy pursuit. To the surprise and consternation of her circle, Freda Baronby eventually accepted him.

What he only discovered after his marriage was that behind the poised manner, the fine, classical features and mask-like beauty of his bride lay an inordinate appetite for gin. When the early months of their marriage had passed, the serious and high-minded young Chancery barrister took refuge from the increasingly frequent scenes and tantrums at home by burying himself in his work, spending nights and weekends poring over the mass of legal papers which in a gradually increasing flood flowed into his chambers. That important and lucrative work came to him so early in his career was due to the Baronbys' family solicitor, Stephen Plater, a man many years Robert's senior who had always admired the famous athlete. His was a leading firm in the City of London, and he was happy to promote the career of his young sporting hero.

At the start of the marriage Freda found his dedication to his work tiresome and complained frequently. But it was not long before she found it a relief. For the physical passion soon faded and without it the two had little in common. In winter she began to spend more and more days hunting with the Quorn and, when she did come to London, in entertaining her friends and being entertained at dinners and parties from which she and the other hostesses happily excused her husband. Her friends, especially her women friends, now expressed quite openly their opinion about this *mésalliance*, and they became more and more condescending whenever they encountered him. He found them frivolous and contemptible; they found him a bore and a joke.

As soon as the London season was over, Freda took a party to the villa near Cap Ferrat which she had inherited on the death of her parents and she remained there until late September. During their first years Robert visited for a few days but soon never, spending his holidays in the Highlands in Scotland walking with his brother, a doctor in Edinburgh, and his brother's family. There were no children of the marriage. Within a very few years they had grown to dislike each other intensely. But not for a moment did the strictly Calvinistic Robert Murray consider divorce. She did, but when she was approaching forty, she had an accident in the hunting field. She fell awkwardly on her neck, injuring her spine. From then on she was paralysed from the waist down and confined to a wheelchair.

Her smart friends faded away; the villa in the South of France was sold and her bedroom in the country house moved to the first floor. Later a lift was installed – and her drinking increased. Much of her money had gone on wild extravagance, whereas he was now earning very substantially at the bar. So she abandoned any thought of divorce. Robert moved to a flat in Lincoln's Inn and only visited her one weekend each month.

At the Chancery bar his career went from strength to strength. He took silk early and after a few successful years he was appointed to the Chancery bench. He was a dour and solitary man and played no part in any of the social life of the profession. To the relief of the benchers of Lincoln's Inn, he declined appointment as Treasurer. It was not long, however, before he was promoted to 'Vice Chancellor', the Head of the Chancery Division, and such was his prowess as a judge and a lawyer that it was prophesied that it would not be long before he skipped appointment to the Court of Appeal and be elevated to the most senior judicial rank as a Lord of Appeal in Ordinary with a peerage and a seat in the House of Lords.

On the bench he cut an awesome figure, renowned for his impatience with counsel who had insufficiently prepared themselves in the law, or who were long-winded, or who persisted in arguments which the Vice Chancellor had made clear he rejected. There was rarely any question of his being persuaded to change his mind or alter the view he formed early in the case, a view often formed solely from his perusal of the papers and before counsel had even uttered a single word in court. He was also very jealous of the prerogatives of the Chancery Division and had a marked objection to any counsel, even an experienced silk, straying from the Queen's Bench or Family Divisions and appearing in his court. Thus when he heard that in the proceedings for ejectment which he was to try between Fleur Caverel, the plaintiff, and Francis Peregrine Caverel by his guardian *ad litem*, Andrea, Baroness Caverel, defendant, a Common Law silk, Mordecai Ledbury QC whom he had heard of but never met, was briefed for the infant, he had looked – so Robertson, his clerk, had told Braythwaite's clerk – more grim than usual; and when he put on his plain black gown in his room on the morning of the start of the Caverel claim, that look had not altered. Mr Ledbury, Robinson suspected, was going to have a difficult time at the hands of his lordship.

This, then, was the man for whom everyone in the court was waiting when there arose a sudden commotion at the right-hand door which led to the court from the corridor. A voice was heard, an angry voice. Those standing beside the rows of benches were seen to be falling back, stumbling and pushing at each other.

Percy turned to Welby. 'Ledbury,' he said. 'He's cut it fine.'

27

Moving like a crab, thumping his sticks on the ground, ordering the spectators to make way and barging through them, Mordecai Ledbury made his entrance into the court. When he reached the front row, he flung his sticks on the desk with a clatter and levered himself along the bench, while his clerk deposited his brief and untied the pink tape.

'Morning, Ledbury,' Percy said, smiling. Mordecai looked at him grimly and nodded and then fell back on to his seat.

Oliver Goodbody, accompanied by Andrea and Nicholas, followed and they took their seats in the bench in front of Mordecai, separated only by a few feet from Michael Stevens and Fleur. Andrea was dressed in a floral dress with a black velvet head band. She looked to her right and caught Fleur's eye. Fleur immediately lowered her gaze to her hands in her lap.

'Silence,' cried the usher, and everyone rose as the Vice Chancellor swept into court and took his seat on the bench.

Andrea looked up at the severe face under the grey, bobbed wig. She was surprised that he wore only a plain black gown. Somehow she had thought he would be in scarlet and ermine with a full-bottomed wig. But he looked impressive enough even in his plain robes and bob wig, although ill-tempered, she thought, and cross.

And Sir Robert Murray was cross. Chancery business did not often attract a crowd, and certainly not the numbers that had flooded into his court on this summer morning so eager to hear the claim about which there had been so much publicity. After everyone had resumed their seats, there was silence and then a slight noise of whispering began which ceased abruptly when the judge said loudly, 'Sir Percy, you are accustomed to this court. Do you not find the place over-hot?'

Percy got to his feet but before he could answer the judge went on, 'I find it inordinately hot. Too many people, far too many people.'

'It is certainly very close, my lord,' Percy said agreeably. 'It's a warm morning and I gather it's likely to get warmer. Would your lordship like me to get the usher to turn up the air-conditioning – '

'I find it tolerable enough,' interjected Mordecai from his seat, 'but then unlike my friend, I'm a cold-blooded fish. But if my learned friend and your lordship – '

The judge, ignoring him and looking fixedly at Percy Braythwaite, went on, 'I was saying to you, Sir Percy, that I found the court inordinately hot, due I presume to the number of people who are present.'

He tapped with his pencil and bent down over the bench to the usher. 'Require the engineers to improve the ventilation.' He looked up. 'The persons presently standing in the passage-way along the sides of the court must find seats, and if they cannot, they must stand still and to one side in order to allow easy passage to those who have business with the court. Above all I warn everyone to keep quiet during the proceedings.' Then to the Associate, he said, 'Call the case.'

The Associate stood and called out, 'Caverel v. Baron Caverel of Ravenscourt.'

'Who are the counsel engaged, Sir Percy, beside yourself? You are for the petitioner and who else?' the judge asked.

'I appear with Mr Harold Welby for the petitioner, Miss Fleur Caverel; and the infant, Lord Caverel, is represented by my learned friends Mr Mordecai Ledbury and Mr James Beatty.'

'How do you spell that name?'

'L-E-D-B-U-R-Y.' Mordecai spelt it out loudly from where he sat.

Again the judge ignored him. 'Sir Percy, I was asking you the name of the other counsel.'

'Mr Mordecai Ledbury – '

'Yes, I have that. But how is it spelt?'

From his seat Mordecai again spelt out loudly, this time both names. M-O-R-D-E-C-A-I L-E-D-B-U-R-Y.

'Spell it for me, please, Sir Percy,' said the judge.

A flush spread over Mordecai's saturnine face. Oliver turned and put his hand out in a gesture to restrain him. Mordecai glared at him. Percy repeated the spelling.

'Thank you, Sir Percy. Very well, you may now commence your opening, and I trust you will be able to do so', and for the first time he turned his head and looked directly at Mordecai Ledbury, 'without interruption.'

Standing very straight, his notes on the stand in front of him, Percy Braythwaite began.

As he spoke Andrea half turned to look at him from over her left shoulder. She saw how tall he was and she liked the sound of his agreeable voice and his attractive looks under his grey wig. Very different, she thought, from the man Oliver Goodbody had chosen to represent them. She knew Nicholas had taken an intense dislike to their counsel from the moment they'd met. Nicholas had told her that Oliver had only briefed him because he believed he was the best person to deal with those whom Oliver invariably called 'the conspirators'. Nicholas had said he thought there was some rule about counsel not interviewing witnesses but Oliver said of course she, as Francis' guardian *ad litem*, might meet counsel, but he did not recommend it. Ledbury, he said, was a difficult man and made a point of rarely agreeing to meet those he represented. So the first Andrea had seen of Mordecai Ledbury was for a brief moment in the corridor when she was introduced to him before she and Nicholas had followed him into court. She, like so many, was startled by his ugliness and the distortion of his body. Now as she watched and listened to Percy Braythwaite she wished that it was he who was their champion.

She cast another quick glance at Fleur sitting so demurely in front of Sir Percy. Andrea remembered the scene on the staircase at Ravenscourt. Play-actress, she said to herself, playing the innocent! In the corridor, Andrea had seen her with the man who'd brought her to Ravenscourt last September. She hoped he was going to be a witness, and she hoped she'd be in court when their ugly QC cross-examined him. For the first time she thought of Mordecai Ledbury with approval. She turned back and looked up again at the judge.

Sir Robert Murray was sitting back in his tall chair, now and then leaning forward to make a note or to take up one of the documents before him. How harsh and stern he looked, she thought. But would he be deceived by the lies the girl and her friends would tell him? From his face she could tell that no one would receive any sympathy from him. There'd be no sentiment on account of her and Francis' situation. He looked the kind for whom human sympathy did not exist. But would the girl fool him, as she had fooled the press and the public? Was he the kind to be taken in by a pretty face? Already she was uneasy. Clearly the judge approved more of the other barrister; he had already snubbed theirs.

She bent her head and tried to concentrate on what the barrister was saying.

Percy Braythwaite was explaining that although he submitted that the court at the end of the day must find that the Claimant was the lawful and legitimate child of Julian, the elder son of Walter the 15th Baron Caverel, and thus the rightful heir, he wanted to make plain on behalf of the Claimant that when the younger son, Robin Caverel, had purported to succeed to the barony neither he nor any of the family nor their advisers knew of the existence of the true heir. There was no suggestion that Robin Caverel or his wife, Andrea, or Mr Goodbody, the solicitor to the family, had behaved with anything other than complete propriety. The Claimant herself had no idea of her true identity until two years ago when she had her attention drawn to an advertisement in the Paris edition of the *Herald Tribune*. That had led her to return to Charleston in South Carolina which she had left as a child of fourteen, although she then looked older, and it was only at the age of twenty-six that she had discovered who were her real parents. It had been as much of a surprise to her as it had to the family. Her complaint, if she had a complaint, was that the widow of Robin Caverel had so peremptorily rejected the truth of what she was alleging.

'My client well appreciates', he said, lowering his voice a little and speaking kindly and sympathetically, 'how hard it is for a mother, especially a recently widowed mother, to be confronted suddenly and unexpectedly with a stranger of whom no one had ever heard, a stranger who was now asserting a superior right to all that the widow thought had belonged to her husband and on his death had passed to her small son. Here was a stranger who claimed she was the true owner of the great house and estate where the bereaved widow had so recently made her home.' He paused and looked towards where Andrea was sitting and bowed slightly. 'The lady', he said, 'deserves every sympathy in the painful position in which she now finds herself. That she should feel resentment, even anger, is understandable.'

He turned a little to face the judge. 'But, my lord, when you have heard the facts of Fleur Caverel's birth and parentage and when you have heard her story, I submit that the court will have no alternative but to find that this unfortunate lady never was the Lady Caverel and never had any right to Ravenscourt. She is only the widow of the younger son of the 15th Baron whose true heir was and remains, my client, the Claimant, Miss Fleur Caverel.'

Harold Welby stirred. This was the kind of nonsense that made him dislike appearing in court, this clap-trap, this rhetoric. Braythwaite shouldn't bother with it. Murray wasn't a jury. He'd not be affected by sympathy or generosity. The woman and her family had only themselves to blame for their present plight. Or if not they, then certainly their lawyers. They should have taken more trouble to discover what had happened to the elder son, Julian, before allowing the woman and her husband to take up the inheritance. And that, Welby felt sure, was what Murray would be thinking.

Willoughby Blake, however, was pleased. He liked the expression of sympathy for the family. The serious press would like it. It demonstrated the Claimant's reasonableness and generosity.

Percy now did what Welby thought he should have done earlier; he turned to the facts about Walter, 15th Baron Caverel and his first marriage which had been terminated by divorce. But before that divorce, Percy emphasised, the then Lady Caverel, Walter Caverel's wife, had given birth to the son, Julian, who, he would demonstrate, was the father of the Claimant.

On the bench Robert Murray made a show of attention. As was his rule he had read with care all the documents in the case, and in his chambers over the preceding evenings had made an extensive note of the facts alleged and the likely propositions of law. If counsel now addressing him at such length had been less senior and less respected than Sir Percy, Murray would have told counsel to get on with it. But Percy was a contemporary and a fellow Bencher of Lincoln's Inn so Robert Murray allowed him licence while he himself turned his attention to observe the five persons sitting below him immediately in front of counsel.

To his left was the silver-haired Oliver Goodbody, looking as usual, Robert Murray thought acidly, like a member of the bench of bishops, a species of which he, with his Wee Free associations, did not approve. Next to him was a military-looking man with a moustache, presumably a member of the family. He looked to be of the same ilk as the woman beside him who, presumably, was the mother of the infant respondent. She, he noted irritably, never kept still, fidgeting continually. Above all she looked typical of those upper-class Englishwomen with the manner and style of his wife and her friends, the type of woman who had so condescended to him when he was a young man and whom he so intensely disliked. Indeed in appearance she was a little like the young Freda herself, with the same English looks and, doubtless, the same superior and arrogant manner. When preparing himself for the case in his usual thorough manner he had looked up the Caverel family and seen that the mother of the infant had been born an Aberdower, only daughter of Lord Aberdower, Captain RN retired. Freda's family would doubtless have been friends of the Aberdowers. Freda would have known them, as she would have known the Caverels. Perhaps she was even related to them? At the thought of Freda and her family and her friends and of how they'd treated him there surged up in him the resentment he never could suppress. As he examined Andrea Caverel, he echoed the thoughts of Harold Welby. She should have found out more about the older son before she and her husband had rushed into assuming the inheritance. She had only herself to blame.

He shifted his gaze along the row to where the Claimant was sitting, noting her dark skin but fine, delicate features and the poise with which she kept so perfectly still, her eyes lowered on her hands. The man next to her, her solicitor presumably, whispered something in her ear and he saw her smile, a sudden, radiant smile. He liked the look of her as much as he disliked the look of the other.

When Robinson had told him that the Claimant's solicitors

were Stevens and Co., he'd enquired and been told about them. Why and how, he wondered, had she got into their hands? She herself looked personable enough – indeed, he thought, she looked bonny. A black hereditary Baroness in the House of Lords, Robert Murray ruminated, among the English Caverels and the Aberdowers, alongside the family of his wife, the Baronbys. The prospect gave him not a little grim satisfaction.

Percy Braythwaite had now reached the part of the story when the girl of fourteen had run away from her home in South Carolina and the woman who at that time she thought was her real mother. Murray looked up at the clock.

'We'll rise now for the luncheon adjournment,' he said. 'Two o'clock.'

While the court was emptying, Mordecai stayed in his place. Oliver, Andrea and Nicholas stood in front of him. Mordecai looked over his shoulder. When he was certain no one could overhear him, he said savagely, 'Where the devil is he?'

'He should be here soon,' Oliver replied.

'Soon! What does that mean? When did you last hear from him?'

'A message a week ago, a telephone call from Istanbul. I haven't spoken to him personally for a fortnight.'

'We face an offensive and hostile judge, the time for evidence is approaching and you have supplied me with not an iota of material with which to cross-examine.'

Andrea was next to Oliver, listening. Mordecai looked up and saw the anxious expression on her face. He stretched out his hand and took hers in his. His twisted face broke into a smile, one of those rare smiles which few were fortunate enough ever to witness. It was as though the sun had suddenly broken through a bank of black cloud.

'Don't look so worried, Lady Caverel,' he said gently. 'It will be all right. I promise it will be all right.' He patted her hand. 'Go now and have a glass of wine. But don't be back late, or that rude Scotsman will be angry.' And he smiled again.

On their way out Andrea said to Nicholas, 'He's very extraordinary. When he smiles, everything changes.'

'For the better, I hope. It could hardly be for the worse. The judge doesn't like him.'

'I do,' she said. 'When he smiles.'

In court, Oliver said to Mordecai, 'I have booked an interview room across the corridor.'

'You promised me that the little man would be here when the case began,' Mordecai said as he struggled out of the bench. 'He's not. And you said he was the best.'

'He is the best, and he will be here.'

On the table in the interview room, Freeman, Goodbody's clerk, had left a plate of sandwiches, a large thermos and three cups. Oliver poured the coffee. Mordecai took a flask from the inside pocket of his court coat and added the liquor to his coffee. Oliver cocked an eyebrow.

'Do you think that wise?'

'It'll help me keep my temper with that confounded Scotsman.' Mordecai drank and fell back into a chair. 'And face the task you'd landed me with – using up time until your wretched little man gets here, if he ever does. The Scotsman won't like it, he won't like it at all. Our only hope is that windbag Braythwaite won't cut anything short. With any luck he'll last out the afternoon.'

When the court resumed, Percy Braythwaite dealt only sketchily with that part of the Claimant's life between her arrival in Europe and the advertisement in the newspaper which led to her return to Charleston. All he said was that as a child she had been a talented singer and, after some training as a dancer in Atlanta and New Orleans, she had commenced a career on the stage in the cities of Europe. She was driven to scrape a living by performing in clubs.

It was this part of Fleur's story that had always troubled him. He knew Robert Murray would not look happily on anyone who performed in night-clubs, so he had decided to leave the details to be described, in what Stevens hoped would be a sanitised form, by Fleur herself. She, Percy believed, would be better able to charm Sir Robert Murray. So he passed on rapidly to the advertisement in the *Herald Tribune*, Fleur's return to Charleston, the old lawyer, the revelations in her mother's letter and the steps that had been taken to verify her parents' marriage and her own birth. He took his time, and it was towards the end of the afternoon session before he concluded. He then told the judge that before he called the Claimant to elaborate on her history he would be calling various official witnesses who would produce documents proving the marriage of Walter Caverel to Julian's mother and the decree of divorce which had terminated that marriage.

The judge interrupted him. 'Have not these matters been agreed between the parties?'

'No,' Percy replied. 'Everything has to be proved. The respondent has agreed to nothing.'

'Why not?'

Mordecai answered him from his seat. 'Because there is primary, better evidence of Walter Caverel's marriage than – '

Murray swung his head round and interrupted angrily. 'If you wish to address me, Mr Ledbury, please have the good manners to do so when standing and not when you are seated.'

Mordecai struggled slowly to his feet, making an even greater show of the effort. For a moment he stood, swaying slightly and supporting himself with both hands on the desk in front of him, his large head bowed. There was complete silence in court which seemed to last a long time before he raised his head and very slowly began to speak.

'As I have not previously appeared in your lordship's court nor had the pleasure of your lordship's acquaintance, your lordship may not have noticed that I do not have the great good fortune, so particularly enjoyed by your lordship, of having sound limbs.' Murray flinched and a slight flush came over his craggy features. Mordecai went on remorselessly, 'The highest judges in the land, sitting in the Judicial Committee of the House of Lords or in the Privy Council, have the consideration to appreciate that for me to stand to object or to reply promptly is not always possible because of the time it unfortunately takes me to get to my feet. They invariably show consideration of my disability, for which courtesy I, as a cripple, am always greatly obliged.'

He emphasised the word cripple, and the flush on the judge's face deepened. In his wish to put the interloper from the Queen's Bench Division in his place, he had been over-hasty. He had not realised how disabled Ledbury was.

'Mr Ledbury,' he said, for once hesitantly, 'I, I didn't appreciate. I'm sorry – '

145

'As your lordship can surely observe, it takes time and effort for me to raise myself to my feet.'

Murray realised the depth of his mistake and that he'd have to make amends. 'Of course, of course, Mr Ledbury. I quite understand. I should not have interrupted you. As I said, I did not appreciate your difficulties. What was it you wished to say?'

Mordecai bowed. The judge's obvious discomfiture had given him an opening. He had one eye on the clock. This could take up time, at least sufficient time to postpone the start of any evidence until the next day.

'I wished to explain to your lordship that if Sir Percy is going to tender a witness to produce documents to prove the celebration and then the termination of Walter Caverel's marriage, there is better evidence, first-hand evidence, available to him. For there is present in this court a person who from her personal experience can give direct evidence of both those events.'

Then he said loudly, without turning, jerking up an arm behind him, the sleeve of his black robe fluttering, his finger pointing to where the Senora was sitting, 'I refer to the lady sitting behind Sir Percy, the lady who married Walter Caverel and was divorced from him.'

Everyone turned to look at her and the Senora gave a little squeak and turned and buried her head on Mrs Campion's shoulder, to that lady's considerable embarrassment.

Mordecai went on, 'She is seated in the fourth row near to a Mr Willoughby Blake, a notorious publicist who before the cause has come to trial has been orchestrating the public campaign to promote the claim of the plaintiff and to denigrate the family.'

Percy leaped to his feet. 'My learned friend', he said, 'has no right to say such a thing. He has no right to make such offensive allegations. It is quite improper.'

'It was a statement of fact,' Mordecai snarled at him.

'It is merely abuse, and grossly unfair. And as to what witness I choose to call, that is a matter for me, not for him.'

Murray saw the chance to re-establish his bruised authority. He tapped gently on his desk with his pencil. 'Gentlemen, please restrain yourselves.' He turned to Mordecai and for the first time addressed him with civility.

'Mr Ledbury, I think you will agree that Sir Percy has the

right, within of course the rules, to select whichever method he chooses to present his evidence. The choice is his. What attention or weight I may give to the fact that he may have declined to call a particular witness who might have been able to give more direct evidence will be a matter for me.'

'If you please,' said Mordecai, and sat down.

His purpose had been to sting Braythwaite into calling the grandmother as his first witness and before the formal witnesses. If Braythwaite did, then there would be no worry over using up time until Mr Rogers arrived because the evidence of the grandmother and her cross-examination would inevitably be lengthy.

It was four o'clock and Murray was known to be prompt to rise at the end of a session, not because he wanted to get away to his own amusements but because he could then spend several hours in his room studying the law, or reading the documents, or even preparing a judgement in another case. 'As you have completed your opening, Sir Percy,' he now said, 'this seems a convenient time to rise. You may begin the evidence tomorrow. Ten thirty, tomorrow morning.'

'Is he here yet?' Mordecai hissed to Oliver.

'No,' Oliver replied, 'not yet.'

Mordecai cursed. 'Then we must pray that Braythwaite decides to call the grandmother as his first witness. If he doesn't, we're in trouble.'

He made his stumbling way out of court, waving aside all those in his path with his stick.

'What was all that about?' Andrea said to Nicholas.

'I haven't the slightest idea.'

'I thought our QC was right to say what he did.'

Nicholas took her arm. 'Perhaps. Let's have tea at my club, after we've braved the mob at the entrance.'

In the taxi when they reached Admiralty Arch, Andrea said, 'I want some air, so I'll walk from here. I don't want any tea. I'll see you tonight for dinner.'

She hurried off into St James's Park, went across the bridge over the lake and walked towards the Palace on the path beside Birdcage Walk. She made her way to Hyde Park Corner, then through the tunnel into the park. She walked along the Serpentine towards Kensington Gardens where she would pick up a taxi to take her to her cousin Fay in Egerton Gardens where she was staying.

The late afternoon was warm and sultry. She pulled off her hair band and thought about Nicholas. She knew how much she relied on him at Ravenscourt, and she knew how much Ravenscourt meant to him. If they lost the case, he would be bereft, but he wouldn't have to leave his home. The dower house was his, inherited from his mother whose father, the last great Caverel, had bequeathed it to her. It was not part of the estate.

Andrea stood for a moment by the Serpentine, watching the rowers on the lake and thinking of her own childhood in London before she went to Africa. If they lost the case Oliver had warned there'd be very little money. Robin had left none. What then would Francis' childhood be? When the thunderbolt of the claim had fallen she'd been in a bad way. But when the woman journalist had insulted her and the campaign in the press against the family had been mounted and she'd discovered that some of her own servants were betraying her, she'd become angry. This was Francis' and her battle. Now she'd fight for Francis like a tigress. She thought of her grandfather whom she had loved so dearly, murdered in Kenya. He'd have told her to fight, fight to the end.

As she searched for a taxi she thought over the day in court and of the two barristers. Theirs so handsome and personable; mine so ugly and twisted. The Princes of Light and Darkness. But however nice theirs might be, she knew he was on the side of Darkness. Hers, for all his ugliness, was the Prince of Light.

But it was the judge who worried her most. For all his learning, his appearance of strength and sternness, he was just the kind to be taken in by a pretty face. He'd like the Claimant, she knew he would; and she knew he wouldn't like her. She'd sensed that from the way he'd been looking at her. Why? Probably he hates people like us and what we stand for. Now only the ugly, crippled barrister can save us from him. She thought of the smile which lit up the twisted face, and the memory of it made her feel better.

*

After court, Oliver returned to his office in Lincoln's Inn Fields and spent several hours on the telephone. One call was to the Maritim Grand Hotel in Berlin. That was as close as he came to tracing Mr Rogers. After leaving Berlin, Mr Rogers had gone back to Istanbul. Where he had stayed when he was there, no one knew. And that was over a week ago.

It was after eight before he got to Anne's flat and she gave him his whisky-and-soda.

'When must he get here?' she asked after Oliver had told her why he was so late.

'When the young woman gives her evidence.'

'Will that be tomorrow?'

'Yes.'

'And if he's not?'

Oliver drank from his glass. 'It will be the end,' he said. 'The end for the Caverels – and the end of Ravenscourt.'

He didn't add what she knew he was thinking – the end also for himself.

28

When he left court, Percy Braythwaite was not so happy as he had been two hours earlier. Murray's snapping at Ledbury and Ledbury's effective response would oblige Murray to be more polite to him from now on, and the advantage Percy had as a regular practitioner in Murray's court had been reduced. He consoled himself by remembering Ledbury's reputation – sooner or later there'd be a quarrel. Any truce between Ledbury and Murray would not last.

What was concerning him more was Murray's hint over the inference he might draw if the 'best' or 'primary' evidence of Walter's marriage and Julian's birth, that is to say the evidence of the grandmother, was not tendered early on, and as Percy walked to the robing-room he pondered whether he ought not to call the old lady before the formal witness who would produce the certificates of Walter Caverel's marriage, the birth of Julian and the divorce.

In the robing-room he spoke to Welby, but Welby shrugged. He was, he claimed, totally ignorant about 'the arcane devices of advocates', and hurried away to confer with the Church Commissioners.

The only other person with whom Percy might discuss the question was Michael Stevens, but Percy had never felt at ease with Stevens. His behaviour had been impeccable. He had prepared an excellent brief; he was deferential and candid about his inexperience in Chancery law and practice, and quiet and sensible when he had brought his client to conferences. Nevertheless there was something about him that made Percy uncomfortable. It may have been his manner. It was too ingratiating, too smooth. That might be due to the fellow's experience in dealing with clients and lawyers in the criminal courts, but whatever it was, there was something about him that Percy felt was not quite straight.

As he strolled to his chambers in Gray's Inn in the warm late afternoon sunshine, he came to a decision: he would definitely call the grandmother as his first witness. But when he got to his chambers, his clerk said that Mr Stevens had preceded him; he was in the waiting-room.

'Give me three minutes, then bring him in. I'll ring when I'm ready.'

Percy's was a large, important room; the walls were lined with leather-bound volumes of the Law Reports and, above the books, some handsome eighteenth-century prints. He hauled up the sash windows to let in as much air as possible, changed out of his dark coat, and put on a fresh white shirt, dark tie and white linen jacket. He sat at his desk and rang the bell.

As soon as Stevens was shown into the room he began. 'The grandmother, Sir Percy, Senora Martinez, are you intending to call her as a witness?'

'Of course. I have decided to call her as my first witness.'

Stevens looked grave. 'I thought you might, Sir Percy, and that is why I have come.'

'Why? Is there a problem?'

Michael Stevens cleared his throat. 'I fear it is the Senora herself who has what is called a problem.' He paused. 'She drinks.'

Percy leaned forward. 'What do you mean?'

'She's a very heavy drinker. We have to be very careful with her.'

'Do you mean she might turn up in court intoxicated?'

'It is quite possible.'

'I know I live in the rarefied world of the Chancery courts, but are you saying that she might be drunk at ten o'clock in the morning?'

Stevens nodded. 'I'm afraid she might. Her problem first came to my attention when she created a scene at a press conference before proceedings had begun – '

'I'd heard about that, but I understood it was because she'd been outrageously provoked and insulted by some questions from someone in the audience and lost her temper.'

'That was so but she was also, I regret to say, inflamed by drink. I understood that recently she's got better – she's been in a nursing home after a bad fall. But I don't think we can altogether rely on her. I recommend that the case for the petitioner is firmly established before you call her to give evidence.'

'Are you solemnly telling me that you cannot guarantee to keep one of our most important witnesses from getting at the liquor bottle on the morning when she's due to be called as a witness?'

'I have had a lady very experienced in these cases looking after her, but somehow or other she seems able to get hold of liquor. Alcoholics, Sir Percy, are notoriously cunning and resourceful in getting their hands on drink and when drunk they can be very unpleasant. I do not know what she might not say.'

Percy fiddled with the papers on his desk. Ledbury had in effect challenged him to call the grandmother immediately. 'We shall have to call her at some time,' he said. 'She's the only member of the family supporting our case.'

'I appreciate that, but I suggest it would be safest to hold her back until after Miss Caverel has given her evidence. It would be unfortunate if she was called at the start of our case and before Miss Caverel gave her evidence and she made . . .' He paused and then went on, 'made an unfortunate impression.'

Percy was still thinking of what Ledbury had said and he remembered that Ledbury had also said something about somebody else.

'What part in this case is Willoughby Blake playing?' he asked abruptly.

'Mr Blake has befriended the petitioner from the start. He was one of the first who was convinced by her story and he has been prominent in demonstrating his confidence in her claim.'

'How?'

'By speaking widely to his many friends, soliciting their support. He is an influential man and he has been insisting that she is the rightful heir.'

'Is he connected with the media?'

'Not directly.'

There was silence for several moments. Then Percy said, 'Is he what they call a publicist?'

'In a manner of speaking. But the Caverel claim is for him a matter of conviction. He is convinced of its rightness and he is determined to see that Miss Caverel gets justice.'

When, many months ago, Percy had been retained, he had wondered how the claim was being financed but his clerk had told him that Stevens had assured him he had ample funds. Was the publicist the source of those funds? He shifted a little uneasily in his chair.

Stevens said, 'I have never regarded Mr Blake as being a potential witness.'

'No, but if he is, as you say, a publicist, I presume he's been drumming up support in the press. Of all judges this judge is the last who would appreciate that, as he would be the most offended by a drunken witness. And God forbid that Ledbury should have the chance of getting at either of them. Especially at the grandmother when she's not in a fit state to appear!'

He rose and walked around the room, pausing to lean against the wall by the window, looking down on to the square below. The story set out in his brief was perfectly straightforward. Naturally it all depended upon the genuineness of the Claimant, and when he had met her she had seemed honest and truthful. He had liked her. But Blake? What exactly was his role? What was his relationship to her? Were there, then, some murky shadows being cast over the case which cross-examination might reveal? But Blake had not invented the Claimant. She, Percy was convinced, was genuine. It was her claim, not Blake's nor the drunken grandmother's, and it was hardly Fleur's fault that the

152

old woman was an alcoholic. As he stood looking down out of the window he kept telling himself that he believed in and trusted Fleur Caverel. He knew he could win the case for her. All he had to do this evening was to decide the best order of witnesses. And having heard what Stevens had said, he certainly could not take the risk of calling the grandmother before Fleur. He would ignore Ledbury's challenge and revert to his first plan: to call at the start the formal witnesses to produce the certificates; and follow them with Fleur.

He turned back to Stevens. 'Very well,' he said, 'I shall call the grandmother later. But it's up to you, Mr Stevens, to see that, when I do call her, she's sober and capable of giving evidence. And keep Willoughby Blake out of this. Right out of it.' He pressed the bell on his desk. 'Until tomorrow then. Good evening, Mr Stevens.'

In the taxi on his way back to his office, Stevens thought of Braythwaite's instructions to keep Willoughby Blake out of it, and smiled. As if that were possible! Nevertheless Michael Stevens was satisfied with the result of the interview. Presumably Ledbury must have had some information about the Senora's drinking and that was why he had tried to get Braythwaite to get her into the box. And he'd nearly succeeded.

Stevens had been told that the Vice Chancellor was a judge who made up his mind about a case very quickly and once it was made up, rarely changed it. What was necessary, therefore, was to prove the marriages and births quickly; then call Fleur who would make an excellent impression and captivate the judge.

The first of the formal witnesses was an official from Somerset House and the Divorce Registry who would produce certificates proving the Senora's marriage to Walter Caverel, Julian's subsequent birth, and the Senora's divorce from Walter. After him came the vital witnesses – Jed Blaker's men from South Carolina, who would produce documentation to prove Julian's marriage and the birth of Fleur. Much expense and effort had been devoted to obtaining this evidence with the assistance of Richard Jameson, and it was on this evidence, Stevens reckoned, that the action would be decided. Unless the family could show the documents were forgeries or were able to cast doubt on their authenticity, he was certain that the claim would succeed.

On their arrival in London he had lodged the Americans well out of the way in an hotel near Heathrow. Today he had brought them to an hotel close to the Law Courts and kept them on call but out of sight. When it had become clear they would not be needed today, they had been sent back to their hotel at Heathrow. After they had given evidence and been released from further attendance at the court, a part of their reward was three days in Paris before they flew home, to which he knew they were much looking forward. Once the evidence of marriage and birth was established, followed by a good performance by Fleur, Stevens was sure that victory would be theirs.

In the hotel in Kensington Willoughby was sitting with Fleur. They were alone. Willoughby had opened a bottle of champagne. 'I thought Braythwaite's performance today first-class,' he said expansively. 'He's an attractive fellow, and he made an excellent fist of the story.'

Fleur was perched on the sofa. 'What were they quarrelling about at the end?'

'Lawyers' nonsense. The other fellow was a bit cheeky about the Senora – '

'And about you.'

Willoughby laughed. 'I don't care a fig what they say about me. I don't matter. It's you who matters.' He raised his glass. 'Here's to tomorrow, Fleur, the most important day in your young life. Stevens believes the case hinges on the American witnesses and . . .' He rose and glass in hand came over and stood smiling down at her. 'And on you.'

He handed her a glass which she put untouched on a low table in front of her. Willoughby rested his hand gently against her cheek. 'Scared?' he asked.

'A little.'

'There's nothing to be scared about. All you have to do is tell your story in your own words. Our man will help you along – '

'And then the other one goes for me.'

'What can he do? He can only suggest you're not telling the truth, but as you are what's there to worry you? I was watching the judge. I don't think he thinks much of her ladyship. But you, I also saw him looking at you.' He laughed. 'I think he likes the look of you. Behind all that Scots Presbyterian gravitas, there's a horny old man wanting to get out.'

Fleur grimaced. Willoughby sat beside her and took her hand. 'We're nearly there, Fleur. It's nearly over. Soon that toffee-nosed woman and her child will be out and we'll be in.' He patted her hand. 'A great new life will start for all of us. You can do what you like with your share, raise the wind on the house and the estate, sell the silver and the pictures – or whatever you're able to do. You'll be rich. You can go where you like, over the seas, into the sun – although God knows it's warm enough here at the moment.'

He got up again and taking off his jacket hung it round the back of a chair. She saw the damp marks on his shirt round the armpits and thought of Paul and the night in Paris when he'd seen the advertisement and it had all begun. It had been hot that night too. She missed Paul. For all his grossness, he'd been kind and true. He should be here now, when it was approaching the climax.

By the window Willoughby was on the telephone to Jameson at the hotel at Heathrow. Fleur was glad Jameson wasn't with them. Paul had never liked him. He's a gangster, Paul had said.

'Are the Yanks happy?' she heard Willoughby ask. 'Well, make sure they've everything they want. But not too many mint juleps.' He laughed his hearty, man-of-the-world laugh. 'Stevens says they'll be on the stand tomorrow, so see they get to bed early – if you can.'

He replaced the receiver. 'You're a trouper, Fleur, you've been one since you were a child. Think of tomorrow as a performance, like the performances you've given so many times before.'

She looked at him. 'Stark naked?' she said.

'That would be a sensation! But you're as pretty with your clothes on as I'm sure you are with them off. No, seriously, think of tomorrow as a show. You know your lines and – '

'I've never had lines to say before.'

'Perhaps not, but you're used to standing up in public and having people stare at you and that's half the battle. Think of the box as a stage. You'll do fine. All you have to do is to tell them the truth.'

She thought of how many lines she had, all those pages of large type in what Stevens called her 'proof'. She had to

155

remember them all, otherwise the man with the ugly face would try and catch her out. In the past weeks, as the date of the trial approached, she'd often lain in bed thinking about it, imagining standing in the box giving evidence. Some nights she got into a panic and wanted to run away and hide, abandon it as she had wanted to just after Paul's death. And Greg, he too had suggested she chuck it. He'd asked her why she was going on with it, why it was so important, was it worth it? Did she have to go on? What would she do with that enormous place, living in the gloom and the rain with people turning up their noses at her?

But by the time she'd met Greg, it was too late to turn back. He didn't, he couldn't, understand.

She liked Sir Percy. That was her comfort. He was so polite and so reassuring. He'd told her that he had complete confidence in her. Just as she had in him. Paul would have liked him. He was the kind of English lawyer that Paul would have expected.

Tonight she couldn't get Paul out of her mind. She thought of all the times they'd had together, of his kindness and support. She thought of Paul's wife, now his widow. She hoped she was all right. They'd only met once when she and Paul had been having lunch in a small restaurant on the left bank. She'd looked up and seen a worn, white-faced woman standing in front of their table. Paul had got to his feet and introduced her. My wife, he'd said, and asked her to sit with them and poured her wine. As the woman drank, she'd asked Fleur her name and where she came from, so many questions that Paul had become irritated and said they had to leave, they had to get back to the club for a rehearsal. That had been long before the advertisement in the *Herald Tribune*.

'You'll have that judge eating out of your hand, Fleur,' she heard Willoughby say. 'I know you will. And I know we're going to win. Now have some champagne. It'll do you good.'

She sipped from her glass and thought of Greg. He'd been so good over the money. She hadn't treated him well, but what could she have done? Willoughby was too jealous. She knew she'd have to wait until the case was over. Then she'd explain – about Paul and about how it had all begun. She knew what Greg felt for her. The sex hadn't been for him as it had been for her, a release from the tension of the past months. For Greg it had been serious, important, and she knew he'd suffered when she'd forbidden him even to try to see her again until the case was over. She wondered if he would come to court. She hoped he would.

'I'm going to bed,' she said.

'It's still light,' Willoughby protested. 'You must have something to eat.'

'Soup,' she said, 'just send up some soup later. And the sleeping pills. Tonight I want to sleep.'

But not, she hoped, to dream.

Nicholas was waiting for Andrea and her cousin, Fay, when they arrived at Wilton's for dinner. In his club he had looked up the judge in *Who's Who*. He'd married Freda Baronby, he told them. Andrea had known the Baronbys, but not Freda although she knew about her. 'She was crippled in a hunting accident,' she said.

'Perhaps that's why the judge was so mortified when he went for Ledbury.'

Andrea shook her head. 'No, he just knew he shouldn't have said what he did. He's not a kind man. I saw him looking at the woman. She'll fool him. I'm sure of it.'

'Ledbury won't let her. He'll show her up. That's what he's best at, Oliver says. He'll frighten the life out of her. He's ugly enough.'

'Not when he smiles,' she said.

In the taxi back to Egerton Gardens with Fay, Andrea said, 'When I found out about Robin's affair in Rome, I thought I could never again feel such unhappiness and despair. But I did, when he died. And I do tonight.'

'You mustn't. It'll be all right. They won't win, they can't.'

'If they do, I'll have to go to Nicholas until I find somewhere. Where that'll be, I don't know. I'll have very little money.'

'Won't you have what Robin left?'

'There wasn't much, in fact hardly any. They'll have to disentangle the little of his from what he inherited. All the entailed property, Oliver says, will be the woman's. His father left all his free property and his money to the Frenchwoman. What Robin had was very little. So I shall be very poor.'

'It won't happen,' Fay said. 'I know it won't.'

I think it will, Andrea thought.

Before he went to bed, Sir Robert Murray took several turns around the gardens of Lincoln's Inn. He had a flat at the top of one of the eighteenth-century houses beside the Hall. He walked briskly, striding along like the athlete he had once been. He watched his weight and he was careful with his diet. A little malt whisky in the evening was all the liquor he allowed himself and he kept in good shape. He was still angry with himself for having snapped at Ledbury. He had not realised how crippled the man was. He shouldn't have spoken as he had. Tomorrow he'd make a point of being especially polite.

As he marched round New Square, he thought also about the two women: on the one side the bonny lass, the Claimant, so quiet and modest; and on the other the woman of the kind he'd encountered when he was in love with Freda, before he knew about the gin. There'd be some startled English faces, he thought, if, or rather when, as he was presently inclined, he decided for the Claimant.

Oliver Goodbody was woken by the telephone just after 5 a.m. It was dawn. Half an hour later he was at Albany in Piccadilly and the night porter led him along the centre path under the glass canopy. Ledbury, in a flowered dressing-gown over striped pyjamas and one stick in his hand, opened the door. They went to the dining-room and Ledbury disappeared, returning with a coffee pot and three cups. They sat in silence, waiting.

A little before six thirty, Ledbury answered the door again. Mr Rogers followed him into the dining-room.

'I leave for court at ten,' Ledbury said, sitting down. Mr Rogers sat opposite and took from his case a sheaf of documents.

'I had most of it typed before the flight. There are some notes in my handwriting which I wrote on the aeroplane.'

Ledbury took the papers from him, spread them out on the table and began to read.

'We have three hours,' he growled.

'And a half,' added Mr Rogers pouring himself some coffee.

29

As was his habit, Percy entered the Law Courts from the back entrance in Carey Street and so he did not encounter the crowd at the main entrance in the Strand. It was even greater than yesterday, swollen by the publicity the case had received in the press and on television, and the prediction that today the Claimant herself would be giving evidence.

In the Vice Chancellor's court, Percy sorted the papers on his stand; on the top he placed the proof of the witness from the registry in Somerset House; beneath it those of the witnesses from Charleston.

Stevens and Fleur took their seats. Fleur smiled shyly. Today she looked prettier than ever.

'It won't be long now, Miss Caverel,' Percy said, smiling in return, 'and the sooner you start your evidence, the sooner it'll be over. First, we have some formal evidence. After that, you'll be in the box. I expect you're feeling nervous,' he went on, 'but it'll pass as soon as you begin. I'll lead you through your statement and we'll take it slowly.'

'The grandmother will not be coming to court,' said Stevens over his shoulder as he laid out his papers. 'She's indisposed.'

The Senora had come into Mrs Campion's room in the middle of the night very drunk. It had taken two hours to quieten her and get her back into bed.

'Gastric trouble,' Stevens went on. 'Nothing serious. She'll be well enough by the time we need her.'

Percy was relieved. The witness was ill. Now he could genuinely avoid Ledbury's challenge.

Andrea and Nicholas came to their places. She looked very drawn and tired. Percy bowed slightly but they ignored him. Can't blame them, he thought. They have too much at stake. Ledbury, he supposed, would make another late entrance with as much fuss as possible. But whom was he trying to impress? There was no jury. A trial before the Vice Chancellor was very different from trial by jury. If Ledbury kept the judge waiting, the war would be resumed before the truce had ever begun.

Judge Blaker and his team of three, all in a uniform of seersucker jackets and bright ties, made their entrance, shuffling noisily into the seats reserved for them, smiling to each other, looking around the old-fashioned court-room with the panelling and the high ceiling and the barristers in their eighteenth-century wigs. 'Like the movies, Jed,' one said loudly to Blaker who smiled and pulled at his white moustache.

Percy dabbed at his face with his red silk handkerchief. The air-conditioning had not been on for long enough and he was already warm in his robes. He heard the clatter of Ledbury's progress into court, the thumping of his walking-sticks and the orders to stand aside, but he did not look up. One snub was enough. When Percy did glance to his right, he saw that Oliver Goodbody was absent.

He leaned forward and tapped Stevens on the shoulder. 'Are the witnesses ready?'

Stevens did not turn. 'Of course,' he snapped.

'Then make sure that the first,' Percy looked at his note, 'Mr Steadman, is by the steps to the box.'

'My clerk has seen to it. The witness is already there.'

It was almost rude. No 'sir', no 'Sir Percy', very different from his former respectful manner. Why, Percy wondered. Then he noticed Stevens' hand as he opened his files. It was shaking. But what had Stevens to be nervous about? All he had to do was to sit and listen. Stevens' work was done.

Indeed it was, and because his work had been done, Stevens was thinking about the Americans. Would they stand up to cross-examination? He could not be calm until this evidence was over and the Americans safely away. Whichever way it went, triumph or disaster, their evidence, he believed, would be crucial.

Percy looked round again to catch a glimpse of Eleanor. She was in the fourth row back and he caught her eye. She smiled and mouthed 'Good luck'. He smiled back. Today she was not next to the smart, grey-haired woman she'd sat beside yesterday but to the sun-tanned man with white hair who kept getting to his feet and smiling. Willoughby Blake.

'All rise,' the usher called out and the Vice Chancellor took his seat. The Associate announced, 'Caverel versus Baron Caverel of Ravenscourt, part heard.'

Percy rose. Murray nodded to him but before Percy could begin Ledbury called out as he struggled to his feet.

'My Lord.'

'Yes, Mr Ledbury?' Murray said with what served him for a smile. 'You wish to address me? Please take your time.'

That's better, thought Mordecai.

'I want to bring to your attention', he said when he had got to his feet, 'the presence of a mob which has gathered outside the forecourt of the Strand entrance to the courts. They are shouting at everyone who enters and waving placards and threatening anyone they think has anything to do with the respondents.'

'I am very sorry to hear it,' the judge replied. 'Are there no police controlling them?'

'An inadequate number.'

'If they remain on the pavement and outside the forecourt, there is little I can do.'

'It is a blatant attempt to intimidate the witnesses for the family,' Ledbury went on. 'I ask your lordship to use your authority to bring their behaviour to the attention of the Police Commissioner.'

'Very well,' said Murray. 'I shall do what I can.'

There was silence as he scribbled. When he had finished he motioned to his clerk in the chair beside him and handed him the note. As the clerk disappeared through the door behind the judge's chair, Murray said, 'I have written to the City Police Commissioner asking him to do what he can. I will not permit witnesses, or indeed any person, to be intimidated.'

Mordecai bowed and subsided on to his seat with a crash. Every minute that served to postpone Fleur's appearance in the witness box counted. But if Braythwaite had fallen for his bait of yesterday and called the grandmother as his first witness, his worries were over. There was much he could ask her, and his cross-examination could properly take them well into the afternoon.

'Now, Sir Percy,' said the judge, 'you may begin.'

'The witness Mr Ledbury referred to yesterday, the Senora Martinez,' Percy said, 'who is the grandmother of the Claimant and Walter Caverel's first wife and the mother of Julian Caverel and whom I had considered calling as my first witness is, I am sorry to say, indisposed. My first witness therefore is Mr William Steadman from the Registry at Somerset House.'

Oliver and his senior clerk, Freeman, were in the interview room across the corridor outside the court. Oliver looked grey, older, the skin on his cheeks taut. He took the watch on its chain from his bottom waistcoat pocket. 'They'll have begun. You go in, Freeman. I'll wait here.'

Oliver glanced again at the documents Mr Rogers had brought to Albany. After a few minutes, there was a knock on the door and Mr Rogers entered.

'Well?' Oliver enquired.

'Two hours at the earliest. More likely, the afternoon. We're doing our best.'

Oliver nodded. 'Ledbury will have to do what he can. It won't make him popular.' He examined Mr Rogers, who had taken a chair. 'You look exhausted.'

You don't look too good yourself, Mr Rogers thought. 'I am,' he said. 'How long before they get to her?'

'If they don't call the grandmother, she could be in the box this morning. Ledbury will do what he can to delay it for as long as possible.'

'I'd better stay here and wait.' Mr Rogers placed his bowler hat on the table in front of him. 'I should like to be in court, however, when she takes the oath.'

'You shall. One of my clerks is to be stationed at the Carey Street entrance to keep a look-out. Before he does he'll bring you a thermos of coffee and the sandwiches for Ledbury's lunch.' Oliver walked to the small window which overlooked a grimy internal court-yard. 'The next twenty-four hours will settle it. Tonight at least you'll sleep in your own bed.'

Mr Rogers looked at Oliver. 'And sleep the sleep of the just?'

There was a note of interrogation in his voice. For a moment neither spoke. Then Oliver said, 'You have done what was asked of you. But you gave us a fright when you didn't call in. As you yourself pointed out, these people are not over-scrupulous.'

'All was only settled at the last moment and I couldn't telephone during the flight. There were no seats in first-class or club. I was next to a mother with an infant which yelled all night so I had very little rest. But it gave me the opportunity to write up my notes.'

'What matters is that you are here.' Oliver was leafing through the papers.

'I have insisted on affidavits. Your office are seeing to it.'

'Good.'

'It was an interesting task you set me. I only hope it achieves the result you want.'

'That depends on Murray.'

They exchanged looks.

'I'll go into court now,' Oliver said. He left Mr Rogers sitting in his chair, his eyes shut, smiling.

When Oliver took his place beside Andrea, Percy had just completed his examination-in-chief of Mr Steadman. Mordecai heaved himself up even more slowly than usual, with the cumbersome twisting which eventually got him on to his feet. He was still cursing at the absence of the Senora whose evidence would have given him the time they needed so badly. Now he'd have to do what he could with the formal witnesses – and there was precious little he could. Murray would soon twig and get irritated. Mordecai braced himself for trouble.

He looked up at Steadman balefully from beneath his black eyebrows. 'Mr Steadman,' he began at last. It sounded like an accusation and as he spoke his mouth seemed to slip to one side, the lips almost to the edge of his jaw. Steadman, though conscious that nothing in his evidence was in the least controversial, felt a twinge of apprehension.

'You may not be able to help me and if you can't please say so.' Mordecai paused. 'If you can't, I'll have to wait for the evidence of the lady who was a party to this marriage and divorce but who, we have been told, is at present indisposed.' He looked at Percy, who ignored him. 'So, Mr Steadman, I shall have to content myself with asking you some questions. From your records, did the marriage between Walter, Lord Caverel, and Lucy, Lady Caverel, née Bull of Clapham, take place at Chelsea Register Office on 26th June 1946?'

'It did.'

'He has already told us that,' Murray said pleasantly. Mordecai bowed. 'Do they also show that the marriage was terminated in October 1950 when the wife was granted a decree of divorce on the grounds of her husband's adultery?'

And he's already told us that too, Murray was tempted to say but stopped himself.

'They do.'

'Lady Caverel, whose maiden name was Bull, didn't originate the divorce proceedings, did she?'

'No, they were originated by Lord Caverel, her husband. He filed a petition. However the wife eventually obtained a decree on her cross-petition.'

'Thus the proceedings were commenced by the husband filing a petition for a decree in which he sought a divorce on the grounds of his wife's adultery with a co-respondent, a man called Alfredo Leiter. Did Lord Caverel at the same time seek the exercise of the court's discretion?'

'That is so.'

'That means, does it not, that he admitted his adultery during the course of the marriage?'

This time Murray could not keep silent. 'Whereas a jury would not understand the meaning of the prayer for the exercise of the court's discretion, Mr Ledbury, I do,' he said with his wintry smile.

Mordecai inclined his head. 'Of course, your lordship, of course.' He turned back to the witness. Now he had to move on to more dangerous ground.

'In Lord Caverel's original petition, did he allege that during the course of the marriage the wife had given birth to a son, Julian?'

'He did.'

'And did the husband, Lord Caverel, claim that his son was not a child of the marriage?'

'That is correct.'

'In the wife's answer and cross-petition, did she in reply swear that Julian, born on 11th January 1949, was a son of the marriage?'

'She did.'

'And she sought, and was eventually granted, a decree of divorce on the grounds of the husband's adultery?'

164

Murray again intervened, still marginally affable but with a note of impatience. 'That was because the husband abandoned his petition which was dismissed. He did not defend the cross-petition and the wife was granted a decree. Is that not correct?'

'It is,' repeated Mr Steadman, smiling nervously.

'Thus the husband's assertion that the son Julian was not his son was rejected by the court,' Murray continued, 'and the wife's claim that Julian was a son of the marriage was upheld.'

Mordecai had begun to stump up and down the bench. Oliver half turned and whispered over his shoulder, 'Patience, Mordecai, patience.'

Murray was going on. 'Remind me of what the order drawn up by the divorce court says with regard to the financial settlement for the wife and the custody and the maintenance of the son, Julian.'

'The order, my lord, recites that by agreement a sum of one hundred thousand pounds was to be settled on the wife by the husband; she was granted custody of Julian with maintenance at two thousand pounds per annum until he was twenty-one on 11th January 1970. On attaining his majority Julian was to receive a life annuity of two thousand pounds. The husband was also ordered to pay the costs.'

'And this order was drawn up in 1950?' the judge added.

'Yes.'

'Considerable sums for those days.'

Mordecai could restrain himself no longer. 'Has your lordship finished? If you have, may I now resume?'

Oliver lowered his head and rested his chin on his hands. Why does he have to be so aggressive?

Murray bridled. There was an ominous pause before he laid down his pencil and said shortly, 'You may.'

'Thank you.' Mordecai turned to the witness. 'Have you any note in the papers which can tell us the date of the death of Julian Caverel?'

'No.'

'None at all?'

'No.'

'Well, as doubtless we shall hear from another source, Julian died on 28th September 1978 in San Francisco, of, I believe, what is now known as Aids and – '

Percy was on his feet. 'That is a most improper observation. My friend has no right to say that – '

'I withdraw the question,' Mordecai said quickly.

'It was not a question. It was a statement.'

Before the judge could intervene Mordecai went on rapidly, 'At any rate, as we shall hear, shall we not, at the date of the death of Mr Julian Caverel in the United States, Walter, the 15th Lord Caverel was still alive?'

The witness remained silent.

'You can't help us over that?'

'No.'

'Well, at least you have been able to say from the records you produce that at one time Walter Caverel was claiming that Julian was not his son and – '

Robert Murray's earlier resolution to be polite had deserted him. He was now thoroughly irritated. 'That is yet another statement and not a question. The matter as to the legitimacy of the son, Julian, speaks for itself.'

Mordecai bowed his head. He appeared to be about to speak but apparently thought better of it and sank back into his seat. He took up some of his papers and shuffled them noisily. Oliver again half turned and whispered over his shoulder, 'Don't tangle with him, Mordecai. Remember, we need time.'

'Tangling with judges', Mordecai whispered back, 'takes up time.'

'There's no need,' whispered Oliver.

'No,' Ledbury replied. 'But no harm either.'

'I'm not so sure,' Oliver whispered.

Percy had risen. Murray said, 'If you thought of reverting to the legitimacy of Mr Julian Caverel which Mr Ledbury has for some reason known only to himself been exploring, there is no need, Sir Percy. The position in law is quite clear. The divorce court found that Julian Caverel was the child of the marriage. He was the elder son of the 15th Lord Caverel by the first wife. Robin Caverel was the younger son of Walter Caverel by his second wife. As I understand it, Julian having pre-deceased his father, the younger son, in ignorance of any alleged heir, assumed the inheritance on his father's death. I should have thought that even a practitioner in the Common Law courts

166

would have been well aware of the effect of those simple conclusions of law.'

Percy bowed. The judge went on. 'That is all there is to it. The point in question is whether the late Mr Julian Caverel had any legitimate issue. Please proceed.'

A hum rose in the court. Murray tapped angrily with his pencil. 'Silence,' called out the usher. Willoughby nodded his head happily and looked at Jameson who ignored him. Stevens turned to Fleur, a half-smile on his face.

'My next witnesses', Percy said, 'are from Charleston, South Carolina, and they will be producing formal records about the marriage of Julian in the United States and the birth of Miss Caverel. Mr Jeremiah Blaine, please.'

In the interview room Mr Rogers was drinking coffee, watched by Oliver's junior clerk. 'What's the judge like?' Mr Rogers enquired.

'My senior, Mr Freeman, says he's a bloody old tartar. Don't stand no nonsense, Mr Freeman says.'

Mr Rogers considered this gravely. 'I suppose it depends on what he thinks is nonsense.'

The young clerk sniggered. 'Mr Freeman says this judge thinks anything out of the ordinary, nonsense.'

'What is nonsense? What is ordinary?' Mr Rogers mused, both hands around his cup. 'Indeed what is truth, said Jesting Pilate, an observation, my young friend, made by another judge in another and more famous trial nearly two thousand years ago.'

The young clerk smirked. 'I'll leave you now. I'll be at the rear door in Carey Street.'

He left Mr Rogers alone in the room, waiting.

Jeremiah Blaine, his agreeable southern American accent pronounced, gave his evidence in a deep, sonorous voice which carried easily around the whole court. After he'd taken the oath he had turned towards the spectators in the body of the court and winked at Judge Blaker who shook his head but smiled. Fortunately Murray had not noticed.

Percy took Jeremiah Blaine through his evidence. Yes, he had with him and now produced from the registry at St John's, Lakeside, certified copies of the certificate of marriage at the Chapel of the Coming Kingdom on 16th August 1971 of Mr Julian Caverel, of London, England, bachelor, to Miss Florence Wilson, spinster, of the parish of St John's, Lakeside in the County of Radstock, South Carolina.

'Was that a marriage recognised as lawful by the State of South Carolina?'

'It sure was, sir.'

'And do you also produce from the same registry a certified copy of the birth to Mrs Florence Caverel of a daughter, named Fleur Sarah, on 26th December 1971?'

'I sure do, sir.'

'I want to ask you now about the hurricane in 1989 when St John's suffered such severe damage.'

Mordecai tapped Oliver on the shoulder and whispered in his ear, 'Have you anything for me about the certificates?'

Oliver shook his head unhappily. 'There is only the hurricane. You must do what you can with that.'

'It was bad, sir,' Jeremiah Blaine said from the witness box, 'mighty bad. It was a regular tornado.'

'When this tornado struck Southern Carolina so severely in 1989 and your town in particular,' Percy asked, 'did the registry at St John's among many other buildings suffer considerable damage?'

'It sure did, sir, severe damage, like as did the whole township. The registry is in the Town Hall, sir, and the roof was sliced off as neat as if it'd been done with a knife.'

'Were any of the records in the registry lost or defaced as a result of the damage during the tornado?'

'Some documents went, from wind and water as well as fire. Later when she'd blown herself out, we collected others from all over.'

'With regard to the records, certified copies of which you are now producing, and which relate to Mr Julian Caverel and Miss Fleur Caverel, what happened to them?'

'Them, sir? Oh, them were among those that were all right. They were fine. So we could take from them the certified copies which I have here.'

'Is there any doubt as to the authenticity or accuracy of the certified copies you are producing to this court?'

'None whatsoever, sir.'

Percy sat.

Mordecai lumbered to his feet. Oliver had always claimed that any evidence of the records at John's would be fabricated, but he had produced nothing to support his allegation. Oliver might be right, but all Mordecai could do was probe. There was only what he might make of the hurricane and the damage to the records.

'Where did you find the documents, or rather the originals of the documents, copies of which you produce to this court? You said you found some documents from the registry all over. Where did these come from?'

'From the registry.'

'You said the registry was destroyed.'

'He said nothing of the kind,' said Murray sharply. 'He said the registry was damaged not destroyed.'

Mordecai was glowering. 'But many documents in and from the registry were destroyed. Is that not right?'

'Correct.'

'But not these?'

'No, sir, not these.'

'Where were they found?'

'How do you mean?'

'I mean what I asked. Where were these documents found?'

'You mean these – '

'Of course I mean these! Where did you find these, or the originals from which you have taken these copies? You say you retrieved some from all over, whatever that means.'

'Some of the documents, not these.'

'Well, where did you find the documents that had been blown out of the registry?' Mordecai looked about him theatrically. 'Were they floating in the ditches or in the drains, or blown up on to the church steeple?'

Mr Blaine laughed pleasantly. He was not put out by the sarcasm. 'I guess I understand, sir, I get the drift. No, sir, there sure were some documents scattered around but not actually on the church steeple. Some were jest scattered when the roof went or in the flood which followed and were damaged by water or fire and defaced. Some were picked up, but some of the records were safe in the registry, like these here, the certified copies of which I have here.'

'How many documents were lost?' Mordecai persisted.

'I can't tell you that, sir.'

'Try. Try and tell me how many were lost? Millions, thousands, hundreds?'

'Scores, but that's a shot, as good a shot as I can reckon.'

'And, lo and behold, out of the scores destroyed, the originals of these two documents were miraculously saved?'

'Correct, sir, correct. These records were intact. They were all right. But it weren't no miracle. Would you like to know, sir, why these here records were intact?'

'Of course I would.'

'Well, you see, sir, it was because the originals of these here copies were on microfiche.' Blaine paused and grinned. 'That's how we stored some.' He grinned again at Mordecai before he went on. 'The microfiche was in steel cabinets. They were OK and these entries were on microfiche. Do you wanna see the original microfiche, sir?'

Mordecai paused. Oliver folded his hands on the table in front of him and gripped them tight. Blaine had deliberately held back that these copies were taken from microfiche. He had been playing with Mordecai. Game, set and match to Mr Blaine.

Stevens held his breath. The witness had not only survived; he had triumphed.

Murray did not disguise his satisfaction. He smiled one of his wintry smiles at Jeremiah Blaine. He turned to Mordecai. 'Yes, Mr Ledbury, anything more to ask the witness?'

Mordecai knew he'd been worsted and changed tack. 'Who first asked you to locate these documents and produce certified copies?' he growled.

Mr Blaine scratched his head. 'Let me see if I can recollect who it was. Why yes, I reckon it was old Isaac Walker, who first asked. He's passed away now, poor old soul.'

'Was he the lawyer on Station Street?'

'He was, sir.'

'And when did this lawyer ask you to locate the originals of these documents?'

Jeremiah Blaine looked across the court towards ex-Judge Blaker.

'Who are you looking at?' Mordecai spat out.

'I was looking at no one in particular, sir. I was jest looking and thinking.'

'Who is that man?' Mordecai pointed at Jed Blaker. 'The man in the fourth row with whom you were sitting before you came into the witness box?'

'Him?' said Mr Blaine easily. 'Why, that's Jed Blaker, Judge Blaker as we still call him. He used to be our judge, sir. But he ain't a judge now, he's – '

'What's his business here?'

'He brought us over, sir, he conducted us over here and – '

'He came with you from Charleston? He's with you?'

'In a way. He's – '

Judge Blaker was on his feet. 'I was associated with the late Mr Isaac Walter in some pieces of his law business, your honour,' he called out. 'I was instructed to try and locate the documents, and – '

'Please sit down,' said Murray, but he spoke pleasantly, not apparently as offended as might have been expected. 'You must not interrupt the proceedings.'

'I'm sorry, your honour, I was only trying to help.'

'I understand, and if you're called as a witness, you can of course explain.'

'One judge bawling out another!' Mordecai said to Oliver. Murray heard and turned on him. 'Please do not interrupt, Mr Ledbury, but since you have, will you, please, explain to me the purpose of these questions. Are you challenging the validity of the documents this witness has produced or not?'

'I am seeking to investigate how and why these documents were saved. I'm enquiring into the strange coincidence that out of the . . .' Mordecai paused. It was using up time but it couldn't go on much longer. The judge was by now thoroughly incensed. 'The coincidence,' Mordecai continued, 'that out of the hundreds of documents destroyed or lost in 1989, these so conveniently survived.'

'What do you mean by so conveniently? Convenient for whom?'

'For the Claimant, obviously.'

'It is not obvious to me. I ask you again, Mr Ledbury, are you challenging the documents as not true copies of the originals?

Or are you saying that if they are true copies, the originals are false?'

From the bench Mordecai picked up the bundle of pleadings bound together by small bows of green tape. 'Has your lordship read the pleadings?'

'Of course I have read the pleadings.' Murray was even angrier now. Either Ledbury was being obtuse or he was deliberately wasting time. 'It's my invariable practice, as you ought to know, to read and study the pleadings in every case in my court before I try the case. If you are suggesting I haven't read them in this case, that is impertinent.'

'Then of course I apologise.' Out of the corner of his eye Mordecai saw that a clerk had approached Oliver and was bent beside him, whispering in his ear. 'I was led into the error by your lordship's question about the purpose of my cross-examination. Your lordship will have seen from the pleadings that the defence to this claim on behalf of the infant Lord Caverel' – here his voice became particularly slow and solemn – 'denies the legitimacy of Julian Caverel; denies that he was ever married; denies that he was the father of a daughter; denies the legitimacy of any child said to be his. Indeed,' he added more quietly, 'the defence challenges everything about the claim – and everything about the Claimant.'

He paused. Oliver turned and slipped a note on to the desk in front of him. Mordecai glanced down. 'We are ready.' He looked up at the judge. 'But in view of your lordship's pertinent comments and my misinterpretation of your lordship's practice, I shall conclude my cross-examination of this witness and, if it's any assistance to my learned friend, I shall not cross-examine any other witness that my friend might call upon this issue.' He sat down, with the usual noisy clatter.

Murray turned to Jeremiah Blaine. 'Thank you,' he said with another of what passed for him as a smile. 'You have been very helpful and I am much obliged to you.'

'Only too pleased to be able to oblige.' Blaine picked up his papers, went down the steps from the witness box and made his way to his seat beside Jed Blaker, who clapped him happily on the back.

'Well done, old cock,' Willoughby whispered. 'You did fine.'

Percy rose. 'In view of what my friend has just said, I understand that he accepts the authenticity of the documents.' He paused and looked at Mordecai who ignored him. Percy went on, 'As he does not dispute what I have just said, I have no re-examination of the witness and I shall call no further witness to confirm the authenticity of these certified copies.'

Murray nodded. 'Very well. Let us get on.'

'My lord, this witness and the other gentlemen who have been brought here to prove these documents have come from the United States and are anxious to return to their official duties as soon as possible. As the challenge to their evidence has been withdrawn, I ask that they be released from further attendance.'

Stevens had turned and was looking up at Percy expectantly.

'Very well,' Murray repeated. 'These witnesses – '

There came a rumble from Ledbury in his seat.

'If you please.' He hauled himself to his feet. 'The evidence in the case has only just begun and I suggest as a point of principle that it is unwise to release witnesses at such an early stage in the trial. I submit you should not order their release.'

Stevens had turned and, anxious again, was looking towards Mordecai.

'Why?' said Murray abruptly. 'Why should you object? You have completed your cross-examination and you have said that you do not seek to cross-examine any other witness about these documents.'

'That is so,' Mordecai said, 'but I submit it's never wise to release any witness who has come from a distance and cannot be easily recalled until all the evidence has been completed.'

'What evidence are you referring to?'

Mordecai looked at him. Some seconds passed.

'All the evidence,' Mordecai replied. 'There will be much evidence and many witnesses before this case is concluded. So until your lordship has heard all the evidence, I suggest that no witness should be released.' There was another pause. 'By evidence, I mean not only evidence for the Petitioner but also evidence for the Respondent.' Again he paused.

Stevens was looking down at his papers, biting his lip. 'It could be disastrous, leading to costly adjournments, if, for any reason, either party or your lordship yourself required their presence and these witnesses had been released and were three thousand miles away and outside the jurisdiction of the court which would have no power to ensure their return.'

For a time Murray said nothing. He knew that Ledbury was right in principle, but the man had succeeded in thoroughly exasperating him, not only by his attitude to the bench but also by his slowness and irrelevance. Moreover Ledbury had not really challenged the certificates, so how could there arise circumstances in which the American witnesses would be further required? It was a risk, but he'd take it.

He looked down at his notebook. 'The application', he said at last, 'is granted. The witnesses dealing with this part of the Claimant's case are released.' He looked up at the clock. 'I shall adjourn now,' he said. 'Two o'clock,' and he swept out of the court.

Percy rested his hand for a moment on Stevens' shoulder. The knuckles of Stevens' fists on the table were showing white. Julian's birth, Julian's marriage and Fleur's birth were now in evidence. The expense, and the trouble, had been worthwhile. 'Thank you,' he said to Percy.

'Thank Ledbury. His cussedness did it for us. For all his reputation, he's not a very skilful cross-examiner or today he's not in very good form.' Percy smiled at Fleur. 'You've very little to worry about when you're in the box this afternoon,' he said.

In his room Murray was having a twinge over how wise he'd been to release the Americans. He couldn't conceal from himself that the reason he'd decided as he had was principally his antipathy to Ledbury. For a brief moment he pondered whether it might not be wiser to change his decision but it was now probably too late. The witnesses might have already left. And he'd be quite unable to tolerate the look of satisfaction it would bring to the face of Mordecai Ledbury.

When the judge had made his ruling about the witnesses, Willoughby had grasped Jameson's hand under the bench and squeezed it.

'We've done it, old son,' Willoughby whispered.

In the corridor he caught up with Jed Blaker and put his arm round his shoulder. 'Nice doing, old cock. Now you can be off.'

174

'I expected we'd be here until the end of the week. We're booked into *Sunset Boulevard* on Friday evening and we're not on a flight to Paris until Saturday morning.'

'Then stay around and be our guests. Let's have a glass to celebrate. Jeremiah did very well, very well indeed. He made their lawyer look an ass. We're nearly there, old cock. Now it all depends on Fleur.'

30

She did brilliantly, speaking in a low attractive voice which could be heard throughout the court-room, her eyes flickering from counsel to judge and up to the public gallery above her. She looked stunning in a smart black and white outfit, her raven dark hair glistening under the sunshine steaming in from the windows high above her.

'Sit if you wish, Miss Caverel,' the judge said when she entered the witness box. She replied she'd rather stand, so he ordered the usher to bring a chair and place it behind her so that if she grew tired she could sit. She was only a few feet from him to his right and he rarely took his eyes off her.

As soon as she had climbed the steps into the witness box and taken the testament in her hand, she saw Greg. He was sitting in the last row at the back of the court, leaning forward, his elbow on the desk and smiling. So he had come. Now she knew she'd do well.

At first she was solemn and serious but, as she grew in confidence, every now and then a smile lit her face, especially when she spoke of the elderly woman whom she believed to be her mother and who had raised her as Sarah Wilson; and of the gentle, white-haired man she called father, although somehow she never really believed he was. Years ago he had been a conductor on the 'Orange Blossom' Express, the famous winter train from New York Grand Central station to West Palm Beach, and when, after a lifetime with the railroad, he had retired, he and his wife lived comfortably enough some miles out of town. They kept very much to themselves. There were no other children, and Fleur rarely went to school. The old man taught her to read using his Bible, and did simple sums with her. She was very ignorant until she came to Europe and began to devour every book she could lay her hands on. 'I'm self-educated,' she said.

She had loved them both but they were old, and she was lonely. And when she was fourteen, she had taken some dollars from the tea caddy in the kitchen where the old woman kept the housekeeping money and caught the bus and left.

'I never told them where I'd gone,' she said. 'Secretly I suspect they were glad I had run away. It couldn't have been easy for them at their age raising a teenage girl.'

She smiled, and it was an infectious smile which made even the correct and decorous Sir Percy smile in return as he shepherded her through the story of her life. The craggy features of the Vice Chancellor noticeably softened when she looked at him. Andrea watched the judge watching Fleur. I knew, she said to herself, I knew.

Willoughby Blake was preening himself. She was doing well; and the longer she was in the box, the more confident he became. Today he was savouring the culmination of the months of endeavour, of planning, of grooming and training – and of expensive cultivation of the press. Today he was harvesting the return on his investment.

Fleur had reached the time in her story when she'd arrived in Paris after a year or two in Atlanta and then New Orleans. This was the part of her story which had caused Percy concern, fearing the effect the night-club background might have on the prudish Nonconformist elder of the kirk. But he had no need. Fleur had been told that it would be up to her to make the judge understand and sympathise when she spoke of being driven to appear on the stage in those places, so at this point she turned to face the judge and there were no smiles as gravely, even sadly, she explained that she had run away from the old couple because she had no friends of her own age who lived near their home and she'd always dreamt of going on the stage and becoming a famous singer. Since she'd been small, at home she'd danced and sung while the old man played his fiddle and the old woman clapped her hands. Music, she told the Vice Chancellor who nodded gravely, was her love. She supposed she inherited this from her father because, as she later came to learn, he had been a musician, a professional pianist.

When she'd run away, she'd gone to the house in Atlanta of a much older girl she'd met on one of the family's few visits to the Chapel of St John's at Lakeside. This girl had come as a member of a visiting choir and she and Fleur had talked at the supper after the service and afterwards had gone for a long walk together along the bank of the river. Fleur had told her new friend about her dreams and ambitions and the friend had given Fleur her address in Atlanta. So she had not been altogether surprised when Fleur turned up on her doorstep. The girl and her flat-mate had let Fleur sleep on the sofa in the living-room and a few days later they took her to the manager of a piano-bar for an audition. But in Atlanta they'd only been interested in her figure not her voice, and they made her into a dancer – although, Fleur said, smiling at Murray, at first she was not very good. But they taught her to do what they called bump and grind and strike poses in time to the music.

When she said this, Mordecai leaned forward to Oliver. 'She means, of course, her Attitudes,' he said in his penetrating stage whisper, 'the modern Attitudes of a modern Emma Hamilton.'

Murray looked at him, frowning but not catching the words, only aware that counsel for the defendant must have said something derogatory.

After about two years in Atlanta, Fleur continued, she got the chance to go to New Orleans where she stayed for eighteen months. Then she'd been offered an engagement in Paris which she'd accepted eagerly. Since she'd left home, she'd never told the old people where she was but used to send them postcards without any address. From Paris she sent them one of the Eiffel Tower so that they would know she was in France. But no message, and again no address.

It turned out to be a hard life in the clubs, she said, two shows a night, very long hours, no glamour. Just work. And management often exploited the dancers, failing to pay what they'd promised so they were driven to take any engagement wherever it was offered, which meant travelling to cities all over Europe. But she never wanted to go home. She'd always felt she was different, she said. She did not know why, although she knew she had a lighter skin. Once she'd arrived in Paris, she felt far more European than American. Placing a hand to her throat and looking directly at the judge, she said, 'I hope you'll understand when I say this, but for the first time I felt more white than black.'

There was a stir among some of the spectators in the gallery, and Percy hurried her along to the time, after many years touring from city to city, when she'd been told about the advertisement in the *Herald Tribune*.

'How did that come about?' Percy asked.

'It was in Paris. A friend who'd helped me in my career called Paul Valerian told me about it. Paul came from Warsaw in Poland. Originally his family had come from Russia. They were White Russians. He owned the club in Paris where I was dancing. He showed the advert to me and said it must be me they were looking for.'

'Where had you met Mr Valerian?'

'In Instanbul where I was working, and then later in Berlin. He was very kind because when I was stranded in Berlin after the club there folded, he brought me to Paris and engaged me to dance in his club.'

'Was he a married man?'

'He was. I'd met his wife with him.'

'Will you, please, look at this.' Percy handed a newspaper to the usher, who showed it to the witness. 'Is that a copy of the advertisement Mr Valerian showed you?'

'Yes,' she said. 'It is.'

'Will you read out what it says?'

Fleur read. 'If Sarah Wilson, last heard of in Paris, France, will get in touch with Mr Isaac Walker, attorney-at-law, of 387 Station Street, St John's, Lakeside, Charleston, South Carolina, USA, she will learn something to her advantage. A reward of fifty dollars will be paid to anyone who can inform the above-named Mr Isaac Walker of the whereabouts of Miss Sarah Wilson or of her last known address.'

'What did you do when you first read that in the newspaper?'

'I talked about it with Mr Valerian and – '

'Before you tell the court more, can you say what happened to Mr Valerian?'

She hesitated and looked down at her hands folded on the edge of the witness box. 'He was killed in a terrible accident in

London last year.' She fumbled in her bag and brought out a small handkerchief.

'Take your time,' said the judge solicitously.

Don't spoil it, Fleur darling, Willoughby thought. You're doing so well. Don't let the bloody Pole ruin it. Don't overplay. And she didn't. She just held the handkerchief in her hands twisting it round her fingers but not raising it to her eyes.

'He tripped and fell in front of a train in the subway during the rush hour and was killed. I'm afraid he'd been drinking.'

'Were you in London at the time?'

'Yes, he'd come with me to London to help me.'

'The death of the man who had helped you in the past and was helping you at that time must have been a great shock as well as a great loss.'

'She's more than capable of telling her own story without you putting words into her mouth,' growled Mordecai. 'Don't lead.'

Murray heard him. 'Technically it may have been a leading question,' he said sternly, 'but – '

'It was a statement,' said Mordecai.

'Perhaps it was, but it was hardly appropriate for an objection.'

Mordecai shrugged and swivelled in his seat until he had turned sideways on away from the judge and sat with his hand over his eyes muttering to himself. Murray watched him. There was a pause. Murray turned to the witness.

'Pray continue.'

'Paul was a dear friend. As I said, he'd helped me in the past, saved my life almost in Berlin, and when he showed me the advert he wanted me to do something about it. But I didn't want to. I knew the old people back in South Carolina had very little money and I wasn't going to do anything about it. But Paul insisted I find out what it was all about and he'd lend me the money to go to see Mr Walker. So I did. My foster mother had died just before I arrived – it was because she was so ill they'd thought of the advertisement. The old man had died some years before. It was then that I learnt who my real parents were.'

The court was very quiet, people leaning forward in their seats to catch every word she spoke. Except Mordecai, who remained sitting with his back almost to the witness box and the judge, looking bored and cynical. In front of him Andrea, white-faced and agitated, looked mostly at the witness, but sometimes turned to look at Percy Braythwaite, or behind her at Mr Rogers who had slipped into a place by the aisle several rows back.

'How did you learn about your real mother?'

'The old lawyer gave me a letter from my real mother which my foster mother had kept to give me when I was grown. But I'd run away and she didn't know where I was, except that I was in France. So when she became very ill, the lawyer had advised her to put an advert in the Paris *Herald Tribune*.'

'Where is the letter your real mother wrote?' Braythwaite asked.

'I don't know. Mr Walker gave it to me when I came to see him and I read it in his office in front of him. But later I couldn't find it. I know Mr Walker didn't have it. He told me so when I asked him before he too died. I must have lost it on my journeys.'

'What happened after you'd returned to Paris?'

'I spoke to Paul and he urged me to go to London. He said I ought to get from my father's family what he called my rights. So we came to London and Paul found me Mr Stevens, my solicitor, who made my claim for me.'

Percy next took Fleur in detail over the meeting with Walker and in even greater detail over the missing letter, before turning to her arrival in London. The letter Stevens had written to the family, telling them of her existence, was produced.

'Was none of even the formal correspondence agreed?' Murray asked Percy.

'No, my lord, none.'

'Why not?'

'I cannot help your lordship about that.'

'This is a perfectly proper and ordinary letter from a lawyer advising the family of the existence of the young lady. Why was not this agreed?'

'All I can tell your lordship is that none of the correspondence, none of the documents, nor the marriage and birth certificates were agreed, all have to be proved. Only the formal letter before action which commenced the legal proceedings has been agreed.'

Murray looked over his spectacles at Mordecai, who still had his shoulder turned towards him. There was a pause. The judge waited. Mordecai said nothing.

'Have you anything to say, Mr Ledbury?'

Mordecai rose. 'Only that as Mr Justice Mellor once said, when the matter is in the hands of attorneys on one side or the other, it's not worth a farthing.'

'Mr Justice Mellor?'

'Yes, the late Mr Justice Mellor, a judge in the nineteenth century who was one of the judges in the great trial at bar of the Tichborne Claimant, of which your lordship has possibly heard.'

Murray stared hard at Mordecai, before at last replying, 'I certainly have heard of that trial, at the conclusion of which, as I remember, the counsel for the defendant was disbarred because of his conduct towards the bench. Now I repeat, why were none of the formal documents agreed?'

Mordecai shrugged. 'I have no idea,' he said and sat.

After a pause Murray went on. 'I am offered no explanation. Very well. I shall make a note of that. Please proceed, Sir Percy.'

Fleur then told of the refusal of the family to have anything to do with her, except for Julian's mother who was living in BA in the Argentine and who had immediately come to London to support her. Then Percy asked, almost casually, 'Who is Mr Willoughby Blake?'

'He's a great friend of Mr Stevens and after Mr Valerian had been killed, he supported me. He was convinced of the rightness of my claim and offered to help. So when my grandmother arrived I went to live at the Kensington Park Hotel with her and her companion.'

'Who paid for that?'

'Mr Blake.'

'Who is providing the funds for you to bring your claim to court?'

'Friends, people who believe in me and want me to get my rights. Mr Blake organised it. He has been very kind. In September he even drove me down to Ravenscourt on one of the open days so that I could see where my ancestors lived. But when we got there, Lady Caverel ordered us from the house.'

'Do you see the lady here in court?'

'Yes, she's sitting there.' Fleur pointed.

'She did what?' asked Murray.

'She told us to get out.'

Murray looked at Andrea who stared straight ahead of her. Murray picked up his pen. 'I was ordered from the house,' he said as he wrote, 'by the lady calling herself Lady Caverel.'

Mordecai began to struggle to his feet. One of his sticks fell from the desk with a crash. Murray looked up, surprised by the noise. Mordecai, his normally saturnine face flushed, said thunderously, 'The lady sitting in front of me rightly calls herself the Lady Caverel. She does so because she is the Lady Caverel, and it was as Lady Caverel that the witness spoke of her. Your lordship, however, purporting to quote the witness, wrote down in your notebook, "the lady calling herself Lady Caverel". Is your lordship minded at this stage of the trial when your lordship has heard only a part and a small part of the evidence, to call her anything other than the Lady Caverel?'

Startled, Murray replied, 'I thought that the witness had referred to the lady as calling herself Lady Caverel?' He looked at Percy, who shook his head.

'Apparently I was wrong,' Murray said at last.

Mordecai remained on his feet. 'The shorthand writer will have a note of what the witness said.'

Murray was ruffled. 'I appear to have made a mistake, Mr Ledbury. Please do not take it as any indication of how my mind was working. Of course, Lady Caverel. I have corrected my note. I am sorry if any wrong impression was gained.' He paused. 'Now may we go on?' he said mildly.

'Very well,' Mordecai said, staring hard at the judge before once more slumping down. 'He had better be more careful,' he said to Oliver in his stage whisper. Murray heard but ignored him.

Oliver's junior clerk came into court and spoke to Freeman who tapped Mr Rogers on the shoulder. Mr Rogers slipped from his seat which was taken by Freeman to keep for him until he returned. In the conference room, Mr Rogers said to the junior clerk, 'I was sorry to have to leave court. It was becoming rather entertaining.'

In court, Percy saw from the clock that the time for the adjournment was approaching. He did not want to expose Fleur to cross-examination when she'd been in the witness box for some hours. It was better she face Ledbury in the morning when she was fresh, so he took her slowly over the rest of the story, even going back over some parts until Murray announced he was rising for the day.

182

As the judge got to his feet, Ledbury said, 'The witness is under examination and – '

Murray interrupted. 'I know that, Mr Ledbury,' he said testily. He looked towards Percy. 'Although she is not under cross-examination, it would be better for the witness not to speak to anyone about the case during the adjournment.'

In his room he flung his wig on to the table. Once again he was angry with himself. As he strode up and down his room, he promised himself to keep a better guard on his tongue. What on earth had led him to make that stupid mistake over what the witness had said? What was it about that fellow Ledbury that had the effect of driving him into making slips?

He was, he admitted to himself, greatly taken by the evidence of the Claimant. She was giving her evidence well and proving an impressive witness, and it had already been established that there was a daughter, born in wedlock, of the elder son. That could be the end of it. She was the rightful heir. Was it, then, his present inclination to accept the plaintiff's evidence that had led him into the mistake of referring to the other woman as 'the lady calling herself Lady Caverel'? Or was it his irritation at the sight of her fidgeting, her apparent inability to keep still, while at the same time looking supercilious with her disapproving nose stuck in the air? The more he watched her, the more she reminded him of those friends of Freda's. And today Freda was much on his mind for tomorrow, Friday evening, he was due to pay one of those visits to her which he so greatly disliked. His annoyance with himself and his gloom at the prospect of the weekend made him dislike the other woman even more. But he must, he knew, be more careful. When the evidence was complete and when he gave judgement that would be the time when he could say what he liked. Until then, he must check himself.

In the corridor outside the court Mordecai had taken Andrea's hand.

'Tomorrow will decide the matter, Lady Caverel. So you must be prepared.' He smiled. 'Now Oliver and I have work to do. Tomorrow, then, we shall meet at Philippi.' He stumped off, leaving Andrea marvelling once again at the change that came over his twisted face whenever he smiled.

When Fleur had come out of court with Stevens, Willoughby

darted up to her and embraced her. 'Marvellous, darling,' he breathed in her ear, 'you were quite marvellous.'

'You'd better not speak to her. She must go home alone. I'll take her to the car.' Stevens bustled Fleur on. Turning the corner in the corridor, they came face to face with Greg. He was leaning against the wall. Fleur halted.

'I hoped you would come,' she said simply.

'I was in at the beginning when you first arrived, so I thought I had a right to be here at the end. I just wanted to wish you luck.' He stared at her and then turned on his heel and disappeared down the stairs.

She watched him go. 'You needn't come with me,' she said to Stevens.

'There'll be a crowd at the entrance. I'll see you to the car.'

'Very well, but then I want to be alone.'

At Hyde Park Corner she told the car to stop and took a taxi. Ten minutes later Greg let her into his apartment. Without a word he seized her in his arms.

31

It was mid-morning when Mordecai Ledbury began his cross-examination. He clambered to his feet more slowly, more elaborately and more noisily than usual and stood leaning against the bench, his head lowered, taking his time, one hand on a stick, the other playing with the papers on the desk in front of him.

For a moment Murray was tempted to order him to get on with it, but he remembered his vow to keep quiet. Instead he began to rehearse in his mind what he would say in his judgement about the conduct of the respondent's counsel; and it wouldn't be complimentary.

Fleur was paler, looking more tired than she had the day before. She was dressed in the same outfit because she had not been back to the hotel. Her pallor, Robert Murray decided, suited her.

Without needing to look, she knew Greg was sitting in the same place at the back of the court and the knowledge of his presence comforted her even more than the sight of him had on the day before. 'However much he tries to provoke you, all you have to do is to stay calm and tell the truth,' Greg had said as they lay in bed. 'He can't harm you.'

When late that night there had been no sign of her, Willoughby had telephoned Stevens who told him where he thought she was. 'Leave them alone,' Stevens had said. 'Tomorrow is too important.'

Mordecai raised his head and stared at the witness.

'What is your name?' he began.

She had not expected that. 'My name?' she said hesitantly.

'Yes, your name. What is your name?'

'Fleur Caverel, of course.'

'Why of course?'

'Because it is. You know it is.'

'Do I? When did you first call yourself by that name?'

'When I learnt that it was my true name.'

'When was that?'

'When I'd seen Mr Walker and he gave me my mother's letter.'

'Where is that letter?'

'I don't know. I said, I've mislaid it.'

'Mislaid it! You've mislaid the letter which, if what you say is true, would change the whole of your life, the important letter which told you of your parentage – and of your expectations?'

'I didn't then know what to expect. All I know is that I don't know where the letter is now.'

'So, you're telling us that the letter has gone. And the lady who wrote it has gone; and the lady who kept it and brought you up has gone; and the lawyer is gone. All dead. Doesn't that sound very convenient?'

'I am not inventing it.'

'We have only your word that the letter ever existed, isn't that right?'

'Yes, only my word.'

'And the integrity of your word, madam, I'm going to challenge. Do you understand?'

'Of course. It's your job.'

A titter ran around the court which Murray made no attempt to quiet. He even allowed himself a nod and a faint smile.

'And your job, madam, or rather your duty under the oath

185

you've taken,' Mordecai said savagely, 'is to tell the truth.' Murray was about to intervene but Mordecai did not give him the chance as he went on rapidly, 'Were you calling yourself Fleur Caverel when you first returned to Paris from Charleston and your interview with the lawyer?'

'No.'

'Why not?'

'I didn't until I had talked to my friend, Paul Valerian.'

'You wanted his advice?'

'Yes.'

'What were you calling yourself when you returned to Paris from seeing Mr Walker?'

'Sarah, Sarah Wilson.'

'And was that the name Paul Valerian knew you by?'

'Yes.'

'Always?'

'Yes, always.'

'From the first moment you and he had met?'

'Yes. When we met I thought Wilson was my name.'

'All the time you knew him he never called you anything else?'

'Never, always Sarah.'

'And he called you Sarah Wilson when you were alone together and when you met his friends and he introduced you to them?'

'Yes.'

'Were you and Paul Valerian lovers?'

She looked at Murray. 'Is this relevant, Mr Ledbury?' Murray asked coldly.

'It is.'

'Then you must answer,' said Murray gently.

'We were, years ago, for a very short time. Later we were just friends, very good friends.'

'The love affair was over when you worked for him at his club?'

'Yes. That was many months later.'

'After the end of the love affair, he helped you to get engagements in Berlin and then gave you work himself?'

'Yes. I told you, we were friends.'

'And from first to last he called you Sarah, Sarah Wilson?'

'Yes.'

'Even when you were lovers?'

'Yes.'

Mordecai paused. 'You've been called by other names, haven't you?'

'What do you mean?'

'Was the question so difficult? What other names have you been known by?'

There was a silence. 'Stage names,' she said quietly.

'Please speak up,' Mordecai said, his cane thumping on the floor. At the noise, Murray looked up angrily from his notebook but said nothing. 'What was your answer?'

'I said stage names, sometimes I've used stage names.'

'Why?'

'We all did. Sometimes we called ourselves different names when we were in different countries.'

'Who are we?'

'My friends, the other dancers.'

'Tell the court what were these other names that you have used.' There was a pause. He waited. 'Perhaps I can help you,' he went on. 'Ella Moreau. Is that a name you remember?'

'Yes,' she said. 'I believe it is.'

'Believe!' Mordecai leaned forward, wagging his head. 'Don't you know? Don't you recognise the name, Ella Moreau?'

'Yes. That was a name I sometimes used on the stage.'

'Only on the stage?'

'No, not always. When we were in some countries we used different names. Sometimes we didn't want people to know our real names.'

'Why not?'

She shrugged. 'There were men who tried to get off with us, who pestered us.'

'Does the name Lila or Leila Houseman mean anything to you?'

'Yes, that's a name I used.'

'Anna St Martin, was that another of the names you went under?'

'Yes, it was another stage name.'

Mordecai paused. 'Who chose the name, St Martin?'

'I did.'

187

'How did you pronounce it? In the English way or in the French?'

'The French way.'

'Why did you choose that name?'

'I don't know. It was just a name, a made-up name for the stage.'

'But St Martin is a place. Have you not heard of St Martin?'

'No.'

'It is an island in the Caribbean, is it not, in the group of islands known as the Lesser Antilles, near to Guadeloupe? Does that mean anything to you?'

'No, why should it?'

'Have you ever been to St Martin?'

'No.'

'Have you any family there?'

'No, of course not.'

There was a long pause, Mordecai standing very still, looking at Fleur.

'Yes, Mr Ledbury,' said Murray at last. 'Continue.'

Mordecai switched his gaze from Fleur to Murray. 'Very well,' he said menacingly, 'very well. I shall return to that name St Martin, and that place St Martin, a little later.' He turned to face Fleur. 'These names you used, can you remember which name you used in which city?'

She thought. 'No,' she said, 'I can't.'

'Let me see if I can jog your memory. You performed at a club called the Amigo in Venice. What name did you use there?'

'Ella, I think, Ella Moreau.'

'And at Jack's Club in Antibes in the South of France?'

'The same, I think.'

'And at the Vie en Rose in the Campo dei Fiore in Rome?'

She thought. 'St Martin, I think Anna St Martin.'

'The Kleine Nachtrevue in Berlin?'

She paused. 'Anna St Martin,' she said at last. 'Anna St Martin.'

'Both on stage and off?'

'Yes.'

'And in your friend's club in Paris, Valerian's club, what name did you go under there?'

'Leila Houseman.'

'On stage and off?'

'On stage, although I used that name off stage for some people. Not for all.'

'But not for your old friend, Paul Valerian?'

'No, as I said, he called me Sarah, always Sarah.'

'Even when you were performing at his club under the name of Leila Houseman?'

'Yes.'

'You first met the Pole when you were performing what you call your poses at the Minaret Club in Istanbul?'

'By the Pole, I presume you mean Mr Valerian?' said Murray acidly.

Mordecai was looking towards Fleur. He didn't turn to the judge. 'Of course,' he said curtly and continued, still facing Fleur, 'We needn't be shy about the nature of your poses or act on stage, need we?'

'Not as far as I'm concerned.'

'It involved you stripping off your clothes and standing or strutting about the stage under a spotlight stark naked?'

She nodded.

'Please speak. The shorthand writer has to take a note. Yes or no?'

'Yes.'

'You were a stripper?'

'Yes.' Then she said fiercely, 'I said yesterday that I had no money and when management didn't pay the dancers the money they owed us, I had to take any job that was going.'

'Dancers? What dancing had you done?'

'I started in the chorus. Then I did solos.'

'Posing without any clothes on?'

She was silent. Then she said softly, 'I haven't pretended.'

'No. I accept you have not pretended about that.' There was a pause before Mordecai repeated, 'I fully accept you haven't pretended about that.'

Percy rose to his feet. 'I'm always reluctant to intervene during a cross-examination – '

'Then don't,' snarled Mordecai.

Percy looked at him icily and went on to the judge, 'That was a statement by counsel, not a question.'

'Do not make statements, Mr Ledbury,' said Murray shortly. 'Ask questions.'

189

Mordecai stared at the judge under his black eyebrows. He took a deep breath and said slowly, 'Oh, I shall. I shall be asking many questions.'

'Then ask them,' said the judge.

Mordecai bent his head, his mouth twisted. Oliver turned and caught his eye, appealing. Mordecai turned back to Fleur. 'I'll put it to you in the form of a question. You have not told the court the truth, have you?'

At the back of the court Willoughby, smiling at the reporters' bench, shrugged his shoulders and sighed elaborately. Earlier he had turned to stare at Greg sitting behind him. Greg had his head now between his hands, his elbows on the desk in front of him. Please God, he prayed, she keeps her cool.

'I have told the truth.'

'Some of what you've told us is, I suggest, a lie?'

'About what?'

Mordecai stared at her. She had been answering his questions with her head turned away, speaking directly to the judge. Now she half turned and faced him. Suddenly he said very loudly, 'About who you are.'

'I don't know what you mean.' A flush had come to her face. 'I am Fleur Caverel.'

'Are you?'

'Of course I am.'

'Are you? Or is Fleur Caverel just another of the names you have adopted, like Leila or Lila Houseman and Anna St Martin – and Sarah Wilson?'

'I thought Sarah Wilson was my name until I found out my real name. The others were stage names I sometimes used.'

'Are you saying, swearing, that Ella Moreau was not your real name, that it was a false name, an invented name?'

'I am.'

Mordecai, his head lowered, limped a few paces up and down the bench before suddenly he changed tack. 'Tell me about your friend, Mr Blake. He's what they call a publicist, isn't he?'

'I don't know. Mr Stevens introduced me to him.'

'But you know now, don't you? Doesn't Mr Blake manage would-be pop stars, young actors and actresses, and promote them and get their names into the press?'

'I told you, I don't know.'

'What exactly is Mr Blake's role in this case, this claim made by the lady' – here he looked hard at Murray – 'calling herself Fleur Caverel?'

'I don't know what you mean.'

'I think you do. Hasn't Mr Blake taken you on in order to publicise you and promote your claim in the hope of getting money – for you and for him?'

'I don't understand.'

'Why do you say you don't understand? Didn't you attend a press conference he staged last year?'

'He arranged it. He said it was all right because no legal claim had begun.'

'Did he? But what was the point of holding a press conference?'

'To put my side of it, he said.'

'Your side of what?'

'Of the story.'

'The story you've invented – or the true story?'

'The true story. I've invented nothing.'

'I suggest that the purpose of Mr Blake's press conference, as you know perfectly well, was to promote you and to put pressure on the family by stirring up public opinion in the hope they'd buy you off and there'd be money for you and your friends. Isn't that right?'

'Mr Ledbury,' said Murray. 'The witness said that it was Mr Blake who arranged the press conference.'

'I know perfectly well what the witness said,' Mordecai replied. 'But she took part in it. She knew why it was being staged.'

'I did not,' Fleur said.

'Are you telling the court you had no idea what was the purpose of the press conference in which you played a part?'

'I thought it was to put before the public my side of the story. The family's rich and powerful and . . .'

'And you and Mr Blake are weak and poor? Is that what you are saying?'

'I'm saying the press conference was to give my side of the story but I never spoke because there was a scene.'

'There certainly was. The lady who calls herself' – he looked again at Murray – 'your grandmother, the one-time Lady Caverel

191

born Lucy Bull, got drunk and threw glasses at the audience. Isn't that right?'

'She is my grandmother and she's not well.'

'To put it bluntly, what you and Willoughby Blake are after, are you not, is money?'

'No. I want my rights.'

'Your rights! Your rights to what? The barony of Caverel? If you win this case, do you intend to petition the Crown and become the Baroness Caverel?'

She paused. 'I'm not sure. I . . .'

'No, you're not sure, are you, because what you and those backing you are after is money?'

'No, it's because I'm not interested in titles. I don't know anything about that sort of thing. I just want my rights, the rights that are mine as the daughter of my father.'

'The son of the lady born Lucy Bull in Clapham?'

'What's wrong with being called Bull or coming from Clapham? Why do you keep sneering at that?'

Mordecai saw his mistake and went on rapidly, 'Who are the friends who are contributing to the costs of this claim?'

'I don't know. Mr Blake arranged it.'

'And what do these friends expect to get out of it if you succeed?'

'They'll be paid back.'

'What they've loaned?'

'Yes.'

'Only paid back what they've loaned? Is that all?'

She hesitated and he saw her hesitation. 'No profit on their investment, no cut from the proceeds? They're just putting up cash out of a chivalrous desire to help a young maiden in distress?'

'Really!' Percy said, half rising from his seat.

Once again Mordecai hurried on. 'Let's return to your friend, Paul Valerian. Tell us again what name you were using when you first met him?'

'I've told you time and time again, Sarah Wilson, the name I was raised with.'

'Sarah, the name he called you by?'

'Yes, I told you.'

'Always?'

'Yes.'

'On every occasion and to everyone?'

'Yes.'

Mordecai stared at her in silence. 'Sarah Wilson,' he repeated almost to himself. Suddenly he swung round, his back to the judge, facing the door of the court, and flicked his fingers.

'What are you doing, Mr Ledbury?' Murray said icily. 'Is this a part of your cross-examination?'

Mordecai swung back. 'It is. I am calling for a certain person to come into court and be identified by the witness. This person will be the first of many.'

A noise arose in the court-room like the branches of trees rustling in the wind. People turned to each other, whispering. The swing-door opened slowly, and Mr Rogers ushered in a small, elderly woman, shabbily dressed with a tired, worn face. She stood a few feet inside looking confused and bewildered. Mr Rogers gently took her by the arm and gestured for her to go further inside. She took a few more steps and Mr Rogers pointed in the direction of the judge and then at Fleur in the witness box.

Mordecai turned back to face Fleur. 'Do you recognise this lady?'

Fleur stared down at the woman, one hand to her throat in the same gesture she'd used when she'd been telling the judge she felt more white than black.

'Yes,' she whispered.

'Who is she?'

'She's Paul's wife.'

'The widow of the man who knew you as Sarah Wilson?'

Before Fleur could reply, from the bench Murray said abruptly, 'It is after one o'clock. I shall rise now.' He gathered up his papers.

'No,' Mordecai protested angrily. 'This part of the evidence should be concluded before there is any adjournment. It is important this should be done without any interruption and before the witness has a chance to – '

'I decide when my court shall rise, not you, Mr Ledbury. I said I shall rise now. It is past one o'clock.'

Murray rose. Mordecai thumped the table with his stick. 'The witness should be warned – ' he began.

'It is common knowledge that no one is permitted to speak to a witness under cross-examination,' said Murray coldly. 'I trust you're not suggesting that Sir Percy or anyone else would do such a thing.' He disappeared.

When he had gone, Mordecai turned to Percy. 'I hold you personally responsible to see that no one, no one, speaks to the witness.'

'There is no need to threaten me, Ledbury.'

'Then what arrangements will you make?'

'Miss Caverel will be escorted to the cafeteria for her lunch. You can send a clerk with them if you wish.'

'I certainly do.'

Oliver spoke to Freeman who went across the court and stood beside Stevens.

'I don't want anything,' Fleur called from the witness box. 'I'll stay in the court.' She stepped down and came to the seat beside Stevens where she'd been sitting before she had begun her evidence. 'Bring me a glass of water, please,' she said to the usher.

Freeman remained beside her.

Outside, Willoughby came up to Stevens as he emerged alone. 'Where's Fleur?'

'She's staying in court. She doesn't want anything.'

'The woman who was brought in? What's she going to say?'

Stevens shrugged and Willoughby flung away.

Mordecai and Oliver joined Mr Rogers in the conference room. 'The others?' Mordecai asked. Mr Rogers nodded. Mordecai poured some liquor from his flask into his coffee cup and ignored the sandwiches. Oliver watched but said nothing.

When the court resumed, Fleur was back in the box, the woman standing where she had been before the adjournment.

Murray nodded curtly. Mordecai turned to Fleur. 'You have been granted some time in which to think about what you know I am going to ask.'

'That is not a question,' said Murray.

Before Mordecai could reply Fleur said, 'I have no idea what you're going to ask me.'

'Haven't you?'

'No.'

'Where have you met this lady before?'

'In Paris.'

'When?'

'Two or three years ago.'

'When you met her, it was many months, perhaps a year before you saw the advertisement for Sarah Wilson in the *Herald Tribune*. Isn't that correct?'

'Yes.'

'And many months after you had first met Paul Valerian in Istanbul?'

'More than months, a year or more.'

'Did you meet this lady, Mr Valerian's wife, now widow, in a restaurant in Paris in the Rue Montparnasse where you and Paul were having lunch?'

'Yes.'

'She came to your table and spoke to her husband. Did he introduce you?'

'Yes.'

'He said to you, I suppose . . . This is my wife?'

'Yes.'

'And what did he say to her about you? How did he introduce you?'

'I cannot remember.'

'Try.'

Fleur shook her head. She had the small handkerchief in one hand rolled in a ball and she began passing it from one hand to the other. At the back of the court Greg shifted in his seat, in agony for her.

'You told us that Paul knew you as Sarah Wilson, that he always called you Sarah. Well, was that the name he called you when his wife came over to the table in the restaurant in Paris?'

Still she did not reply. Mordecai answered for her. 'He didn't, did he? Nor did he say, this is Leila Houseman, the name you were using at his club, did he?' Mordecai waited for her answer but as she didn't reply, he went on, 'He called you Ella Moreau, that's what he called you, didn't he? Not Sarah Wilson. It wasn't Sarah Wilson he called you when he introduced you to his wife, was it?'

195

'I don't know. I can't remember.'

'I repeat. Did he not say to his wife that you were Ella, Ella Moreau?' Mordecai waited but she did not reply.

'If this lady when she comes to give evidence says you were introduced to her as Ella Moreau, would you deny that?'

'No. I suppose he may have.'

'Why should he have called you Ella Moreau when you've told us he always referred to you on all occasions as Sarah Wilson?'

'If he did, I don't know why.'

'Do you think that this lady, if she says her husband called you, introduced you as, Ella Moreau, could be mistaken?'

'No, but – '

'You and she had quite a long talk on that occasion, did you not?'

'We talked.'

'She joined you and Paul, and asked you about yourself and you told her?'

'She did ask about me.'

'And you told her you were Ella, Ella Moreau and' – he went on rapidly – 'that your mother came from the island of St Martin near Guadeloupe in the Caribbean and that your father was a steward off an American tourist ship?'

Fleur leaned forward over the edge of the witness box. 'That is not true,' she said, 'that is not true.' She had raised her voice almost to a shout. 'I never said that.'

'So if this lady were to say you did, she would be lying?'

'She would, she would be lying. I may have said my name was Ella – I did use that name. I've told you it was one of my stage names but I never said anything to her about my mother or my father. That's a lie, a lie.' Tears had come into her eyes and she dabbed them with the handkerchief.

Mordecai turned to the woman standing below the witness box. She was looking even more bewildered than she had when she had entered the court. '*Merci, madame,*' Mordecai said. '*Asseyez-vous maintenant, s'il vous plaît.*'

'What was that?' said Murray. 'What did you say?'

'I told her in my imperfect French that she may sit.' Mordecai looked around. 'I think she may prefer to leave the court and

196

wait outside. But she'll be back, to give evidence when she is needed.'

Mordecai nodded to Mr Rogers who led the woman out through the swing-door.

Murray saw Fleur's distress. 'Would you like to sit?' he asked her.

'Yes,' she said. The usher pushed up the chair and Fleur sat. Only her head and her folded hands in which she still held the balled handkerchief could be seen over the rim of the witness box.

'Continue,' Murray said.

'At the date when you met the lady who has just left court, what was the name on your passport?'

'I can't remember.'

'When you first came to Europe, what kind of a passport did you have, from what country?'

'The United States.'

'In what name?'

'Sarah Wilson.'

'Where is that passport?'

'It was stolen.'

'Where?'

'In Istanbul. I was lodging in the Pera. I left my bag on the bar counter for a moment and – '

'Did you report the loss or theft to your embassy?'

'No.'

'Why not?'

'I thought I might get into trouble.'

'Why?'

'I thought they might think I sold it. People were doing that at that time, and anyway I had another.'

'Another passport?'

'Yes.'

'How was that?'

'Paul got me one.'

'He got you another American passport?'

'No, it was German.'

'How did he get you that?'

'I don't know.'

'In what name?'

'He said the name had to be German-sounding so it was in the name of Leila Houseman.'

'One of your so-called stage names?'

'Yes.'

'Have you still got that passport?'

'No.'

'Was that passport stolen too?'

'No. I gave it back to Paul.'

'What passport have you now?'

'An American passport.'

'In what name?'

'Sarah Wilson.'

'Where did you get that?'

'From the embassy in Paris. I told them I'd lost the original.'

'When did you get this new passport?'

'Just before I went to Charleston.'

'For the first or the second time?'

She looked at him, biting her lip. 'The first time. When I went to see Mr Walker about the advertisement.'

'You made a second trip to Charleston and not long before this trial commenced, did you not?'

'I did.'

'Why was that?'

She hesitated. 'I needed to remind myself.'

'About what?'

'About where I'd spent my early life.'

'And you needed to remind yourself?'

'Yes.'

'Or was it so that you could see for the first time the places where Sarah Wilson spent her childhood so that you, Ella Moreau, could the better lie when you came to court?'

She struck the edge of the witness box with the hand holding the handkerchief. 'That's not true. I went because I . . . because I just wanted to see the place again, to remind myself and . . .' Her answer petered out.

Mordecai stared at her, waiting. Then he said, 'I shall return to that second, recent, mysterious visit, the visit which you say was to remind yourself, a little later in my cross-examination. For the moment let me ask you about your first visit to Charleston. In

Paris you applied for a new passport in order to go and see the lawyer who had placed the advertisement in the *Herald Tribune*?'

'Yes.'

'By applying at the embassy for a replacement passport, didn't you fear there might be trouble, as you had feared when you were in Istanbul?'

'No.'

'And you applied as Sarah Wilson?'

'Yes.'

'And using that passport you went to Charleston to see the lawyer and showed him that passport to identify yourself as Sarah Wilson?'

'Yes.'

'And it was many months later that you returned to Charleston in order, you say, to remind yourself?'

'Yes.'

There was a long pause. Suddenly Mordecai asked, 'Have you ever been to Budapest?'

'Yes. I've worked there.'

Mordecai turned and nodded to Mr Rogers who held open the door of the court.

This time the noise from the spectators in the gallery which greeted the new entrant through the court door was louder. 'It's Dukie,' someone cried from the gallery, 'it's Dukie Brown.'

When he heard the cry as he came into court, Dukie Brown, bronzed and sun-tanned, wearing an electric blue jacket and white trousers, hand in hand with Clem in the shortest of miniskirts, looked up at the gallery, grinned and waved with his free hand.

'Who shouted that?' Murray said from the bench. 'Have that person removed immediately.'

The usher stood, looking up at the gallery. In the body of the court, Willoughby half rose to his feet. Dukie saw him and raised two fingers at him.

'Who are these people?' said Murray.

'I shall ask the witness,' said Mordecai. 'But I'm only interested in the man, not his companion.'

'She's with me,' said Dukie cheerfully.

'Be quiet,' Murray said, a querulous note now in his voice. For

199

the first time in his judicial experience he seemed to be in danger of losing control of his court. Ledbury, it was all Ledbury's doing.

Mordecai went on, 'Do you recognise this man?'

Fleur was staring at Dukie. 'Yes,' she whispered.

'He's a singer, isn't he, a pop star?'

She nodded. 'What's his name?'

'Dukie Brown.'

'Do you remember meeting Mr Brown in Budapest in 1992?'

'Yes.'

'You spent the weekend of 16th to 18th December 1992 with him' – Mordecai held up a piece of paper and read from it – 'at the Grand Hotel, Corvinus Kempinski, isn't that right?' He lowered the piece of paper. She nodded. 'Please answer, yes or no.'

'Yes.' It was a whisper.

'What name did you call yourself when you spent that weekend with Mr Brown?'

'I don't remember.'

'Think.' He waited. 'It wasn't Sarah Wilson, was it?'

'I don't know.'

'When Mr Brown comes into the witness box and if he swears that you were then calling yourself Ella Moreau, would you deny it?'

'No. I could have.'

'Could have? You could have called yourself anything. What were you calling yourself in 1992?'

'Ella Moreau, sometimes. It was my stage name.'

'During your weekend with Mr Brown do you remember talking with him about the Caribbean and the islands – and in particular the island which is one half Dutch and the other French, the island called St Martin from which you came?'

'That's not true. That's a lie.'

'And did you tell him that you knew the island of St Martin well?'

'I did not, I did not.'

'So if this gentleman says you did, he too would be a liar, like the lady who has just left the court. Is that it?'

'Yes.'

'About a year after your weekend with Mr Brown, you told Paul Valerian's wife your name was Ella Moreau?'

'If I did, I told you it was my stage name.'

'So to Madame Valerian and to Mr Brown you said your name was Ella Moreau – not Lila or Leila Houseman, not Anna St Martin, not Sarah Wilson but Ella Moreau.'

'I keep telling you. It was my stage name.'

Mordecai paused. Then he said very quietly, 'It was more than your stage name, wasn't it?'

'What do you mean?'

'You know very well what I mean. You called yourself Ella Moreau to Paul Valerian's wife and to Duke Brown, because Ella Moreau was your real name, because Moreau was your mother's name. You took her name, didn't you, the name of your mother who never married the steward off the tourist ship. You were, and always have been Ella Moreau. The other names, including Sarah Wilson, were names you have assumed. Isn't that the truth, Miss Ella Moreau?'

She had got to her feet and was bending over the rail of the witness box, the tears now rolling down her face.

'No, no, it's not true. I am Sarah Wilson – I mean I was Sarah Wilson until I discovered my real name was Fleur Caverel.'

Greg had his head again in his hands. Dukie Brown was pointing at Willoughby, raising two fingers again and laughing.

'What is that man doing?' said Murray.

Mordecai turned to Mr Rogers. 'Take them out,' he said.

As Dukie and Clem left, giggling, Mordecai turned once again to the back of the court. He pointed to an elderly black woman with grizzled, grey hair.

'Please stand,' he said. The woman did. Fleur had sunk down on to the chair behind her.

'Who is the woman now standing in the back of the court?'

Fleur had her hands over her eyes. 'Please look at the lady standing in court behind me. Who is she?'

Fleur dropped her hands and looked across the court. 'I don't know.'

'Don't you know who she is? Don't you recognise this lady? Perhaps if you stood, you might be able to see her better.'

Fleur stood. 'Who is she?' repeated Mordecai.

'I don't know,' said Fleur. 'I don't know her.'

Mordecai turned to the woman standing behind him. 'Will you, please, come forward and stand below the witness box where the witness can see you clearly.'

The woman came to where Mordecai had directed.

Mordecai said to Fleur, 'You can see the lady quite well now. Who is she?'

'I told you. I don't know her.'

Mordecai gestured and the woman went back to her seat. Fleur sat, the tears falling down her cheeks.

'Why are you weeping?'

Percy got to his feet. 'The witness is weeping because she's distressed. My friend can see that perfectly well and – '

'Oh yes,' Mordecai said savagely. 'I can see she's distressed. She's distressed, as you call it, because she knows . . .' He raised his arm and pointed at Fleur in the witness box, his robe flapping, looking, Mr Rogers thought, like a great black raven. '. . . she knows that after all these months of lies and imposture, she's being confronted with the truth.'

Fleur, her hands in her lap, was rocking to and fro on her chair, now and again dabbing her eyes with the balled handkerchief.

'The truth,' repeated Mordecai, 'she is being confronted with the truth.' He paused. 'I ask you again. Who is the woman who was standing just below you?'

Still Fleur rocked back and forward, sobbing, shaking her head.

'You don't answer because you don't know, do you? But if you were who you say you are, you would know. The real Sarah Wilson would know who that lady is and she'd be able to tell us. For the last time, I ask. Who is she?'

There was no reply.

'Then let me tell you what I suggest that lady will say when she gives evidence before the court. She'll say she is the niece of the woman who brought up Sarah Wilson, the niece Sarah Wilson used to call Aunt Tess, the niece whom fifteen years ago, during Sarah Wilson's childhood, Sarah Wilson saw at the Wilsons' home in St John's near Charleston in South Carolina day in and day out, week in, and week out for years on end.'

202

'That's not true, it's not true,' Fleur sobbed. 'It's a lie.'

'No, madam, it is you who are the lie. You have been living a lie ever since you and your friend Paul Valerian conceived the plot that you should adopt the name and role of the real Sarah Wilson – '

'Then where is Sarah Wilson?' Fleur said, suddenly standing. 'If I'm not her, where is she?'

Mordecai looked at her. For a time he remained silent. Then he said, 'As you've asked that question, let me answer it.'

He turned again to Mr Rogers who was now sitting in one of the seats at the back of the court. Mordecai nodded and Mr Rogers put his hand on the arm of a plump woman seated beside him. The woman looked at Mr Rogers. She was dark-skinned, but no darker than Fleur and younger than the woman whom Mordecai had called to stand beneath Fleur in the witness box.

Mr Rogers gestured for the woman to rise and she did so, smiling slightly.

'You asked where Sarah Wilson is. If this lady, when she comes to give evidence, says she was with a young woman, a dancer at a club whom she knew as Wilson, when that young woman lay dying – she thought of diphtheria – in . . .' Again he picked up another sheet of paper. '. . . in a lodging near the Galata Köprüsü, or bridge, by the ferry to Usküda in Istanbul in May 1994, would you say she also was a liar?'

Murray burst in. 'This is most irregular, Mr Ledbury, most irregular.'

'It is, most irregular, but it's most irregular for a witness to lie and lie and lie on oath, as this witness has done in this court ever since she entered the witness box.'

'It is you are lying, not me,' Fleur burst out. 'You are all lying.' She turned to face Murray. 'I tell you it's not true.' She put her hands to her face. 'They're trying to trick me.'

'Oh, no, madam,' said Mordecai, 'it is you who have been trying to trick the court. It is you, you who have been living a lie – '

'I've said what's true.'

'You know perfectly well, do you not, that Sarah Wilson died in 1994?'

'No. no.'

Mordecai shook his head. He lifted the stick he'd been leaning on and laid it beside the other on the desk in front of him. Then he leaned forward, both hands on the desk.

'Shall I suggest to you what is the truth?' He waited and when she shook her head he went on, 'The truth is that when Sarah Wilson died, probably from drugs and not diphtheria but died, she owed your friend Paul Valerian a great deal of money. And when Valerian learnt she was dead, he thought he would never see any of his money again. Then he came upon the advertisement and thought Sarah Wilson might have inherited something in Charleston, and he persuaded you to pretend to be Sarah Wilson and go to the lawyer in Charleston and find out what it was.'

Fleur was staring at him, shaking her head. 'No,' she said, 'no.'

Mordecai went on. 'And he made you get that passport in Sarah Wilson's name and sent you to Charleston. But when you came back and told him what you'd learnt about Sarah Wilson's real mother, Paul Valerian saw there could be far more to it than a few hundred dollars, that there might be a great estate and hundreds of thousands of pounds. And as you had successfully carried off the imposture in Charleston with the lawyer, Paul Valerian decided you should go on with it. Isn't that the truth?'

'No, it's not. It's not true.'

'By then, you were compromised, weren't you? You had obtained that passport in Wilson's name from the embassy in Paris and you had visited the lawyer pretending to be Wilson. So, willingly or unwillingly, you went along with what Paul Valerian planned?'

'That isn't true. It isn't true. You're inventing this.'

Mordecai shook his head. 'No, Miss Moreau, I'm inventing nothing. It is not I who is making things up.'

He paused, and then said very gently, 'Do you remember the doctor in Bucharest?'

'Doctor? I don't remember a doctor.'

'Think. Didn't you consult a doctor when you were working in Bucharest in Romania in 1994?'

'I could have. I have been to doctors.'

'Look around the court. Do you see the doctor from Bucharest you consulted here today?'

She stood up and looked around her, wide-eyed, trembling. 'Take your time,' Mordecai added. She shook her head, her handkerchief pressed to her mouth.

'Ask the doctor to stand, please.'

Mr Rogers leaned across the dark woman who had stood when Mordecai had been asking about the death of Sarah Wilson and tapped the arm of a grey-haired man in a blue suit and striped tie sitting beside her. The man looked at Mr Rogers who whispered to him. The man got to his feet.

'Do you recognise Dr Dubrescu?'

Fleur stared at the man standing at the back of the court. 'I may . . .' she began. 'Yes, I think, it could be.'

'It's more than could be. It is. It is Dr Dubrescu whom you consulted in Bucharest in October 1994. You went to his office near . . .' He studied another piece of paper. '. . . near to Herăstrău Park, close to the Herăstrău Country Club?'

'I may have seen a doctor when I was there. I had woman trouble.'

'That may have been one of the reasons for your first visit to the doctor, but there were other visits, were there not? Did you not later tell him of what you called your other troubles, your nervous attacks, your migraines, your day-dreams and night-dreams and fantasies which arose from your visits to seances and fortune-tellers?'

'No, it was nothing like that. I never said anything of that. It's not true. I went because of woman trouble.'

'It wasn't only woman trouble, was it?' Mordecai was speaking now very quietly, his manner soft and gentle, very different from what it had been at the start of his cross-examination. 'At that time, were you on drugs?'

'Drugs? No, of course I was not.'

'Are you sure?'

'Yes.'

'I'll ask you again. At the time when you consulted the doctor were you on drugs?'

She looked at Murray, biting her lip. 'Sometimes, a little, in the clubs I used to, but . . . I did sometimes.' She stopped.

Mordecai went on even more quietly, 'Didn't the doctor tell you that you must stop the cocaine, you must stop the fantasising and the invention of stories, that it was making you disturbed and unbalanced? Didn't he advise you to see a psychiatrist and seek treatment? And did you tell him about – '

'What are you talking about? A psychiatrist? Treatment? The doctor never said anything like that. What are you saying?'

'Didn't the doctor tell you that you were more ill than you knew? Didn't he warn you that you must stop taking the drugs and cease acting and pretending and be yourself or you would have a breakdown and would end in an asylum?'

She was staring at him, her hand to her mouth. 'An asylum? End in an asylum?'

'Didn't that doctor warn you that you were heading for a complete mental collapse and that – '

'That's not true. He never said anything of the kind. No one said anything about an asylum. It's a lie, it's all lies.'

She sank back into the chair and buried her face in her hands and again rocked to and fro. 'Leave me alone, leave me alone,' she cried through her hands.

Mordecai stood very still, looking at her. Murray sat rigid, both hands gripping the sides of the desk in front of him. Willoughby had his head resting on one hand.

Fleur lowered her hands and stared back at Mordecai. Then she stood up. 'It's all lies, they're all telling lies about me,' she whispered. 'I'm not ill, I'm not mad, I'm not mad.'

She turned to Murray, and suddenly shouted, 'Tell them to leave me alone, tell them to stop.'

Murray looked down at his notebook on the table in front of him. He was about to speak when Fleur turned back to face Mordecai and began to shout at him, leaning over the edge of the witness box. 'The doctor is lying. I'm not mad.' She put her arm in front of her eyes. 'I can't stand this. I can't stand your lies and your bullying and accusing.' She pointed at Mordecai. 'You've brought these people here to lie about me.'

'All of them?' he said very gently. 'All of them? Is that what you are saying, Ella?'

'Yes, all of them. You're wicked. You're evil.'

Suddenly she turned, knocking over the chair behind her with a crash. She ran down the steps of the witness box to the floor of the court and then towards the door.

'Where are you going? What are you doing?' Murray said, bewildered.

The spectators in the gallery were standing, craning forward. Greg clambered noisily across the people in the back row of the court in order to get to her. 'Let me through,' he said, 'let me through.'

He caught Fleur as she reached the door and put his arm around her. He pushed open the door and they disappeared. For a moment there was dead silence. Then the noise broke out. 'Silence,' shouted the usher, 'silence.'

Percy got to his feet. 'The witness, my lord, my client,' Percy said, 'she's obviously very distressed.'

'Disturbed,' said Mordecai quietly, 'you mean she's very disturbed.'

Percy ignored him. 'The cross-examination, my lord, was very severe. I'll send a doctor to her. I'm sure she'll recover. She needs a little time.'

Mordecai had remained standing, his head bowed. Percy went on, 'Since it is nearing the end of the afternoon and it is Friday, perhaps your lordship would adjourn while I make enquiries and get a doctor to her? There'll be time over the weekend for her to recover. I'm sure she'll be well enough to resume by Monday.'

Robert Murray was as anxious as Braythwaite to bring the session to an end. He had never before experienced such an afternoon in court. He turned to Mordecai.

'Mr Ledbury – ' he began.

Mordecai cut him short. 'There's nothing I can say, is there? I haven't a witness to cross-examine. And I have a great deal more to ask.'

Murray looked at him balefully. That such a scene should occur in his court! In a court of Chancery! It was all Ledbury's fault.

'I will adjourn now,' he said. 'Sir Percy, see that your witness is back on Monday or that I have a medical report.'

As soon as the judge was through the door, Oliver turned and put both hands on Mordecai's arms. Mordecai fell back into his seat. Oliver looked over his head at Mr Rogers and smiled. Mr Rogers nodded.

32

The journalists had scampered from their bench in an ugly rush when Fleur ran from the witness box, but it was only after the judge had disappeared that the court erupted in an explosion of noise. People stood and argued and jostled each other as they slowly forced their way out into the corridor.

In the emptying court, Andrea, Nicholas and Oliver, joined by Mr Rogers, faced Mordecai who had slumped into his seat, his wig askew on his forehead and the sweat running down the deep furrows which led from the side of his nose. The linen of his stiff wing collar and white bands formed a crumpled tangle round his thick neck. He buried his face in a dun-coloured handkerchief and picked up a bundle of documents which he used as a fan. The noise in the court was such that Andrea had to bend to hear him say, 'She's a very accomplished actress – or she is very, very sick.'

'I recognised the man who left with her,' Nicholas said. 'He's an Australian who came to Ravenscourt for the cricket. He'll try and persuade her to come back. How can we stop him?'

'It's all right,' Oliver said. 'It's all over.'

Mordecai hauled himself to his feet. 'She needs a doctor, and I a pint of Bollinger.'

At the door of the court Mordecai stopped and looked at Mr Rogers. 'Your Turkish woman? How certain is she?'

'She is certain that the dying woman she looked after was a dancer called Wilson.'

'Dying from diphtheria?'

'Overdose of drugs, I suspect.'

'Sown in a sack and dumped in the Bosphorus was the traditional fate of a Cyprian in Constantinople.'

Mr Rogers smiled. 'No, she died and was buried. But no one knows where.'

Mordecai took him by the arm and they led the party out of the court into the corridor.

Percy Braythwaite and Harold Welby were sitting on a bench

immediately opposite the court. Mordecai's procession passed them without a glance or a word. An ashen-faced Stevens trotted up to Percy.

'They left in a taxi.'

'You must find them,' said Percy.

'Mr Blake is endeavouring to – '

'No, not Blake. Do not let Blake have anything to do with it. And get a doctor to her. I must have her here in court on Monday, or a medical report.'

Stevens motioned to his clerk who scuttled away.

'Ten minutes in chambers,' muttered Welby, 'and we could have sorted out who she is, without all that arguing and shouting.'

Percy ignored him. 'What do you know about the people Ledbury brought into court?' he asked Stevens.

'Nothing.'

'Find out what you can and about the other names Fleur Caverel was known by. But she's still under oath and under cross-examination and only the doctor can talk to her. You have my telephone number. I shall be back in London on Sunday night. So on Monday, either she, or a medical report, without fail.'

He rose and strode unhappily to the robing-room. An hour later Eleanor collected him in the car. As she threaded her way through the traffic, Percy asked, 'What did you make of it?'

For an answer she took one hand from the wheel and pressed his. 'I felt sorry for her, and for you.'

'Don't worry about me. It's the girl I worry about. For me, it was just a job.'

But Eleanor knew that for him it had been far more than just a job.

'What Ledbury was suggesting, did it sound convincing?' he asked.

'That she is not who she said she was?'

'Yes.'

For a time Eleanor didn't answer. She knew how much Percy had believed in her, how convinced he'd been by her, how anxious he'd been to win the case for her.

'I'm afraid it did,' she said at last. 'She needs help.'

Percy nodded.

What'll you do now?' she went on.

'Wait and see what happens on Monday.'

But he knew in his heart what would happen on Monday. He knew she wouldn't be back.

When Stevens came into his office Willoughby was sprawled on the sofa, smoking an even fatter cigar than usual. Judge Blaker was perched uneasily on the edge of a hard-backed chair.

'You look like death warmed up, old cock,' Willoughby boomed. 'And not warmed up very much.'

Stevens sat at his desk. 'A neighbour saw them leave in Rutherford's car,' he said. 'God knows where they've gone.'

'You won't find 'em.' Willoughby blew a plume of blue smoke into the air. 'Pity. Over the past months I'd grown rather fond of her, and until today I thought we were doing rather nicely. Until that crooked-faced bastard began. It's a rum business yours, Michael. Give me show business every time.'

'All these months of work and preparation to end so suddenly. It's inconceivable.' Stevens had his head in his hands. He looked up. 'She had a fit of hysterics. Perhaps she'll be back on Monday?'

'Not a chance, old son. And if she is, what'll she say to the old Scotch bugger? How'll she explain pushing off like that? And what about all those characters poppin' up and down like jacks-in-a-box, saying she's not who she said she was?' Willoughby shook his head. 'No, she won't be back. She's scarpered with lover-boy. She saw the game was up – the game you and I, Michael, thought was our game and it turns out to have been hers – hers and that bloody Pole's.'

'I can't believe it,' Stevens said, 'I just can't believe it.'

'Well, you'll have to, old cock. She's dropped you and me in the proverbial. And left us a damn sight poorer.'

Stevens was hunched over his desk, his hands folded in front of him.

'Cheer up, old son,' Willoughby said. 'A right pair of Charlies, Michael, that's what we are. Mind you, your Mr Dukie Brown didn't exactly help, turning up like that from Oz and pointing the finger at her – and two fingers at me.' He laughed. 'I rather liked that. Good for Dukie.'

He went to the door. 'I'll be closing down the freebie in the pub in Kensington pronto and we'll have to push off the old lush back to BA.' He turned to Judge Blaker. 'You have your ticket, old son, so I'd skip if I were you.'

'My bill of costs,' said Stevens miserably. 'Counsel's fees and . . .' He looked up at Willoughby. 'Perhaps they've just gone for the weekend? Perhaps her young man will talk her into coming back?'

'The Albert Hall to a china orange he won't even try,' Willoughby said cheerfully. He had his hand on the door-knob. 'No, old cock, it's over. Chalk it up to experience. Someone or something else will turn up. It was a bit of sport while it lasted. Cheerio all,' he said, and left.

In the early evening the heat was still intense; there was no wind and the storm which had threatened all week could not now be long delayed. The forecast said it was coming from the west, and the further west Andrea and Nicholas drove the darker became the sky.

But the nightmare was over. She and Francis were safe. Life could begin again. It had ended so suddenly, so dramatically that she still couldn't quite take it in, and the elation she'd felt in court had already passed. Only now did she realise how tired she was. She closed her eyes and dozed.

Before they arrived at Ravenscourt they heard the first rumble of thunder.

'Will you come in?' she asked Nicholas as they drew up in front of the house.

'No, there'll be a pile of work in the estate office. Then I'll get on home. Will you be all right?'

'Of course.'

'I'll come round tomorrow.'

Francis and Alice were at the top of the great staircase as Andrea came through the front door.

'Mummy,' Francis called, 'you're back, you're back.' He ran down the stairs to the hall and Andrea caught him and hugged him. Alice followed.

'It's a mercy you got here before the storm,' she said. She wanted to ask how the case had gone. She hadn't heard or seen the evening news but she wouldn't ask in front of the child.

Andrea took her arm and whispered, 'They say it's over. We're safe.'

Alice crossed herself. 'Thanks be to God.'

'It's getting very dark,' Andrea said, switching on the lights in the hall. 'Have you had tea?' she asked Francis.

'Hours and hours ago.'

'Well, I'm starving.' She hadn't eaten when the court had adjourned at midday and she led Francis by the hand to the kitchen. 'Where are the Thompsons?' she asked as she filled a kettle. The Thompsons were the successors to the Masons.

'Her father was taken to hospital last night, very bad. So he drove her to Shaftesbury this morning. They've just rung. They don't want to leave her mother, poor old soul, by herself, especially if there's a storm, so they're staying with the old lady tonight.'

'They're quite right.' Andrea poured the tea and cut some bread and spread the butter.

The last time she'd sat here the ordeal of the trial lay ahead. Now it was behind her. She could still scarcely believe it. Francis danced around the table.

'Time for your bath,' Alice said and led him away, protesting.

Andrea finished her tea and strolled into the library. She stood with both hands on the chimney-piece staring at the photograph of Robin in its silver frame. Above was the portrait of Robin's grandfather painted by Frederick Leighton in his Garter robes, the flat velvet cap in his lap. Neither she nor Robin had known the grandfather whom Nicholas had so adored and Oliver so revered.

She picked up Robin's photograph. 'We're all right, darling,' she said, 'we're all right.' Then, to the portrait above, 'You'll be pleased.'

An intensely bright flash of lightning startled her. She counted the seconds before it was followed, not as before by a rumble but by a crack of thunder. The storm was closer now. She wandered round the room, thinking of the afternoon in court and Ledbury's menacing finger pointing and the frightened look on the witness's face. Where was she now? Where had she fled? But at least she wasn't alone. She had her lover. 'Which is more than some of us have,' Andrea said aloud.

She went back to the photograph above the fireplace. Poor

Robin, snared by the Italian when his wife was pregnant and far away. But he wouldn't have betrayed her during the battle. He'd have been the respondent, not Francis, and she'd have been sitting beside him in front of Ledbury and beneath the witness box and the bad-tempered judge. That judge! He'd been so taken by the girl and had so hated her. Why, she wondered?

She closed the library door behind her and climbed the staircase to the nursery. She'd have a bath and go to bed and read. She was dead tired.

The lightning flashes were now more frequent and followed more rapidly by the thunder. In the nursery Francis pretended it was fun but when there was a loud clap he gripped her fiercely.

'You're coming with me, young man,' she said and she scooped him up and carried him to her room. Alice followed. Andrea put him into the great canopied bed. She drew the curtains and put on the side light. 'I'm going to have a bath,' she said.

An hour later the storm was at its height. Andrea was reading in bed with Francis beside her fast asleep when there was a particularly blinding flash followed by the noise of masonry falling from the roof. At the same time the bedside lamp went out and Francis woke. Andrea took him in her arms and with one hand searched in the drawer of the bedside table for a torch but couldn't find it. She heard someone at the door and in the next flash of lightning saw Alice in the doorway.

'The lights have gone out everywhere,' said Alice, sounding remarkably calm. 'I've some matches. There are candles on the dining-room table. That's nearest.'

'I'll come with you,' Andrea said. There was another crash of thunder as she pulled on her dressing-gown and with Francis holding her hand and Alice striking matches and leading the way, they crept down the staircase to the dining-room.

Soon the candles were alight. 'We'll all sleep together,' Andrea decided, picking up the candelabra. 'My bed's big enough.'

The wind had risen and rain was lashing the windows as they went across the hall and mounted the stairs. They had reached the first landing when they heard the bell, the outside bell with the long handle which hung outside the front door. Alice gave a cry.

'It's the wind,' Andrea said. 'Just the wind.'

They stood on the stairs listening. The bell rang again. Then above the noise of the storm they heard the bang of the knocker on the great door.

Alice stared at Andrea. 'I'll take a look from the window by the front door,' she said.

Andrea remained on the landing, holding the candelabra high above her head to light Alice down. With her other hand she gripped Francis.

'I can see the lights of a car at the bottom of the steps,' Alice called. 'Someone's by the door.'

And Andrea knew who it was.

The storm had broken when they were many miles away. As they drew up at the steps beneath the great door, the thunder had lessened but the rain was sheeting down.

'Stay in the car,' she said. 'I won't be long.'

Greg saw her run up the steps. The rain was so heavy that by the time she'd reached the door she was drenched. Peering through the car window, he saw her tugging at the bell and hammering on the door. It opened and she disappeared inside.

In the hall, her hair plastered around her head, the rain-water running down her face and off her clothes to make a pool at her feet, she shook herself like a dog. Alice closed the door behind her and stood against it. She crossed the hall and came to the foot of the stairs.

'Stay where you are,' Andrea called out but she took no notice and began to climb. Then she remembered the dream when she'd been with the Gypsy long before it all began – the hand holding the candle, the wax dropping on her feet and the nails clawing at her face. She stopped several steps below where Andrea was standing with the candelabra in her hand.

'What are you doing here?' Andrea asked.

'I came to see you.'

'Why?'

'To tell you it's over.'

'I know it's over.'

'I wanted to tell you myself.'

'Why?'

The light from the candles and the flashes of lightning from the windows high up in the hall only half lit the staircase and the portraits on the walls.

'Because I wanted you to hear what I have to say. I shan't be going back to the court.'

'Because you've been found out.'

'I have not been found out. But I'm going away and I won't be back, ever. I wanted to tell you to your face that it was all lies. I wanted you to hear the truth from me.'

'Which is?'

'That what they said in court was all lies, nothing but lies.'

'And you want me to believe that, even after you ran away?'

She pushed back her wet hair. 'I couldn't stand any more, the lies, the accusations, the bullying, the talk about my illness and the asylum. That's why I went. But I came here to you because I want you to hear the truth from me.'

'Who are you?'

'Who I said I was.'

'Then why are you running away?'

'Because I want to. Because I want to go away. I hate this country, and its people. The trial was making me ill, the questioning, the shouting.'

'It was you who did the shouting.'

'Was it?' She put her hand to her head. 'I'm not ill, you know. Not in the way they pretended I was ill. But I get migraines, terrible pain, bad, very bad.' Then more fiercely, 'But I'm not mad.' Once again she played with the wet hair around her face. 'I never really wanted to start it,' she said.

'Then why did you?'

'He persuaded me.'

'The man who brought you here in September?'

'No, not him. Paul. It was he who persuaded me.'

The staircase was lit now only by the flickering candle-light, for the storm was moving away. She looked around her and shivered. 'How can you stand living in this place? From the moment Blake brought me and we came through the door and up the stairs and you stood where you're standing now and ordered us out, I hated it. I couldn't live here.'

She looked round her and then down at Alice standing with her back to the front door in the hall below.

'It knows I hate it so it hates me. My father would have hated it, too. He never lived here and I'm glad I never will. I told Blake that, and I told Paul even before I'd seen it. So you're welcome to it. You keep it and live in it, with all its ghosts. It's better for you to have it, you and your little boy.'

Andrea drew Francis closer to her.

She pointed to the portraits. 'My father's ancestors. Take care they don't haunt you.' She pointed at Francis who buried his face in Andrea's skirts. 'His ancestors, his and mine. Our ancestors. Not yours.'

She turned and went slowly down the stairs to the door and stood waiting imperiously for Alice to open it. Alice looked up at Andrea who nodded. Alice swung open the door. The rain blew in a great gust into the hall. She turned and called back to Andrea, 'Tell my little cousin about me when he's older.'

Then she was gone.

Andrea took Francis back to her bedroom. When the child was settled, Andrea said to Alice, 'I'm sorry for her. She's quite mad.'

She tried to telephone but the lines were down so it wasn't until Nicholas came in the morning that Oliver was told of Andrea's visitor of the night before.

Robert Murray's weekend was proving even more disagreeable than usual, Freda even more peevish. She had been reading about the Caverel case.

'I knew them,' she said.

I knew you would, Murray thought.

'The older ones, that is. Old Walter Caverel once made a pass at me in the South of France. Who is this wicked girl?'

'I can't discuss the case.'

'I'm your wife. We're not in court. You can say to me whatever you like and I can say to you whatever I like. It's quite obvious she's a fraud. The TV said she ran out of court when she was being questioned. Doesn't that finish it?'

'I'll be told on Monday.'

'Told what? That she's run away? That she's an imposter? I could have told you that from the start.'

He thought of the young woman in the witness box when she

216

had begun her evidence. A bonny lass was what he'd thought her.

'A child could see through her. But then you were only clever about books – never about people.'

When the Vice Chancellor took his seat on Monday, the witness box was empty. Counsel were in their places, as were Oliver Goodbody, Andrea and Nicholas. No one was sitting in front of Percy Braythwaite.

When he had arrived at his room in the Law Courts, Murray had sent his clerk to find out if the witness was ready to continue. Robinson had told him that he could discover nothing for certain.

'Have counsel expressed a wish to speak to me in chambers before I sit?'

'No, my lord. There'll be a statement in open court. There's talk that it's all over.'

Percy had wanted Ledbury to come with him and see the judge in his private room but Ledbury had refused. 'I'm not going to talk to that brute in private,' Ledbury snapped. 'Say what you have to say in open court.' And he rang off.

In court Murray began. 'Sir Percy, I see that your client, the witness, is not here. Where is she?'

Percy had a sheet of paper in his hand. 'I do not know, my lord,' he said, 'but on my arrival at my chambers this morning there was a fax for me, dated last Saturday morning, from I believe an hotel in Plymouth, and with the first post came a letter signed by my client. The letter and the fax are in identical terms. May I read it to your lordship?'

Murray nodded. Percy read, '"I shall not be returning to court. I am going away. I have dismissed my lawyer, Stevens, and I abandon my claim. I have not lied to the court. I want you to tell the judge that I am not a liar." It is signed', Percy concluded, 'Fleur Caverel.'

The court burst into a rumble of noise. Murray banged with his open hand on the desk while the usher shouted for silence.

'I take it from this, Sir Percy,' Murray said, 'that your client has abandoned her claim.'

'Yes.'

'She writes she is not a liar. Why then has she abandoned her claim and why is she not here to resume her evidence?'

'Because she is a liar,' Mordecai said loudly. He struggled to his feet.

'If she has lied on oath, she is a perjurer,' Murray said. 'She has tried to deceive the court.' And succeeded, he thought. His indignation grew with the memory of how much he had liked her. 'She must be found and prosecuted.'

'I am instructed', Mordecai said, looking down at Oliver who turned and nodded, 'that although the family has suffered grievously, they take the merciful view that the young woman is seriously unbalanced. She is clearly an hysteric and was used by a wicked man, now dead, who induced her to play a part in an audacious fraud.'

'She came to my court, acting a part, telling falsehoods in an attempt to deceive the court.'

'Not that your lordship, I am sure, was taken in for one moment,' said Mordecai silkily. He was enjoying himself. 'Your lordship is far too shrewd a judge of human nature to have been deceived by so obvious a liar, but – '

Murray cut him off. There were two spots of red high up on his cheek-bones. 'She told deliberate falsehoods on oath, Mr Ledbury. That is perjury and perjury cannot be tolerated. The papers in the case should be sent to the Director of Public Prosecutions.'

Mordecai looked at his watch. 'All those who would be required as witnesses for any possible prosecution, namely the persons with whom I confronted the Claimant, are now on their way to Heathrow to board their aircraft for their different destinations overseas, and the family will give no assistance to any prosecution. The unfortunate young woman had a back-ground of mental disturbance and lived in a fantasy world of her own, induced perhaps by drugs and who knows, fuelled by her odd preoccupation with the occult. It is possible she may even have believed that what she was saying was the truth. I was about to go deeper into her medical history in my cross-examination which is why I expect she fled. In these circum-stances, as I say, the family will play no part in any prosecution. It is enough for them that the case over the Caverel inheritance is at an end. Nor do they ask for any order for costs – which in practice there would be little chance of their receiving. But I'm sure your lordship will be glad publicly to acknowledge their generosity.'

Murray listened stony-faced. He could not get out of his mind her beautiful face and how it lit up when she smiled, and the way she spoke and the way she had looked at him. Then he thought of the errors Ledbury had led him into and how this odious man had taken over his court and turned it into a scene of disorder never witnessed before in a court of Chancery. The case, he knew, would do his judicial reputation little good.

He pushed back his chair. 'The claim is dismissed,' he said abruptly, 'with no order as to costs.'

'A boor, to the very last,' Mordecai said to Oliver in his stage whisper, but loud enough for it to carry to the judge's retreating back.

Andrea turned and leaned across the desk dividing her from Mordecai and kissed him on the cheek. 'Thank you,' she said, 'thank you, from me and from Francis.'

He smiled and took her hand and held it. 'To coin a phrase,' he said, 'all's well that ends well.' He lifted her hand and kissed it. 'All I did was to put into words the instructions I received from Mr Goodbody based on the work of this gentleman.' He half turned towards Mr Rogers who had come up to them. 'When we first met, I was doubtful if he'd be able to help but he has ferreted out the truth. So it is he who primarily deserves your thanks. She was a sad, unbalanced young woman but plausible. As I told the judge, I believe that in the end she may have half believed the story herself. It has been a great ordeal for you, Lady Caverel.' He smiled again. 'Now go home, go home to your son, go home to Ravenscourt and, to coin another phrase, live happily ever after.'

Dukie Brown and Clem settled down in row 4, first class Quantas. He patted her knee and raised his glass. 'His face,' he said, 'just to see the bastard's face when we came in, that alone was worth it.'

'And the money,' Clem said as she drank from her glass of champagne. 'What was the name again?'

'Ella something, a French name. The little man told me what it was. I kept forgetting and he kept reminding. Blake's face,' Dukie repeated. 'I'll never forget Blake's face.'

'Aunt' Tess was making for California. She would live on the coast, three thousand miles from her former neighbours. 'Aunt' had been the little man's conceit. It had added, he had said, that extra touch of authenticity.

Madame Valerian, more confused than ever, was escorted via the EuroStar to a home in Soissons where the nuns would see she was looked after to the end of her days.

The Turkish lady flew out of Heathrow on Turkish Airlines and was greeted at Istanbul airport by her husband. Their offer for the sweet-shop and café in Takim, he said wrapping her in a great bear-hug, had been accepted.

Dr Dubrescu went Air France to Paris, settled into the Ritz, had his hair cut, a shampoo and a facial. Then he set forth to buy himself a new wardrobe, starting with six Chavet ties. He had decided he would abandon medicine and invest in his cousin's pharmaceutical business in Philadelphia. One day, he mused, they might even become a members of the Merion Cricket Club.

In Lincoln's Inn Fields Oliver Goodbody had sent his staff home early – to celebrate the conclusion of the most important case the firm had ever conducted. But when they had gone, he was not alone in his room overlooking the gardens. Mr Rogers was seated at a table in the centre of the room. Oliver stood with his back to him looking out of the window.

'They are all safely away?' he asked.

'They are.'

Oliver turned. 'You have the affidavits?'

Mr Rogers pushed the bundle across the table. 'Signed and

sealed.' He knew Goodbody regarded them as his insurance but there was no need to worry. They had been well paid. They would not renege, and if one of them did Goodbody had the affidavits and he himself would be far away.

'The young woman, where is she?'

'She and her friend left for the Continent the night after she visited Lady Caverel. Rutherford also sent a fax before they sailed. To his uncle's office, saying he would not be returning.' Mr Rogers smiled. 'Apparently the news did not unduly distress his relative.'

'Has he any money?'

'His family is very rich. I presume they'll marry or do whatever it is that young people do nowadays.' He folded his hands over his round little stomach. 'He'll take her to Australia. She'll be happier there. She won't trouble you again.' He paused. Then he said softly, 'There remains only your humble and obedient servant.' He got to his feet. 'I shall use the Swiss account. See, if you please, that what we agreed is paid in tomorrow morning.'

'Very well.'

Mr Rogers bowed and left.

The best, as Oliver had always known, never comes cheap. He walked back to the window. What was it that Andrea had told him the woman had said to her? 'It's better for you to have it.' The young woman was right. It was better, far better. It would not have done to have had her presiding over the great table in the dining-room at Ravenscourt surrounded by Blake and his crew and the drunken grandmother. That was why, at great cost, he had done what he had. When Nicholas had complained about the vast sums he had to raise from the estate, Oliver had sold his house at Whitchurch and contributed personally. As for the young woman, he had no regrets. She would have a good life in Australia, a life for which she was altogether more suited.

It was late when he got to Anne Tremain.

'Are you going to the country tonight?' she asked as she brought him his whisky-and-soda.

'No. I shall be remaining in London.'

'So Julian did have a daughter after all?'

He nodded.

'Then it was fortunate you managed to discover she had died.'

Oliver looked down at his glass. 'It was.'

'We should drink to your success – and to Ravenscourt.'

He raised his glass and smiled. 'To Ravenscourt,' he said.

Mr Rogers let himself into the suburban house with the neat front garden in Sanderstead. He tried to shut the door quietly behind him but he was heard.

'Herbert,' the voice called from the kitchen, 'is that you?'

'It is, my dear.'

'Have you had your tea?'

'I have, my dear.'

He hung his bowler hat on the stand and made for the stairs.

'The grass needs mowing.'

'Does it, my dear? I'll just change,' and he climbed slowly up the stairs.

'The Websters are coming at eight to play bridge,' she called after him. 'There's a clean shirt in the laundry cupboard.'

In his room Mr Rogers changed into his lightweight suit, the button of which strained across his stomach. He looked at himself in the looking-glass. A new suit would be his first extravagance.

He put the clean shirt, pyjamas, a toothbrush and a razor into his briefcase, gathered up his passport, the cheque book from Credit Suisse, his well-filled wallet, the books of travellers' cheques and put them into his pockets. Briefcase in hand he went on tiptoe downstairs. He closed the front door quietly behind him and walked briskly to the railway station. At Waterloo he dropped the keys to the house and to the Ford Fiesta into a waste bin and took a taxi to Heathrow.

In the first-class lounge he sipped champagne. He had nothing to do now but enjoy himself. And Mr Rogers was determined that he would. Unlike the past months, the trip on which he was now embarking would, he was determined, last for the remainder of his days. But he was a sensitive soul. So, in all conscience, he felt he should avoid Australia.